Benjamin Franl

# Memoirs of Benjamin Franklin
## Volume 2

Benjamin Franklin

# Memoirs of Benjamin Franklin Volume 2

1st Edition | ISBN: 978-3-75233-278-0

Place of Publication: Frankfurt am Main, Germany

Year of Publication: 2020

Outlook Verlag GmbH, Germany.

Reproduction of the original.

# MEMOIRS
# OF
# BENJAMIN FRANKLIN;
# WRITTEN BY HIMSELF.

VOL. II

# THE WAY TO WEALTH,

*As dearly shown in the practice of an old Pennsylvania Almanac, entitled, "Poor Richard Improved."*

COURTEOUS READER,

I have heard that nothing gives an author so great pleasure as to find his works respectfully quoted by others. Judge, then, how much I must have been gratified by an incident I am going to relate to you. I stopped my horse lately where a great number of people were collected at an auction of merchants' goods. The hour of the sale not being come, they were conversing on the badness of the times; and one of the company called to a plain, clean old man, with white locks, "Pray, Father Abraham, what think you of the times? Will not these heavy taxes quite ruin the country? How shall we ever be able to pay them? What would you advise us to?" Father Abraham stood up and replied, "If you would have my advice, I will give it you in short; for *A word to the wise is enough*, as Poor Richard says." They joined in desiring him to speak his mind; and, gathering round him, he proceeded as follows:

"Friends," said he, "the taxes are indeed very heavy, and if those laid on by the government were the only ones we had to pay, we might more easily discharge them; but we have many others, and much more grievous to some of us. We are taxed twice as much by our idleness, three times as much by our pride, and four times as much by our folly; and from these taxes the commissioners cannot ease or deliver us, by allowing an abatement. However, let us hearken to good advice, and something may be done for us: *God helps them that help themselves*, as Poor Richard says.

"I. It would be thought a hard government that should tax its people one tenth part of their time, to be employed in its service; but idleness taxes many of us much more; sloth, by bringing on diseases, absolutely shortens life. *Sloth, like rust, consumes faster than labour wears; while the used key is always bright*, as Poor Richard says. *But dost thou love life, then do not squander time, for that is the stuff life is made of*, as Poor Richard says. How much more than is necessary do we spend in sleep? forgetting that *The sleeping fox catches no poultry*, and that *There will be sleeping enough in the grave*, as Poor Richard says.

"*If time be of all things the most precious, wasting time must be*, as Poor Richard says, the *greatest prodigality*; since, as he elsewhere tells us, *Lost time is never found again; and what we call time enough, always proves little enough*. Let us, then, up and be doing, and doing to the purpose; so by diligence shall we do more with less perplexity. *Sloth makes all things difficult, but industry all easy*; and *He that riseth late must trot all day, and shall scarce overtake his business at night*; while *Laziness travels so slowly, that Poverty soon overtakes him. Drive thy business, let not that drive thee*; and *Early to bed and early to rise, makes a man healthy, wealthy, and wise*, as Poor Richard says.

"So what signifies wishing and hoping for better times? We may make these times better if we bestir ourselves. *Industry need not wish, and he that lives upon hopes will die fasting. There are no gains without pains; then help, hands, for I have no lands*; or, if I have, they are smartly taxed. *He that hath a trade hath an estate; and he that hath a calling hath an office of profit and honour*, as Poor Richard says; but then the trade must be worked at, and the calling followed, or neither the estate nor the office will enable us to pay our taxes. If we are industrious, we shall never starve; for, *At the workingman's house hunger looks in, but dares not enter*. Nor will the bailiff or the constable enter; for *Industry pays debts, while despair increaseth them*. What though you have found no treasure, nor has any rich relation left you a legacy? *Diligence is the mother of luck, and God gives all things to industry. Then plough deep while sluggards sleep, and you shall have corn to sell and to keep*. Work while it is called to-day, for you know not how much you may be hindered to-morrow. *One to-day is worth two to-morrows*, as Poor Richard says; and farther, *Never leave that till to-morrow which you can do to-day*. If you were a servant, would you not be ashamed that a good master should catch you idle? Are you, then, your own master? Be ashamed to catch yourself idle when there is so much to be done for yourself, your family, and your country. Handle your tools without mittens; remember that *The cat in gloves catches no mice*, as Poor Richard says. It is true there is much to be done, and perhaps you are weak-handed; but stick to it steadily, and you will see great effects; for *Constant dropping wears away stones*; and *By diligence and patience the mouse ate in two the cable*; and *Little strokes fell great oaks*.

"Methinks I hear some of you say, 'Must a man afford himself no leisure?' I will tell thee, my friend, what Poor Richard says: *Employ thy time well, if thou meanest to gain leisure; and, since thou art not sure of a minute, throw not away an hour.* Leisure is time for doing something useful; this leisure the diligent man will obtain, but the lazy man never; for *A life of leisure and a life of laziness are two things. Many, without labour, would live by their wits only, but they break for want of stock*; whereas industry gives comfort, and plenty, and respect. *Fly pleasures, and they will follow you. The diligent spinner has a large shift; and now I have a sheep and a cow, everybody bids me good-morrow.*

"II. But with our industry we must likewise be steady, settled, and careful, and oversee our own affairs with our own eyes, and not trust too much to others; for, as Poor Richard says,

> *I never saw an oft-removed tree,*
> *Nor yet an oft-removed family,*
> *That throve so well as those that settled be.*

And again, *Three removes are as bad as a fire*; and again, *Keep thy shop, and thy shop will keep thee*; and again, *If you would have your business done, go; if not, send.* And again,

> *He that by the plough would thrive,*
> *Himself must either hold or drive.*

And again, *The eye of a master will do more work than both his hands*; and again, *Want of care does us more damage than want of knowledge*; and again, *Not to oversee workmen is to leave them your purse open.* Trusting too much to others' care is the ruin of many; *for in the affairs of this world men are saved, not by faith, but by the want of it*; but a man's own care is profitable; for, *If you would have a faithful servant, and one that you like, serve yourself. A little neglect may breed great mischief; for want of a nail the shoe was lost; for want of a shoe the horse was lost; and for want of a horse the rider was lost, being overtaken and slain by the enemy; all for the want of a little care about a horseshoe nail.*

"III. So much for industry, my friends, and attention to one's own business; but to these we must add frugality, if we would make our industry more certainly successful. A man may, if he knows not how to save as he gets, keep his nose all his life to the grindstone, and die not worth a groat at last. *A fat kitchen makes a lean will*; and

> *Many estates are spent in the getting,*
> *Since women for tea forsook spinning and knitting,*
> *And men for punch forsook hewing and splitting.*

*If you would be wealthy, think of saving as well as of getting. The Indies have not made Spain rich, because her outgoes are greater than her incomes.*

"Away, then, with your expensive follies, and you will not then have so much cause to complain of hard times, heavy taxes, and chargeable families. And farther, *What maintains one vice would bring up two children.* You may think, perhaps, that a little tea, or a little punch now and then, diet a little more costly, clothes a little finer, and a little entertainment now and then, can be no great matter; but remember, *Many a little makes a mickle.* Beware of little expenses; *A small leak will sink a great ship,* as Poor Richard says; and again, *Who dainties love, shall beggars prove;* and moreover, *Fools make feasts, and wise men eat them.*

"Here you are all got together at this sale of fineries and knickknacks. You call them *goods*; but, if you do not take care, they will prove *evils* to some of you. You expect they will be sold cheap, and perhaps they may for less than they cost; but, if you have no occasion for them, they must be dear to you. Remember what Poor Richard says: *Buy what thou hast no need of, and ere long thou shalt sell thy necessaries.* And again, *At a great pennyworth pause a while.* He means, that perhaps the cheapness is apparent only, and not real; or the bargain, by straitening thee in thy business, may do thee more harm than good. For in another place he says, *Many have been ruined by buying good pennyworths.* Again, *It is foolish to lay out money in a purchase of repentance*; and yet this folly is practised every day at auctions, for want of minding the Almanac. Many a one, for the sake of finery on the back, have gone with a hungry belly, and half starved their families. *Silks and satins, scarlet and velvets, put out the kitchen fire,* as Poor Richard says.

"These are not the necessaries of life; they can scarcely be called the conveniences; and yet, only because they look pretty, how many want to have them! By these and other extravagances, the genteel are reduced to poverty, and forced to borrow of those whom they formerly despised, but who, through industry and frugality, have maintained their standing; in which case it appears plainly that *A ploughman on his legs is higher than a gentleman on his knees,* as Poor Richard says. Perhaps they have had a small estate left them, which they knew not the getting of; they think *It is day, and will never be night*; that a little to be spent out of so much is not worth minding; but *Always taking out of the mealtub and never putting in, soon comes to the bottom,* as Poor Richard says; and then, *When the well is dry, they know the worth of water.* But this they might have known before if they had taken his advice. *If you would know the value of money, go and try to borrow some; for he that goes a borrowing goes a sorrowing,* as Poor Richard says; and indeed so does he that lends to such people, when he goes to get it in again. Poor Dick farther advises, and says,

*Fond pride of dress is sure a very curse;*

*Ere fancy you consult, consult your purse.*

And again, *Pride is as loud a beggar as Want, and a great deal more saucy.* When you have bought one fine thing, you must buy ten more, that your appearance may be all of a piece; but Poor Dick says, *It is easier to suppress the first desire than to satisfy all that follow it.* And it is as truly folly for the poor to ape the rich, as for the frog to swell in order to equal the ox.

*Vessels large may venture more,*
*But little boats should keep near shore.*

It is, however, a folly soon punished; for, as Poor Richard says, *Pride that dines on vanity, sups on contempt. Pride breakfasted with Plenty, dined with Poverty, and supped with Infamy.* And, after all, of what use is this pride of appearance, for which so much is risked, so much is suffered? It cannot promote health nor ease pain; it makes no increase of merit in the person; it creates envy; it hastens misfortune.

"But what madness must it be to *run in debt* for these superfluities? We are offered, by the terms of this sale, six months' credit; and that, perhaps, has induced some of us to attend it, because we cannot spare the ready money, and hope now to be fine without it. But ah! think what you do when you run in debt; you give to another power over your liberty. If you cannot pay at the time, you will be ashamed to see your creditor; you will be in fear when you speak to him; you will make poor, pitiful, sneaking excuses, and, by degrees, come to lose your veracity, and sink into base, downright lying; for *The second vice is lying, the first is running in debt*, as Poor Richard says; and again, to the same purpose, *Lying rides upon Debt's back*, whereas a freeborn ought not to be ashamed nor afraid to see or speak to any man living. But poverty often deprives a man of all spirit and virtue. *It is hard for an empty bag to stand upright.*

"What would you think of that prince or of that government who should issue an edict forbidding you to dress like a gentleman or gentlewoman, on pain of imprisonment or servitude? Would you not say that you were free, have a right to dress as you please, and that such an edict would be a breach of your privileges, and such a government tyrannical? And yet you are about to put your self under such tyranny, when you run in debt for such dress! Your creditor has authority, at his pleasure, to deprive you of your liberty, by confining you in jail till you shall be able to pay him. When you have got your bargain, you may, perhaps, think little of payment; but, as Poor Richard says, *Creditors have better memories than debtors; creditors are a superstitious sect, great observers of set days and times.* The day comes round before you are aware, and the demand is made before you are prepared to satisfy it; or, if you bear your debt in mind, the term, which at first seemed so long, will, as it lessens, appear extremely short. Time will seem to have added wings to his heels as well as his shoulders. *Those have a short Lent who owe money to be paid at Easter.* At present, perhaps, you may think yourselves in thriving circumstances, and that you can bear a little extravagance without injury; but

> *For age and want save while you may;*
> *No morning sun lasts a whole day.*

Gain may be temporary and uncertain, but ever, while you live, expense is constant and certain; and *It is easier to build two chimneys than to keep one in fuel*, as Poor Richard says; so, *Rather go to bed supperless than rise in debt.*

"IV. This doctrine, my friends, is reason and wisdom; but, after all, do not depend too much upon your own industry, and frugality, and prudence, though excellent things; for they may all be blasted, without the blessing of Heaven; and, therefore, ask that blessing humbly, and be not uncharitable to those that at present seem to want it, but comfort and help them. Remember, Job suffered, and was afterward prosperous.

"And now, to conclude, *Experience keeps a dear school, but fools will learn in no other*, as Poor Richard says, and scarce in that; for it is true, *We may give advice, but we cannot give conduct.* However, remember this, *They that will not be counselled cannot be helped*; and farther, that, *If you will not hear Reason, she will surely rap your knuckles*, as Poor Richard says."

Thus the old gentleman ended his harangue. The people heard it, and approved the doctrine; and immediately practised the contrary, just as if it had been a common sermon; for the auction opened, and they began to buy extravagantly. I found the good man had thoroughly studied my Almanacs, and digested all I had dropped on these topics during the course of twenty-five years. The frequent mention he made of me must have tired any one else; but my vanity was wonderfully delighted with it, though I was conscious that not a tenth part of the wisdom was my own which he ascribed to me, but rather the gleanings that I had made of the sense of all ages and nations. However, I resolved to be the better for the echo of it; and, though I had at first determined to buy stuff for a new coat, I went away resolved to wear my old one a little longer. Reader, if thou wilt do the same, thy profit will be as great as mine. I am, as ever, thine to serve thee,

RICHARD SAUNDERS.

# ON TRUE HAPPINESS.

The desire of happiness in general is so natural to us, that all the world are in pursuit of it; all have this one end in view, though they take such different methods to attain it, and are so much divided in their notions of it.

Evil, as evil, can never be chosen; and, though evil is often the effect of our own choice, yet we never desire it, but under the appearance of an imaginary good.

Many things we indulge ourselves in may be considered by us as evils, and yet be desirable; but then they are only considered as evils in their effects and consequences, not as evils at present, and attended with immediate misery.

Reason represents things to us not only as they are at present, but as they are in their whole nature and tendency; passion only regards them in the former light. When this governs us, we are regardless of the future, and are only affected with the present. It is impossible ever to enjoy ourselves rightly, if our conduct be not such as to preserve the harmony and order of our faculties, and the original frame and constitution of our minds; all true happiness, as all that is truly beautiful, can only result from order.

While there is a conflict between the two principles of passion and reason, we must be miserable in proportion to the struggle; and when the victory is gained, and reason so far subdued as seldom to trouble us with its remonstrances, the happiness we have then is not the happiness of our rational nature, but the happiness only of the inferior and sensual part of us, and, consequently, a very low and imperfect happiness to what the other would have afforded us.

If we reflect upon any one passion and disposition of mind, abstract from virtue, we shall soon see the disconnexion between that and true, solid happiness. It is of the very essence, for instance, of envy to be uneasy and disquieted. Pride meets with provocations and disturbances upon almost every occasion. Covetousness is ever attended with solicitude and anxiety. Ambition has its disappointments to sour us, but never the good fortune to satisfy us; its appetite grows the keener by indulgence, and all we can gratify it with at present serves but the more to inflame its insatiable desires.

The passions, by being too much conversant with earthly objects, can never fix in us a proper composure and acquiescence of mind. Nothing but an indifference to the things of this world, an entire submission to the will of Providence here, and a well-grounded expectation of happiness hereafter, can give us a true, satisfactory enjoyment of ourselves. Virtue is the best guard against the many unavoidable evils incident to us; nothing better alleviates the weight of the afflictions, or gives a truer relish of the blessings, of human life.

What is without us has not the least connexion with happiness, only so far as the preservation of our lives and health depends upon it. Health of body, though so far necessary that we cannot be perfectly happy without it, is not sufficient to make us happy of itself. Happiness springs immediately from the mind; health is but to be considered as a condition or circumstance, without which this happiness cannot be tasted pure and unabated.

Virtue is the best preservation of health, as it prescribes temperance, and such a regulation of our passions as is most conducive to the well-being of the animal economy; so that it is, at the same time, the only true happiness of the mind, and the best means of preserving the health of the body.

If our desires are to the things of this world, they are never to be satisfied. If our great view is upon those of the next, the expectation of them is an infinitely higher satisfaction than the enjoyment of those of the present.

There is no happiness, then, but in a virtuous and self-approving conduct. Unless our actions will bear the test of our sober judgments and reflections upon them, they are not the actions, and, consequently, not the happiness, of a rational being.

## PUBLIC MEN

The following is a dialogue between Socrates, the great Athenian philosopher, and one Glaucon, a private man, of mean abilities, but ambitious of being chosen a senator and of governing the republic; wherein Socrates in a pleasant manner convinces him of his incapacity for public affairs, by making him sensible of his ignorance of the interests of his country in their several branches, and entirely dissuades him from any attempt of that nature. There is also added, at the end, part of another dialogue the same Socrates had with one Charmidas, a worthy man, but too modest, wherein he endeavours to persuade him to put himself forward and undertake public business, as being very capable of it. The whole is taken from *Xenophon's Memorable Things of Socrates, Book Third.*

"A certain man, whose name was Glaucon, the son of Ariston, had so fixed it in his mind to govern the republic, that he frequently presented himself before the people to discourse of affairs of state, though all the world laughed at him for it; nor was it in the power of his relations or friends to dissuade him from that design. But Socrates had a kindness for him, on account of Plato, his brother, and he only it was who made him change his resolution. He met him, and accosted him in so winning a manner, that he first obliged him to hearken to his discourse. He began with him thus:

"'You have a mind, then, to govern the republic?'

"'I have so,' answered Glaucon.

"'You cannot,' replied Socrates, 'have a more noble design; for if you can accomplish it so as to become absolute, you will be able to serve your friends, you will raise your family, you will extend the bounds of your country, you will be known, not only in Athens, but through all Greece, and perhaps your renown will fly even to the barbarous nations, as did that of Themistocles. In short, wherever you come, you will have the respect and admiration of all the world.'

"These words soothed Glaucon, and won him to give ear to Socrates, who went on in this manner: 'But it is certain, that if you desire to be honoured, you must be useful to the state.'

"'Certainly,' said Glaucon.

"'And in the name of all the gods,' replied Socrates, 'tell me, what is the first service that you intend to render the state?'

"Glaucon was considering what to answer, when Socrates continued: 'If you design to make the fortune of one of your friends, you will endeavour to make him rich, and thus, perhaps, you will make it your business to enrich the republic?'

"'I would,' answered Glaucon.

"Socrates replied, 'Would not the way to enrich the republic be to increase its revenue?'

"'It is very likely it would,' answered Glaucon.

"'Tell me, then, in what consists the revenue of the state, and to how much it may amount? I presume you have particularly studied this matter, to the end that, if anything should be lost on one hand, you might know where to make it good on another; and that, if a fund should fail on a sudden, you might immediately be able to settle another in its place?'

"'I protest,' answered Glaucon, 'I have never thought of this.'

"'Tell me, at least, the expenses of the republic, for no doubt you intend to retrench the superfluous?'

"'I never thought of this either,' said Glaucon.

"'You were best, then, to put off to another time your design of enriching the republic, which you can never be able to do while you are ignorant both of its expenses and revenue.'

"'There is another way to enrich a state,' said Glaucon, 'of which you take no notice; and that is, by the ruin [spoils] of its enemies.'

"'You are in the right,' answered Socrates; 'but to this end it is necessary to be stronger than they, otherwise we shall run the hazard of losing what we have. He, therefore, who talks of undertaking a war, ought to know the strength on both sides, to the end that, if his party be the stronger, he may boldly advise for war, and that, if it be the weaker, he may dissuade the people from engaging themselves in so dangerous an enterprise.'

"'All this is true.'

"'Tell me, then,' continued Socrates,'how strong our forces are by sea and land, and how strong are our enemies.'

"'Indeed,' said Glaucon, 'I cannot tell you on a sudden.'

"'If you have a list of them in writing, pray show it me; I should be glad to hear it read.'

"'I have it not yet.'

"'I see, then,' said Socrates, 'that we shall not engage in war so soon; for the greatness of the undertaking will hinder you from maturely weighing all the consequences of it in the beginning of your government. But,' continued he, 'you have thought of the defence of the country; you know what garrisons are necessary, and what are not; you know what number of troops is sufficient in one, and not sufficient in another; you will cause the necessary garrisons to be re-enforced, and disband those that are useless?'

"'I should be of opinion,' said Glaucon, 'to leave none of them on foot, because they ruin a country on pretence of defending it.'

"'But,' Socrates objected, 'if all the garrisons were taken away, there would be nothing to hinder the first comer from carrying off what he pleased; but how come you to know that the garrisons behave themselves so ill? Have you been upon the place? Have you seen them?'

"'Not at all; but I suspect it to be so.'

"'When, therefore, we are certain of it,' said Socrates, 'and can speak upon better grounds than simple conjectures, we will propose this advice to the senate.'

"'It may be well to do so,' said Glaucon.

"'It comes into my mind, too,' continued Socrates, 'that you have never been at the mines of silver, to examine why they bring not in so much now as they did formerly.'

"'You say true; I have never been there.'

"'Indeed, they say the place is very unhealthy, and that may excuse you.'

"'You rally me now,' said Glaucon.

"Socrates added, 'But I believe you have at least observed how much corn our land produces, how long it will serve to supply our city, and how much more we shall want for the whole year; to the end you may not be surprised with a scarcity of bread, but may give timely orders for the necessary provisions.'

"'There is a deal to do,' said Glaucon, 'if we must take care of all these things.'

"'There is so,' replied Socrates; 'and it is even impossible to manage our own families well, unless we know all that is wanting, and take care to provide it. As you see, therefore, that our city is composed of above ten thousand families, and it being a difficult task to watch over them all at once, why did you not first try to retrieve your uncle's affairs, which are running to decay? and, after having given that proof of your industry, you might have taken a greater trust upon you. But now, when you find yourself incapable of aiding a private man, how can you think of behaving yourself so as to be useful to a whole people? Ought a man, who has not strength enought to carry a hundred pound weight, to undertake to carry a heavier burden?'

"'I would have done good service to my uncle,' said Glaucon, 'if he would have taken my advice.'

"'How,' replied Socrates, 'have you not hitherto been able to govern the mind of your uncle, and do you now believe yourself able to govern the minds of all the Athenians, and his among the rest? Take heed, my dear Glaucon, take heed lest too great a desire of power should render you despised; consider how dangerous it is to speak and entertain ourselves concerning things we do not understand; what a figure do those forward and rash people make in the world who do so; and judge yourself whether they acquire more esteem than blame, whether they are more admired than contemned. Think, on the contrary, with how much more honour a man is regarded who understands perfectly what he says and what he does, and then you will confess that renown and applause have always been the recompense of true merit, and shame the reward of ignorance and temerity. If, therefore, you would be honoured, endeavour to be a man of true merit; and if you enter upon the government of the republic with a mind more sagacious than usual, I shall not wonder if you succeed in all your designs.'"

Thus Socrates put a stop to the disorderly ambition of this man; but, on an occasion quite contrary, he in the following manner exhorted Charmidas to take an employment.

"He was a man of sense, and more deserving than most others in the same post; but, as he was of a modest disposition, he constantly declined, and made great difficulties of engaging himself in public business. Socrates therefore addressed himself to him in this manner:

"'If you knew any man that could gain the prizes in the public games, and by that means render himself illustrious, and acquire glory to his country, what would you say of him if he refused to offer himself to the combat?'

"'I would say,' answered Charmidas, 'that he was a mean-spirited, effeminate fellow.'

"'And if a man were capable of governing a republic, of increasing its power by his advice, and of raising himself by this means to a high degree of honour, would you not brand him likewise with meanness of soul if he would not present himself to be employed?'

"'Perhaps I might,' said Charmidas; 'but why do you ask me this question?' Socrates replied, 'Because you are capable of managing the affairs of the republic, and nevertheless you avoid doing so, though, in quality of a citizen, you are *obliged* to take care of the commonwealth. Be no longer, then, thus negligent in this matter; consider your abilities and your duty with more attention, and let not slip the occasions of serving the republic, and of rendering it, if possible, more flourishing than it is. This will be a blessing whose influence will descend not only on the other citizens, but on your best friends and yourself.'"

## THE WASTE OF LIFE.

Anergus was a gentleman of a good estate; he was bred to no business, and could not contrive how to waste his hours agreeably; he had no relish for any of the proper works of life, nor any taste at all for the improvements of the mind; he spent, generally, ten hours of the four-and-twenty in his bed; he dozed away two or three more on his couch, and as many were dissolved in good liquor every evening, if he met with company of his own humour. Five or six of the rest he sauntered away with much indolence; the chief business of them was to contrive his meals, and to feed his fancy beforehand with the promise of a dinner and supper; not that he was so absolute a glutton or so entirely devoted to his appetite, but, chiefly because he knew not how to employ his thoughts better, he let them rove about the sustenance of his body. Thus he had made a shift to wear off ten years since the paternal estate fell into his hands; and yet, according to the abuse of words in our day, he was called a man of virtue, because he was scarce ever known to be quite drunken, nor was his nature much inclined to licentiousness.

One evening, as he was musing alone, his thoughts happened to take a most unusual turn, for they cast a glance backward, and began to reflect on his manner of life. He bethought himself what a number of living beings had been made a sacrifice to support his carcass, and how much corn and wine had been mingled with those offerings. He had not quite lost all the arithmetic that he had learned when he was a boy, and he set himself to compute what he had devoured since he came to the age of man.

"About a dozen of feathered creatures, small and great, have, one week with another," said he, "given up their lives to prolong mine, which in ten years amounts to at least six thousand.

"Fifty sheep have been sacrificed in a year, with half a hecatomb of black cattle, that I might have the choicest part offered weekly upon my table. Thus a thousand beasts out of the flock and the herd have been slain in ten years' time to feed me, besides what the forest has supplied me with. Many hundreds of fishes have, in all their varieties, been robbed of life for my repast, and of the smaller fry as many thousands.

"A measure of corn would hardly afford me fine flour enough for a month's provision, and this arises to above six score bushels; and many hogsheads of ale and wine, and other liquors, have passed through this body of mine, this wretched strainer of meat and drink.

"And what have I done all this time for God or man? What a vast profusion of good things upon a useless life and a worthless liver! There is not the meanest creature among all these which I have devoured, but hath answered the end of its creation better than I. It was made to support human nature, and it hath done so. Every crab and oyster I have ate, and every grain of corn I have devoured, hath filled up its place in the rank of beings with more propriety and honour than I have done. Oh shameful waste of life and time!"

In short, he carried on his moral reflections with so just and severe a force of reason, as constrained him to change his whole course of life, to break off his follies at once, and to apply himself to gain some useful knowledge, when he was more than thirty years of age. He lived many following years with the character of a worthy man and an excellent Christian; he performed the kind offices of a good neighbour at home, and made a shining figure as a patriot in the senate-house; he died with a peaceful conscience, and the tears of his country were dropped upon his tomb.

The world, that knew the whole series of his life, stood amazed at the mighty change. They beheld him as a wonder of reformation, while he himself confessed and adored the Divine power and mercy, which had transformed him from a brute to a man.

But this was a single instance; and we may almost venture to write MIRACLE upon it. Are there not numbers of both sexes among our young gentry, in this degenerate age, whose lives thus run to utter waste, without the least tendency to usefulness?

When I meet with persons of such a worthless character as this, it brings to my mind some scraps of Horace:

"Nos numerus sumus, et fruges consumere nati,
  ... ... ... ... Alcinoique
  ... ... ... ... . . juventus,
Cui pulchrum fuit in medios dormire dies," &c.

PARAPHRASE.

There are a number of us creep
Into this world, to eat and sleep;
And know no reason why they're born,
But merely to consume the corn,
Devour the cattle, fowl, and fish,
And leave behind an empty dish.
Though crows and ravens do the same,
Unlucky birds of hateful name,
Ravens or crows might fill their places,
And swallow corn and eat carcáses,
Then, if their tombstone, when they die,
Be n't taught to flatter and to lie.
There's nothing better will be said,
Than that *they've eat up all their bread,
Drunk all their drink, and gone to bed.*

---

# SELF- DENIAL NOT THE ESSENCE OF VIRTUE.

It is commonly asserted, that without self-denial there is no virtue, and that the greater the self-denial the greater the virtue.

If it were said that he who cannot deny himself anything he inclines to, though he knows it will be to his hurt, has not the virtue of resolution or fortitude, it would be intelligible enough; but, as it stands, it seems obscure or erroneous.

Let us consider some of the virtues singly.

If a man has no inclination to wrong people in his dealings, if he feels no temptation to it, and, therefore, never does it, can it be said that he is not a just man? If he is a just man, has he not the virtue of justice?

If to a certain man idle diversions have nothing in them that is tempting, and, therefore, he never relaxes his application to business for their sake, is he not an industrious man? Or has he not the virtue of industry?

I might in like manner instance in all the rest of the virtues; but, to make the thing short, as it is certain that the more we strive against the temptation to any vice, and practise the contrary virtue, the weaker will that temptation be, and the stronger will be that habit, till at length the temptation has no force or entirely vanishes; does it follow from thence that, in our endeavours to overcome vice, we grow continually less and less virtuous, till at length we have no virtue at all?

If self-denial be the essence of virtue, then it follows that the man who is naturally temperate, just, &c., is not virtuous; but that, in order to be virtuous, he must, in spite of his natural inclination, wrong his neighbours, and eat, and drink, &c., to excess.

But perhaps it may be said, that by the word *virtue* in the above assertion is meant merit; and so it should stand thus: Without self-denial there is no merit, and the greater the self-denial the greater the merit.

The self-denial here meant must be when our inclinations are towards vice, or else it would still be nonsense.

By merit is understood desert; and when we say a man merits, we mean that he deserves praise or reward.

We do not pretend to merit anything of God, for he is above our services; and the benefits he confers on us are the effects of his goodness and bounty.

All our merit, then, is with regard to one another, and from one to another.

Taking, then, the assertion as it last stands,

If a man does me a service from a natural benevolent inclination, does he deserve less of me than another, who does me the like kindness against his inclination?

If I have two journeymen, one naturally industrious, the other idle, but both perform a day's work equally good, ought I to give the latter the most wages?

Indeed, lazy workmen are commonly observed to be more extravagant in their demands than the industrious; for, if they have not more for their work, they cannot live as well. But though it be true to a proverb that lazy folks take the most pains, does it follow that they deserve the most money?

If you were to employ servants in affairs of trust, would you not bid more for one you knew was naturally honest than for one naturally roguish, but who has lately acted honestly? For currents, whose natural channel is dammed up till the new course is by time worn sufficiently deep and become natural, are apt to break their banks. If one servant is more valuable than another, has he not more merit than the other? and yet this is not on account of superior self-denial.

Is a patriot not praiseworthy if public spirit is natural to him?

Is a pacing-horse less valuable for being a natural pacer?

Nor, in my opinion, has any man less merit for having, in general, natural virtuous inclinations.

The truth is, that temperance, justice, charity, &c., are virtues, whether practised with or against our inclinations; and the man who practises them merits our love and esteem; and self-denial is neither good nor bad but as it is applied. He that denies a vicious inclination, is virtuous in proportion to his resolution; but the most perfect virtue is above all temptation; such as the virtue of the saints in heaven; and he who does a foolish, indecent, or wicked thing, merely because it is contrary to his inclination (like some mad enthusiasts I have read of, who ran about naked, under the notion of taking up the cross), is not practising the reasonable science of virtue, but is a lunatic.

## ON THE USEFULNESS OF THE MATHEMATICS.

Mathematics originally signified any kind of discipline or learning, but now it is taken for that science which teaches or contemplates whatever is capable of being numbered or measured. That part of the mathematics which relates to numbers only, is called *arithmetic*; and that which is concerned about measure in general, whether length, breadth, motion, force, &c., is called *geometry*.

As to the usefulness of arithmetic, it is well known that no business, commerce, trade, or employment whatsoever, even from the merchant to the shopkeeper, &c., can be managed and carried on without the assistance of numbers; for by these the trader computes the value of all sorts of goods that he dealeth in, does his business with ease and certainty, and informs himself how matters stand at any time with respect to men, money, and merchandise, to profit and loss, whether he goes forward or backward, grows richer or poorer. Neither is this science only useful to the merchant, but is reckoned the *primum mobile* (or first mover) of all mundane affairs in general, and is useful for all sorts and degrees of men, from the highest to the lowest.

As to the usefulness of geometry, it is as certain that no curious art or mechanic work can either be invented, improved, or performed without its assisting principles.

It is owing to this that astronomers are put into a way of making their observations, coming at the knowledge of the extent of the heavens, the duration of time, the motions, magnitudes, and distances of the heavenly bodies, their situations, positions, risings, settings, aspects, and eclipses; also the measure of seasons, of years, and of ages.

It is by the assistance of this science that geographers present to our view at once the magnitude and form of the whole earth, the vast extent of the seas, the divisions of empires, kingdoms, and provinces.

It is by the help of geometry the ingenious mariner is instructed how to guide a ship through the vast ocean, from one part of the earth to another, the nearest and safest way, and in the shortest time.

By help of this science the architects take their just measures for the structure of buildings, as private houses, churches, palaces, ships, fortifications, &c.

By its help engineers conduct all their works, take the situation and plan of towns, forts, and castles, measure their distances from one another, and carry their measures into places that are only accessible to the eye.

From hence also is deduced that admirable art of drawing sundials on any place, howsoever situate, and for any part of the world, to point out the exact time of the day, the sun's declination, altitude, amplitude, azimuth, and other astronomical matters.

By geometry the surveyor is directed how to draw a map of any country, to divide his lands, and to lay down and plot any piece of ground, and thereby discover the area in acres, rods, and perches; the gauger is instructed how to find the capacities or solid contents of all kinds of vessels, in barrels, gallons, bushels, &c.; and the measurer is furnished with rules for finding the areas and contents of superfices and solids, and casting up all manner of workmanship. All these, and many more useful arts, too many to be enumerated here, wholly depend upon the aforesaid sciences, namely, arithmetic and geometry.

This science is descended from the infancy of the world, the inventors of which were the first propagators of human kind, as Adam, Noah, Abraham, Moses, and divers others.

There has not been any science so much esteemed and honoured as this of the mathematics, nor with so much industry and vigilance become the care of great men, and laboured in by the potentates of the world, namely, emperors, kings, princes, &c.

*Mathematical demonstrations* are a logic of as much or more use than that commonly learned at schools, serving to a just formation of the mind, enlarging its capacity, and strengthening it so as to render the same capable of exact reasoning, and discerning truth from falsehood in all occurrences, even subjects not mathematical. For which reason it is said the Egyptians, Persians, and Lacedæmonians seldom elected any new kings but such as had some knowledge in the mathematics; imagining those who had not men of imperfect judgments, and unfit to rule and govern.

Though Plato's censure, that those who did not understand the 117th proposition of the 13th book of Euclid's Elements ought not to be ranked among rational creatures, was unreasonable and unjust, yet to give a man the character of universal learning, who is destitute of a competent knowledge in the mathematics, is no less so.

The usefulness of some particular parts of the mathematics, in the common affairs of human life, has rendered some knowledge of them very necessary to a great part of mankind, and very convenient to all the rest, that are any way conversant beyond the limits of their own particular callings.

Those whom necessity has obliged to get their bread by manual industry, where some degree of art is required to go along with it, and who have had some insight into these studies, have very often found advantages from them sufficient to reward the pains they were at in acquiring them. And whatever may have been imputed to some other studies, under the notion of insignificance and loss of time, yet these, I believe, never caused repentance in any, except it was for their remissness in the prosecution of them.

Philosophers do generally affirm that human knowledge to be most excellent which is conversant among the most excellent things. What science, then, can there be more noble, more excellent, more useful for men, more admirably high and demonstrative, than this of the mathematics?

I shall conclude with what Plato says, in the seventh book of his *Republic*, with regard to the excellence and usefulness of geometry, being to this purpose:

"Dear friend—You see, then, that mathematics are necessary, because, by the exactness of the method, we get a habit of using our minds to the best advantage. And it is remarkable that, all men being capable by nature to reason and understand the sciences, the less acute, by studying this, though useless to them in every other respect, will gain this advantage, that their minds will be improved in reasoning aright; for no study employs it more, nor makes it susceptible of attention so much; and those who we find have a mind worth cultivating, ought to apply themselves to this study."

# THE ART OF PROCURING PLEASANT DREAMS.

*Inscribed to Miss * * * *, being written at her request*

As a great part of our life is spent in sleep, during which we have sometimes pleasant and some times painful dreams, it becomes of some consequence to obtain the one kind and avoid the other, for, whether real or imaginary, pain is pain and pleasure is pleasure. If we can sleep without dreaming, it is well that painful dreams are avoided. If, while we sleep, we can have any pleasing dreams, it is, as the French say, *autant de gagné*, so much added to the pleasure of life.

To this end it is, in the first place, necessary to be careful in preserving health, by due exercise and great temperance; for in sickness the imagination is disturbed, and disagreeable, sometimes terrible, ideas are apt to present themselves. Exercise should precede meals, not immediately follow them; the first promotes, the latter, unless moderate, obstructs digestion. If, after exercise, we feed sparingly, the digestion will be easy and good, the body lightsome, the temper cheerful, and all the animal functions performed agreeably. Sleep, when it follows, will be natural and undisturbed; while indolence, with full feeding, occasions nightmares and horrors inexpressible; we fall from precipices, are assaulted by wild beasts, murderers, and demons, and experience every variety of distress. Observe, however, that the quantities of food and exercise are relative things; those who move much may, and, indeed, ought to, eat more; those who use little exercise should eat little. In general, mankind, since the improvement of cookery, eat about twice as much as nature requires. Suppers are not bad if we have not dined; but restless nights naturally follow hearty suppers after full dinners. Indeed, as there is a difference in constitutions, some rest well after these meals; it costs them only a frightful dream and an apoplexy, after which they sleep till doomsday. Nothing is more common in the newspapers than instances of people who, after eating a hearty supper, are found dead abed in the morning.

Another means of preserving health, to be attended to, is the having a constant supply of fresh air in your bedchamber. It has been a great mistake, the sleeping in rooms exactly closed, and in beds surrounded by curtains. No outward air that may come in to you is so unwholesome as the unchanged air, often breathed, of a close chamber. As boiling water does not grow hotter by longer boiling, if the particles that receive greater heat can escape, so living bodies do not putrefy if the particles, so fast as they become putrid, can be thrown off. Nature expels them by the pores of the skin and the lungs, and in a free, open air they are carried off; but in a close room we receive them again and again, though they become more and more corrupt. A number of persons crowded into a small room thus spoil the air in a few minutes and even render it mortal, as in the Black Hole at Calcutta. A single person is said to spoil only a gallon of air per minute, and therefore requires a longer time to spoil a bedchamber-full; but it is done, however, in proportion, and many putrid disorders hence have their origin. It is recorded of Methusalem, who, being the longest liver, may be supposed to have best preserved his health, that he slept always in the open air; for, when he had lived five hundred years, an angel said to him, "Arise, Methusalem, and build thee a house, for thou shalt live yet five hundred years longer." But Methusalem answered and said, "If I am to live but five hundred years longer, it is not worth while to build me a house; I will sleep in the air, as I have been used to do." Physicians, after having for ages contended that the sick should not be indulged with fresh air, have at length discovered that it may do them good. It is therefore to be hoped that they may in time discover likewise that it is not hurtful to those who are in health, and that we may then be cured of the *aerophoba*, that at present distresses weak minds, and makes them choose to be stifled and poisoned rather than leave open the window of a bedchamber or put down the glass of a coach.

Confined air, when saturated with perspirable matter,[1] will not receive more; and that matter must remain in our bodies and occasion diseases; but it gives some previous notice of its being about to be hurtful, by producing certain uneasiness, slight indeed at first, such as with regard to the lungs is a trifling sensation, and to the pores of the skin a kind of restlessness, which is difficult to describe, and few that feel it know the cause of it. But we may recollect that sometimes, on waking in the night, we have, if warmly covered, found it difficult to get asleep again. We turn often, without finding repose in any position. This fidgetiness (to use a vulgar expression for want of a better) is occasioned wholly by an uneasiness in the skin, owing to the retention of the perspirable matter, the bedclothes having received their quantity, and, being saturated, refusing to take any more. To become sensible of this by an experiment, let a person keep his position in the bed, but throw off the bedclothes, and suffer fresh air to approach the part uncovered of his body; he will then feel that part suddenly refreshed; for the air will immediately relieve the skin, by receiving, licking up, and carrying off, the load of perspirable matter that incommoded it. For every portion of cool air that approaches the warm skin, in receiving its portion of that vapour, receives therewith a degree of heat that rarefies and renders it lighter, when it will be pushed away, with its burden, by cooler and, therefore, heavier fresh air, which for a moment supplies its place, and then, being likewise changed and warmed, gives way to a succeeding quantity. This is the order of nature, to prevent animals being infected by their own perspiration. He will now be sensible of the difference between the part exposed to the air and that which, remaining sunk in the bed, denies the air access; for this part now manifests its uneasiness more distinctly by the comparison, and the seat of the uneasiness is more plainly perceived than when the whole surface of the body was affected by it.

Here, then, is one great and general cause of unpleasing dreams. For when the body is uneasy, the mind will be disturbed by it, and disagreeable ideas of various kinds will in sleep be the natural consequences. The remedies, preventive and curative, follow:

1. By eating moderately (as before advised for health's sake), less perspirable matter is produced in a given time; hence the bedclothes receive it longer before they are saturated, and we may therefore sleep longer before we are made uneasy by their refusing to receive any more.

2. By using thinner and more porous bedclothes, which will suffer the perspirable matter more easily to pass through them, we are less incommoded, such being longer tolerable.

3. When you are awakened by this uneasiness, and find you cannot easily sleep again, get out of bed, beat up and turn your pillow, shake the bedclothes well, with at least twenty shakes, then throw the bed open and leave it to cool; in the mean while, continuing undressed, walk about your chamber till your skin has had time to discharge its load, which it will do sooner as the air may be drier and colder. When you begin to feel the cold air unpleasant, then return to your bed, and you will soon fall asleep, and your sleep will be sweet and pleasant. All the scenes presented to your fancy will be, too, of the pleasing kind. I am often as agreeably entertained with them as by the scenery of an opera. If you happen to be too indolent to get out of bed, you may, instead of it, lift up your bedclothes with one arm and leg, so as to draw in a good deal of fresh air, and, by letting them fall, force it out again. This, repeated twenty times, will so clear them of the perspirable matter they have imbibed, as to permit your sleeping well for some time afterward. But this latter method is not equal to the former.

Those who do not love trouble, and can afford to have two beds, will find great luxury in rising, when they wake in a hot bed, and going into the cool one. Such shifting of beds would also be of great service to persons ill of a fever, as it refreshes and frequently procures sleep. A very large bed, that will admit a removal so distant from the first situation as to be cool and sweet, may in a degree answer the same end.

One or two observations more will conclude this little piece. Care must be taken, when you lie down, to dispose your pillow so as to suit your manner of placing your head, and to be perfectly easy; then place your limbs so as not to bear inconveniently hard upon one another, as, for instance, the joints of your ancles; for, though a bad position may at first give but little pain and be hardly noticed, yet a continuance will render it less tolerable, and the uneasiness may come on while you are asleep, and disturb your imagination. These are the rules of the art. But, though they will generally prove effectual in producing the end intended, there is a case in which the most punctual observance of them will be totally fruitless. I need not mention the case to you, my dear friend, but my account of the art would be imperfect without it. The case is, when the person who desires to have pleasant dreams has not taken care to preserve, what is necessary above all things,

A GOOD CONSCIENCE.

[1] What physicians call perspirable matter is that vapour which passes off from our bodies, from the lungs, and through the pores of the skin. The quantity of this is said to be five eighths of what we eat. —AUTHOR.

## ADVICE TO A YOUNG TRADESMAN.

TO MY FRIEND A. B.

As you have desired it of me, I write the following hints, which have been of service to me, and may, if observed, be so to you.

Remember that *time* is money. He that can earn ten shillings a day by his labour, and goes abroad or sits idle one half of that day, though he spends but sixpence during his diversion or idleness, ought not to reckon *that* the only expense; he has really spent, or, rather, thrown away, five shillings besides.

Remember that *credit* is money. If a man lets his money lie in my hands after it is due, he gives me the interest, or so much as I can make of it during that time. This amounts to a considerable sum where a man has good and large credit, and makes good use of it.

Remember that money is of the prolific, generating nature. Money can beget money, and its offspring can beget more, and so on. Five shillings turned is six, turned again it is seven and threepence, and so on till it becomes a hundred pounds. The more there is of it, the more it produces every turning, so that the profits rise quicker and quicker. He that kills a breeding-sow, destroys all her offspring to the thousandth generation. He that murders a crown, destroys all that it might have produced, even scores of pounds.

Remember that six pounds a year is but a groat a day. For this little sum (which may be daily wasted either in time or expense unperceived) a man of credit may, on his own security, have the constant possession and use of a hundred pounds. So much in stock, briskly turned by an industrious man, produces great advantage.

Remember this saying, *The good paymaster is lord of another man's purse.* He that is known to pay punctually and exactly to the time he promises, may at any time, and on any occasion, raise all the money his friends can spare. This is sometimes of great use. After industry and frugality, nothing contributes more to the raising of a young man in the world than punctuality and justice in all his dealings; therefore never keep borrowed money an hour beyond the time you promised, lest a disappointment shut up your friend's purse for ever.

The most trifling actions that affect a man's credit are to be regarded. The sound of your hammer at five in the morning or nine at night, heard by a creditor, makes him easy six months longer; but if he sees you at a billiard-table, or hears your voice at a tavern when you should be at work, he sends for his money the next day; demands it, before he can receive it, in a lump.

It shows, besides, that you are mindful of what you owe; it makes you appear a careful as well as an honest man, and that still increases your credit.

Beware of thinking all your own that you possess, and of living accordingly. It is a mistake that many people who have credit fall into. To prevent this, keep an exact account for some time both of your expenses and your income. If you take the pains at first to mention particulars, it will have this good effect: you will discover how wonderfully small, trifling expenses mount up to large sums, and will discern what might have been, and may, for the future, be saved, without occasioning any great inconvenience.

In short, the way to wealth, if you desire it, is as plain as the way to market. It depends chiefly on two words, *industry* and *frugality*; that is, waste neither *time* nor *money*, but make the best use of both. Without industry and frugality nothing will do, and with them everything. He that gets all he can honestly, and saves all he gets (necessary expenses excepted), will certainly become *rich*, if that Being who governs the world, to whom all should look for a blessing on their honest endeavours, doth not, in his wise providence, otherwise determine.

AN OLD TRADESMAN.

## RULES OF HEALTH.

Eat and drink such an exact quantity as the constitution of thy body allows of, in reference to the services of the mind.

They that study much ought not to eat so much as those that work hard, their digestion being not so good.

The exact quantity and quality being found out, is to be kept to constantly.

Excess in all other things whatever, as well as in meat and drink, is also to be avoided.

Youth, age, and the sick require a different quantity.

And so do those of contrary complexions; for that which is too much for a phlegmatic man is not sufficient for a choleric.

The measure of food ought to be (as much as possibly may be) exactly proportionable to the quality and condition of the stomach, because the stomach digests it.

That quantity that is sufficient, the stomach can perfectly concoct and digest, and it sufficeth the due nourishment of the body.

A greater quantity of some things may be eaten than of others, some being of lighter digestion than others.

The difficulty lies in finding out an exact measure; but eat for necessity, not pleasure; for lust knows not where necessity ends.

Wouldst thou enjoy a long life, a healthy body, and a vigorous mind, and be acquainted also with the wonderful works of God, labour in the first place to bring thy appetite to reason.

## THE EPHEMERA; AN EMBLEM OF HUMAN LIFE.

### TO MADAME BRILLON, OF PASSY.
### Written in 1778.

You may remember, my dear friend, that when we lately spent that happy day in the delightful garden and sweet society of the Moulin Joly, I stopped a little in one of our walks, and stayed some time behind the company. We had been shown numberless skeletons of a kind of little fly, called an ephemera, whose successive generations, we were told, were bred and expired within the day. I happened to see a living company of them on a leaf, who appeared to be engaged in conversation. You know I understand all the inferior animal tongues. My too great application to the study of them is the best excuse I can give for the little progress I have made in your charming language. I listened, through curiosity, to the discourse of these little creatures; but as they, in their national vivacity, spoke three or four together, I could make but little of their conversation. I found, however, by some broken expressions that I heard now and then, they were disputing warmly on the merit of two foreign musicians, one a *cousin*, the other a *moscheto*; in which dispute they spent their time, seemingly as regardless of the shortness of life as if they had been sure of living a month. Happy people! thought I; you are certainly under a wise, just, and mild government, since you have no public grievances to complain of, nor any subject of contention but the perfections and imperfections of foreign music. I turned my head from them to an old gray-headed one, who was single on another leaf, and talking to himself. Being amused with his soliloquy, I put it down in writing, in hopes it will likewise amuse her to whom I am so much indebted for the most pleasing of all amusements, her delicious company and heavenly harmony.

"It was," said he, "the opinion of learned philosophers of our race, who lived and flourished long before my time, that this vast world, the Moulin Joy, could not itself subsist more than eighteen hours; and I think there was some foundation for that opinion, since, by the apparent motion of the great luminary that gives life to all nature, and which in my time has evidently declined considerably towards the ocean at the end of our earth, it must then finish its course, be extinguished in the waters that surround us, and leave the world in cold and darkness, necessarily producing universal death and destruction. I have lived seven of those hours, a great age, being no less than four hundred and twenty minutes of time. How very few of us continue so long! I have seen generations born, flourish, and expire! My present friends are the children and grandchildren of the friends of my youth, who are now, alas, no more! And I must soon follow them; for, by the course of nature, though still in health, I cannot expect to live above seven or eight minutes longer. What now avails all my toil and labour in amassing honey-dew on this leaf, which I cannot live to enjoy? What the political struggles I have been engaged in for the good of my compatriot inhabitants of this bush, or my philosophical studies for the benefit of our race in general! for, in politics, what can laws do without morals? Our present race of ephemeræ will in a course of minutes become corrupt like those of other and older bushes, and, consequently, as wretched. And in philosophy how small our progress! Alas! art is long and life is short! My friends would comfort me with the idea of a name they say I shall leave behind me; and they tell me I have lived long enough to nature and to glory. But what will fame be to an ephemera who no longer exists? And what will become of all history in the eighteenth hour, when the world itself, even the whole Moulin Joly, shall come to its end and be buried in universal ruin?"

To me, after all my eager pursuits, no solid pleasures now remain but the reflection of a long life spent in meaning well, the sensible conversation of a few good lady ephemeræ, and now and then a kind smile and a tune from the ever amiable *Brillante.*

## THE WHISTLE.

### TO MADAME BRILLON.

Passy, November 10, 1779.

\* \* \* \* \* I am charmed with your description of Paradise, and with your plan of living there; and I approve much of your conclusion, that, in the mean time, we should draw all the good we can from this world. In my opinion, we might all draw more good from it than we do, and suffer less evil, if we would take care not to give too much for *whistles* For to me it seems that most of the unhappy people we meet with are become so by neglect of that caution.

You ask what I mean? You love stories, and will excuse my telling one of myself.

When I was a child of seven years old, my friends, on a holyday, filled my pocket with coppers. I went directly to a shop where they sold toys for children; and, being charmed with the sound of a *whistle* that I met by the way in the hands of another boy, I voluntarily offered and gave all my money for one. I then came home and went whistling all over the house, much pleased with my *whistle,* but disturbing all the family. My brothers, and sisters, and cousins, understanding the bargain I had made, told me I had given four times as much for it as it was worth; put me in mind of what good things I might have bought with the rest of the money; and laughed at me so much for my folly, that I cried with vexation; and the reflection gave me more chagrin than the *whistle* gave me pleasure.

This, however, was afterward of use to me, the impression continuing on my mind; so that often, when I was tempted to buy some unnecessary thing, I said to myself, *Don't give too much for the whistle*; and I saved my money.

As I grew up, came into the world, and observed the actions of men, I thought I met with many, very many, who *gave too much for the whistle.*

When I saw one too ambitious of court favour, sacrificing his time in attendance on levees, his repose, his liberty, his virtue, and perhaps his friends, to attain it, I have said to myself, *This man gives too much for his whistle.*

When I saw another fond of popularity, constantly employing himself in political bustles, neglecting his own affairs, and ruining them by that neglect, *He pays, indeed,* said I, *too much for his whistle.*

If I knew a miser, who gave up every kind of comfortable living, all the pleasure of doing good to others, all the esteem of his fellow-citizens, and the joys of benevolent friendship, for the sake of accumulating wealth, *Poor man,* said I, *you pay too much for your whistle.*

When I met with a man of pleasure, sacrificing every laudable improvement of the mind or of his fortune to mere corporeal sensations, and ruining his health in their pursuit, *Mistaken man,* said I, *you are providing pain for yourself instead of pleasure; you give too much for your whistle.*

If I see one fond of appearance, or fine clothes, fine houses, fine furniture, fine equipages, all above his fortune, for which he contracts debts and ends his days in prison, *Alas!* say I, *he has paid dear, very dear, for his whistle.*

When I see a beautiful, sweet-tempered girl married to an ill-natured brute of a husband, *What a pity,* say I, *that she should pay so much for a whistle!*

In short, I conceive that great part of the miseries of mankind are brought upon them by the false estimates they have made of the value of things, and by their *giving too much for their whistles.*

Yet I ought to have charity for these unhappy people, when I consider that, with all this wisdom of which I am boasting, there are certain things in the world so tempting, for example, the apples of King John, which, happily, are not to be bought; for if they were put to sale by auction, I might very easily be led to ruin myself in the purchase, and find that I had once more given too much for the *whistle.*

Adieu, my dear friend, and believe me ever yours very sincerely and with unalterable affection,

B. Franklin.

# ON LUXURY, IDLENESS, AND INDUSTRY.[2]

It is wonderful how preposterously the affairs of this world are managed. Naturally one would imagine that the interest of a few individuals should give way to general interest; but individuals manage their affairs with so much more application, industry, and address than the public do theirs, that general interest most commonly gives way to particular. We assemble parliaments and councils to have the benefit of their collected wisdom; but we necessarily have, at the same time, the inconvenience of their collected passions, prejudices, and private interests. By the help of these, artful men overpower their wisdom and dupe its possessors: and if we may judge by the acts, *arrêts*, and edicts, all the world over, for regulating commerce, an assembly of great men is the greatest fool upon earth.

I have not yet, indeed, thought of a remedy for luxury. I am not sure that in a great state it is capable of a remedy, nor that the evil is in itself always so great as it is represented. Suppose we include in the definition of luxury all unnecessary expense, and then let us consider whether laws to prevent such expense are possible to be executed in a great country, and whether, if they could be executed, our people generally would be happier, or even richer. Is not the hope of being one day able to purchase and enjoy luxuries a great spur to labour and industry! May not luxury, therefore, produce more than it consumes, if without such a spur people would be, as they are naturally enough inclined to be, lazy and indolent? To this purpose I remember a circumstance. The skipper of a shallop, employed between Cape May and Philadelphia, had done us some small service, for which he refused to be paid. My wife, understanding that he had a daughter, sent her a new-fashioned cap. Three years after, this skipper being at my house with an old farmer of Cape May, his passenger, he mentioned the cap, and how much his daughter had been pleased with it. "But," said he, "it proved a dear cap to our congregation." "How so?" "When my daughter appeared with it at meeting, it was so much admired that all the girls resolved to get such caps from Philadelphia; and my wife and I computed that the whole could not have cost less than a hundred pounds." "True," said the farmer, "but you do not tell all the story. I think the cap was, nevertheless, an advantage to us, for it was the first thing that put our girls upon knitting worsted mittens for sale at Philadelphia, that they might have wherewithal to buy caps and ribands there; and you know that that industry has continued, and is likely to continue, and increase to a much greater value, and answer better purposes." Upon the whole, I was more reconciled to this little piece of luxury, since not only the girls were made happier by having fine caps, but the Philadelphians by the supply of warm mittens.

In our commercial towns upon the seacoast fortunes will occasionally be made. Some of those who grow rich will be prudent, live within bounds, and preserve what they have gained for their posterity; others, fond of showing their wealth, will be extravagant and ruin themselves. Laws cannot prevent this; and perhaps it is not always an evil to the public. A shilling spent idly by a fool may be picked up by a wiser person, who knows better what to do with it. It is, therefore, not lost. A vain, silly fellow builds a fine house, furnishes it richly, lives in it expensively, and in a few years ruins himself; but the masons, carpenters, smiths, and other honest tradesmen have been by his employ assisted in maintaining and raising their families; the farmer has been paid for his labour, and encouraged, and the estate is now in better hands. In some cases, indeed, certain modes of luxury may be a public evil, in the same manner as it is a private one. If there be a nation, for instance, that exports its beef and linen to pay for the importation of claret and porter, while a great part of its people live upon potatoes and wear no shirts, wherein does it differ from the sot, who lets his family starve and sells his clothes to buy drink? Our American commerce is, I confess, a little in this way. We sell our victuals to the Islands for rum and sugar; the substantial necessaries of life for superfluities. But we have plenty, and live well, nevertheless, though, by being soberer, we might be richer.

The vast quantity of forest-land we have yet to clear and put in order for cultivation, will for a long time keep the body of our nation laborious and frugal. Forming an opinion of our people and their manners by what is seen among the inhabitants of the seaports, is judging from an improper sample. The people of the trading towns may be rich and luxurious, while the country possesses all the virtues that tend to promote happiness and public prosperity. Those towns are not much regarded by the country; they are hardly considered as an essential part of the states; and the experience of the last war has shown, that their being in possession of the enemy did not necessarily draw on the subjection of the country, which bravely continued to maintain its freedom and independence notwithstanding.

It has been computed by some political arithmetician, that if every man and woman would work for four hours every day on something useful, that labour would produce sufficient to procure all the necessaries of life, want and misery would be banished out of the world, and the rest of the twenty-four hours might be leisure and pleasure.

What occasions, then, so much want and misery? It is the employment of men and women in works that produce neither the necessaries nor conveniences of life; who, with those who do nothing, consume necessaries raised by the laborious. To explain this.

The first elements of wealth are obtained by labour, from the earth and waters. I have land and raise corn. With this, if I feed a family that does nothing, my corn will be consumed, and at the end of the year I shall be no richer than I was at the beginning. But if, while I feed them, I employ them, some in spinning, others in making bricks, &c., for building, the value of my corn will be arrested and remain with me, and at the end of the year we may all be better clothed and better lodged. And if, instead of employing a man I feed in making bricks, I employ him in fiddling for me, the corn he eats is gone, and no part of his manufacture remains to augment the wealth and convenience of the family; I shall, therefore, be the poorer for this fiddling man, unless the rest of my family work more or eat less, to make up the deficiency he occasions.

Look round the world and see the millions employed in doing nothing, or in something that amounts to nothing, when the necessaries and conveniences of life are in question. What is the bulk of commerce, for which we fight and destroy each other, but the toil of millions for superfluities, to the great hazard and loss of many lives by the constant dangers of the sea? How much labour is spent in building and fitting great ships to go to China and Arabia for tea and coffee, to the West Indies for sugar, to America for tobacco? These things can not be called the necessaries of life, for our ancestors lived very comfortably without them.

A question may be asked. Could all these people, now employed in raising, making, or carrying superfluities, be subsisted by raising necessaries? I think they might. The world is large, and a great part of it still uncultivated. Many hundred millions of acres in Asia, Africa, and America are still in a forest, and a great deal even in Europe. On a hundred acres of this forest a man might become a substantial farmer; and a hundred thousand men, employed in clearing each his hundred acres, would hardly brighten a spot big enough to be visible from the moon, unless with Herschel's telescope; so vast are the regions still in wood.

It is, however, some comfort to reflect, that, upon the whole, the quantity of industry and prudence among mankind exceeds the quantity of idleness and folly. Hence the increase of good buildings, farms cultivated, and populous cities filled with wealth, all over Europe, which a few ages since were only to be found on the coast of the Mediterranean; and this, notwithstanding the mad wars continually raging, by which are often destroyed in one year the works of many years' peace. So that we may hope the luxury of a few merchants on the coast will not be the ruin of America.

One reflection more, and I will end this long, rambling letter. Almost all the parts of our bodies require some expense. The feet demand shoes; the legs stockings; and the rest of the body clothing; and the belly a good deal of victuals. Our eyes, though exceedingly useful, ask, when reasonable, only the cheap assistance of spectacles, which could not much impair our finances. But the eyes of other people are the eyes that ruin us. If all but myself were blind, I should want neither fine clothes, fine houses, nor fine furniture.

[2] From a letter to Mr. Benjamin Vaughan, dated at Passy, July 26th, 1784.

## ON TRUTH AND FALSEHOOD.

Veritas luce clarior.[3]

A friend of mine was the other day cheapening some trifles at a shopkeeper's, and after a few words they agreed on a price. At the tying up of the parcels he had purchased, the mistress of the shop told him that people were growing very hard, for she actually lost by everything she sold. How, then, is it possible, said my friend, that you can keep on your business? Indeed, sir, answered she, I must of necessity shut my doors, had I not a very great trade. The reason, said my friend (with a sneer), is admirable.

There are a great many retailers who falsely imagine that being *historical* (the modern phrase for lying) is much for their advantage; and some of them have a saying, *that it is a pity lying is a sin, it is so useful in trade*; though if they would examine into the reason why a number of shopkeepers raise considerable estates, while others who have set out with better fortunes have become bankrupts, they would find that the former made up with truth, diligence, and probity, what they were deficient of in stock; while the latter have been found guilty of imposing on such customers as they found had no skill in the quality of their goods.

The former character raises a credit which supplies the want of fortune, and their fair dealing brings them customers; whereas none will return to buy of him by whom he has been once imposed upon. If people in trade would judge rightly, we might buy blindfolded, and they would save, both to themselves and customers, the unpleasantness of *haggling*.

Though there are numbers of shopkeepers who scorn the mean vice of lying, and whose word may very safely be relied on, yet there are too many who will endeavour, and backing their falsities with asseverations, pawn their salvation to raise their prices.

As example works more than precept, and my sole view being the good and interest of my countrymen, whom I could wish to see without any vice or folly, I shall offer an example of the veneration bestowed on truth and abhorrence of falsehood among the ancients.

Augustus, triumphing over Mark Antony and Cleopatra, among other captives who accompanied them, brought to Rome a priest of about sixty years old; the senate being informed that this man had never been detected in a falsehood, and was believed never to have told a lie, not only restored him to liberty, but made him a high priest, and caused a statue to be erected to his honour. The priest thus honoured was an Egyptian, and an enemy to Rome, but his virtue removed all obstacles.

Pamphilius was a Roman citizen, whose body upon his death was forbidden sepulture, his estate was confiscated, his house razed, and his wife and children banished the Roman territories, wholly for his having been a notorious and inveterate liar.

Could there be greater demonstrations of respect for truth than these of the Romans, who elevated an enemy to the greatest honours, and exposed the family of a citizen to the greatest contumely?

There can be no excuse for lying, neither is there anything equally despicable and dangerous as a liar, no man being safe who associates with him; for *he who will lie will swear to it*, says the proverb; and such a one may endanger my life, turn my family out of doors, and ruin my reputation, whenever he shall find it his interest; and if a man will lie and swear to it in his shop to obtain a trifle, why should we doubt his doing so when he may hope to make a fortune by his perjury? The crime is in itself so mean, that to call a man a liar is esteemed everywhere an affront not to be forgiven.

If any have lenity enough to allow the dealers an excuse for this bad practice, I believe they will allow none for the gentleman who is addicted to this vice; and must look upon him with contempt. That the world does so, is visible by the derision with which his name is treated whenever it is mentioned.

The philosopher Epimenides gave the Rhodians this description of Truth. She is the companion of the gods, the joy of heaven, the light of the earth, the pedestal of justice, and the basis of good policy.

Eschines told the same people, that truth was a virtue without which force was enfeebled, justice corrupted; humility became dissimulation, patience intolerable, chastity a dissembler, liberty lost, and pity superfluous.

Pharmanes the philosopher told the Romans that truth was the centre on which all things rested: a chart to sail by, a remedy for all evils, and a light to the whole world.

Anaxarchus, speaking of truth, said it was health incapable of sickness, life not subject to death, an elixir that healeth all, a sun not to be obscured, a moon without eclipse, an herb which never withereth, a gate that is never closed, and a path which never fatigues the traveller.

But if we are blind to the beauties of truth, it is astonishing that we should not open our eyes to the inconvenience of falsity. A man given to romance must be always on his guard, for fear of contradicting and exposing himself to derision; for the most *historical* would avoid the odious character, though it is impossible, with the utmost circumspection, to travel long on this route without detection, and shame and confusion follow. Whereas he who is a votary of truth never hesitates for an answer, has never to rack his invention to make the sequel quadrate with the beginning of his story, nor obliged to burden his memory with minute circumstances, since truth speaks easily what it recollects, and repeats openly and frequently without varying facts, which liars cannot always do, even though gifted with a good memory.

[3] Truth is brighter than light.

## NECESSARY HINTS TO THOSE THAT WOULD BE RICH.

*Written Anno 1736.*

The use of money is all the advantage there is in having money.

For six pounds a year you may have the use of one hundred pounds, provided you are a man of known prudence and honesty.

He that spends a groat a day idly, spends idly above six pounds a year, which is the price for the use of one hundred pounds.

He that wastes idly a groat's worth of his time per day, one day with another, wastes the privilege of using one hundred pounds each day.

He that idly loses five shillings' worth of time, loses five shillings, and might as prudently throw five shillings into the sea.

He that loses five shillings, not only loses that sum, but all the advantage that might be made by turning it in dealing, which, by the time that a young man becomes old, will amount to a considerable sum of money.

Again: he that sells upon credit, asks a price for what he sells equivalent to the principal and interest of his money for the time he is to be kept out of it; therefore, he that buys upon credit pays interest for what he buys, and he that pays ready money might let that money out to use: so that he that possesses anything he bought, pays interest for the use of it.

Yet, in buying goods, it is best to pay ready money, because he that sells upon credit expects to lose five per cent. by bad debts; therefore he charges, on all he sells upon credit, an advance that shall make up that deficiency.

Those who pay for what they buy upon credit, pay their share of this advance.

He that pays ready money escapes, or may escape, that charge.

>A penny saved is twopence clear,
>A pin a day's a groat a year.

---

## THE WAY TO MAKE MONEY PLENTY IN EVERY MAN'S POCKET.

At this time, when the general complaint is that "money is scarce," it will be an act of kindness to inform the moneyless how they may re-enforce their pockets. I will acquaint them with the true secret of money-catching, the certain way to fill empty purses, and how to keep them always full. Two simple rules, well observed, will do the business.

First, let honesty and industry be thy constant companions; and,

Secondly, spend one penny less than thy clear gains.

Then shall thy hidebound pocket soon begin to thrive, and will never again cry with the empty bellyache: neither will creditors insult thee, nor want oppress, nor hunger bite, nor nakedness freeze thee. The whole hemisphere will shine brighter, and pleasure spring up in every corner of thy heart. Now, therefore, embrace these rules and be happy. Banish the bleak winds of sorrow from thy mind and live independent. Then shalt thou be a man and not hide thy face at the approach of the rich nor suffer the pain of feeling little when the sons of fortune walk at thy right hand: for independence, whether with little or much, is good fortune and placeth thee on even ground with the proudest of the golden fleece. Oh, then, be wise, and let industry walk with thee in the morning, and attend thee until thou reachest the evening hour for rest. Let honesty be as the breath of thy soul, and never forget to have a penny when all thy expenses are enumerated and paid: then shalt thou reach the point of happiness, and independence shall be thy shield and buckler, thy helmet and crown; then shall thy soul walk upright, nor stoop to the silken wretch because he hath riches, nor pocket an abuse because the hand which offers it wears a ring set with diamonds.

# THE HANDSOME AND DEFORMED LEG.

There are two sorts of people in the world, who, with equal degrees of health and wealth, and the other comforts of life, become, the one happy and the other miserable. This arises very much from the different views in which they consider things, persons, and events, and the effect of those different views upon their own minds.

In whatever situation men can be placed, they may find conveniences and inconveniences; in whatever company, they may find persons and conversation more or less pleasing; at whatever table, they may meet with meats and drinks of better and worse taste, dishes better and worse dressed; in whatever climate, they will find good and bad weather; under whatever government, they may find good and bad laws, and good and bad administration of those laws; in whatever poem or work of genius, they may see faults and beauties; in almost every face and every person, they may discover fine features and defects, good and bad qualities.

Under these circumstances, the two sorts of people above mentioned fix their attention, those who are disposed to be happy on the conveniences of things, the pleasant parts of conversation, the well-dressed dishes, the goodness of the wines, the fine weather, &c., and enjoy all with cheerfulness. Those who are to be unhappy, think and speak only of the contraries. Hence they are continually discontented themselves, and by their remarks sour the pleasures of society, offend personally many people, and make themselves everywhere disagreeable. If this turn of mind was founded in nature, such unhappy persons would be the more to be pitied. But as the disposition to criticise and to be disgusted is, perhaps, taken up originally by imitation, and is, unawares, grown into a habit, which, though at present strong, may nevertheless be cured; when those who have it are convinced of its bad effects on their felicity, I hope this little admonition may be of service to them, and put them on changing a habit which, though in the exercise it is chiefly an act of imagination, yet has serious consequences in life, as it brings on real griefs and misfortunes. For, as many are offended by, and nobody loves this sort of people, no one shows them more than the most common civility and respect, and scarcely that; and this frequently puts them out of humour, and draws them into disputes and contentions. If they aim at obtaining some advantage in rank or fortune, nobody wishes them success, or will stir a step or speak a word to favour their pretensions. If they incur public censure or disgrace, no one will defend or excuse, and many join to aggravate their misconduct, and render them completely odious. If these people will not change this bad habit, and condescend to be pleased with what is pleasing, without fretting themselves and others about the contraries, it is good for others to avoid an acquaintance with them, which is always disagreeable, and sometimes very inconvenient, especially when one finds one's self entangled in their quarrels.

An old philosophical friend of mine was grown, from experience, very cautious in this particular, and carefully avoided any intimacy with such people. He had, like other philosophers, a thermometer to show him the heat of the weather, and a barometer to mark when it was likely to prove good or bad; but there being no instrument invented to discover, at first sight, this unpleasing disposition in a person, he for that purpose made use of his legs; one of which was remarkably handsome, the other, by some accident, crooked and deformed. If a stranger, at the first interview, regarded his ugly leg more than his handsome one, he doubted him. If he spoke of it, and took no notice of the handsome leg, that was sufficient to determine my philosopher to have no farther acquaintance with him. Everybody has not this two-legged instrument; but every one, with a little attention, may observe signs of that carping, fault-finding disposition, and take the same resolution of avoiding the acquaintance of those infected with it. I therefore advise those critical, querulous, discontented, unhappy people, that, if they wish to be respected and beloved by others and happy in themselves, they should *leave off looking at the ugly leg.*

## ON HUMAN VANITY.

Mr. Franklin, Meeting with the following curious little piece the other day, I send it to you to republish, as it is now in very few hands. There is something so elegant in the imagination, conveyed in so delicate a style, and accompanied with a moral so just and elevated, that it must yield great pleasure and instruction to every mind of real taste and virtue.

*Cicero*, in the first of his Tusculan questions, finely exposes the vain judgment we are apt to form of human life compared with eternity. In illustrating this argument, he quotes a passage of natural history from Aristotle, concerning a species of insects on the banks of the river Hypanis, that never outlive the day in which they are born.

To pursue the thought of this elegant writer, let us suppose one of the most robust of these *Hypanians*, so famed in history, was in a manner coeval with time itself; that he began to exist at break of day, and that, from the uncommon strength of his constitution, he has been able to show himself active in life, through the numberless minutes of ten or twelve hours. Through so long a series of seconds, he must have acquired vast wisdom in his way, from observation and experience.

He looks upon his fellow-creatures who died about noon to be happily delivered from the many inconveniences of old age; and can, perhaps, recount to his great grandson a surprising tradition of actions before any records of their nation were extant. The young swarm of Hypanians, who may be advanced one hour in life, approach his person with respect, and listen to his improving discourse. Everything he says will seem wonderful to their short lived generation. The compass of a day will be esteemed the whole duration of time; and the first dawn of light will, in their chronology, be styled the great era of their creation.

Let us now suppose this venerable insect, this *Nestor* of *Hypania*, should, a little before his death, and about sunset, send for all his descendants, his friends and his acquaintances, out of the desire he may have to impart his last thoughts to them, and to admonish them with his departing breath. They meet, perhaps, under the spacious shelter of a mushroom, and the dying sage addresses himself to them after the following manner:

"Friends and fellow-citizens! I perceive the longest life must, however, end: the period of mine is now at hand; neither do I repine at my fate, since my great age has become a burden to me, and there is nothing new to me under the sun: the changes and revolutions I have seen in my country, the manifold private misfortunes to which we are all liable, the fatal diseases incident to our race, have abundantly taught me this lesson, that no happiness can be secure and lasting which is placed in things that are out of our power. Great is the uncertainty of life! A whole brood of our infants have perished in a moment by a keen blast! Shoals of our straggling youth have been swept into the ocean by an unexpected breeze! What wasteful desolation have we not suffered from the deluge of a sudden shower! Our strongest holds are not proof against a storm of hail, and even a dark cloud damps the very stoutest heart.

"I have lived in the first ages, and conversed with insects of a larger size and stronger make, and, I must add, of greater virtue than any can boast of in the present generation. I must conjure you to give yet further credit to my latest words, when I assure you that yonder sun, which now appears westward, beyond the water, and seems not to be far distant from the earth, in my remembrance stood in the middle of the sky, and shot his beams directly down upon us. The world was much more enlightened in those ages, and the air much warmer. Think it not dotage in me if I affirm that glorious being moves: I saw his first setting out in the east, and I began my race of life near the time when he began his immense career. He has for several ages advanced along the sky with vast heat and unparalleled brightness; but now, by his declination and a sensible decay, more especially of late, in his vigour, I foresee that all nature must fall in a little time, and that the creation will lie buried in darkness in less than a century of minutes.

"Alas! my friends, how did I once flatter myself with the hopes of abiding here forever! how magnificent are the cells which I hollowed out for myself! what confidence did I repose in the firmness and spring of my joints, and in the strength of my pinions! *But I have lived long enough to nature, and even to glory.* Neither will any of you, whom I leave behind, have equal satisfaction in life, in the dark declining age which I see is already begun."

Thus far this agreeable unknown writer—too agreeable, we may hope, to remain always concealed. The fine allusion to the character of *Julius Cæsar*, whose words he has put into the mouth of this illustrious son of *Hypanis*, is perfectly just and beautiful, and aptly points out the moral of this inimitable piece, the design of which would have been quite perverted, had a virtuous character, a *Cato* or a *Cicero*, been made choice of to have been turned into ridicule. Had this *life of a day* been represented as employed in the exercise of virtue, it would have an equal dignity with a life of any limited duration, and, according to the exalted sentiments of Tully, would have been preferable to an immortality filled with all the pleasures of sense, if void of those of a higher kind: but as the views of this vainglorious insect were confined within the narrow circle of his own existence, as he only boasts the magnificent cells he has built and the length of happiness he has enjoyed, he is the proper emblem of all such insects of the human race, whose ambition does not extend beyond the like narrow limits; and notwithstanding the splendour they appear in at present, they will no more deserve the regard of posterity than the butterflies of the last spring. In vain has history been taken up in describing the numerous swarms of this mischievous species which has infested the earth in the successive ages: now it is worth the inquiry of the virtuous, whether the *Rhine* or the *Adige* may not, perhaps, swarm with them at present, as much as the banks of the *Hypanis*; or whether that silver rivulet, the *Thames*, may not show a specious molehill, covered with inhabitants of the like dignity and importance. The busy race of beings attached to these fleeting enjoyments are indeed all of them engaged in the pursuit of happiness, and it is owing to their imperfect notions of it that they stop so far short in their pursuit. The present prospect of pleasure seems to bound their views, and the more distant scenes of happiness, when what they now propose shall be attained, do not strike their imagination. It is a great stupidity or thoughtlessness not to perceive that the happiness of rational creatures is inseparably connected with immortality. Creatures only endowed with sensation may in a low sense be reputed happy, so long as their sensations are pleasing; and if these pleasing sensations are commensurate with the time of their existence, this measure of happiness is complete. But such beings as are endowed with *thought* and *reflection* cannot be made happy by any limited term of happiness, how great soever its duration may be. The more exquisite and more valuable their enjoyments are, the more painful must be the thought that they are to have an end; and this pain of expectation must be continually increasing, the nearer the end approaches. And if these beings are themselves immortal, and yet insecure of the continuance of their happiness, the case is far worse, since an eternal void of delight, if not to say a state of misery, must succeed. It would be here of no moment, whether the time of their happiness were measured by *days* or *hours*, by *months* or *years*, or by *periods* of the most immeasurable length: these swiftly-flowing streams bear no proportion to that ocean of infinity where they must finish their course. The longest duration of finite happiness avails nothing when it is past: nor can the memory of it have any other effect than to renew a perpetual pining after pleasures never to return; and since virtue is the only pledge and security of a happy immortality, the folly of sacrificing it to any temporal advantage, how important soever they may appear, must be infinitely great, and cannot but leave behind it an eternal regret.

## ON SMUGGLING, AND ITS VARIOUS SPECIES.

Sir,—There are many people that would be thought, and even think themselves, *honest* men, who fail nevertheless in particular points of honesty; deviating from that character sometimes by the prevalence of mode or custom, and sometimes through mere inattention, so that their *honesty* is partial only, and not *general* or universal. Thus one who would scorn to overreach you in a bargain, shall make no scruple of tricking you a little now and then at cards: another, that plays with the utmost fairness, shall with great freedom cheat you in the sale of a horse. But there is no kind of dishonesty into which otherwise good people more easily and frequently fall, than that of defrauding government of its revenues by smuggling when they have an opportunity, or encouraging smugglers by buying their goods.

I fell into these reflections the other day, on hearing two gentlemen of reputation discoursing about a small estate, which one of them was inclined to sell and the other to buy; when the seller, in recommending the place, remarked, that its situation was very advantageous on this account, that, being on the seacoast in a smuggling country, one had frequent opportunities of buying many of the expensive articles used in a family (such as tea, coffee, chocolate, brandy, wines, cambrics, Brussels laces, French silks, and all kinds of India goods) 20, 30, and, in some articles, 50 *per cent.* cheaper than they could be had in the more interior parts, of traders that paid duty. The other *honest* gentleman allowed this to be an advantage, but insisted that the seller, in the advanced price he demanded on that account, rated the advantage much above its value. And neither of them seemed to think dealing with smugglers a practice that an *honest* man (provided he got his goods cheap) had the least reason to be ashamed of.

At a time when the load of our public debt, and the heavy expense of maintaining our fleets and armies to be ready for our defence on occasion, makes it necessary not only to continue old taxes, but often to look out for new ones, perhaps it may not be unuseful to state this matter in a light that few seem to have considered it in.

The people of Great Britain, under the happy constitution of this country, have a privilege few other countries enjoy, that of choosing the third branch of the legislature, which branch has alone the power of regulating their taxes. Now, whenever the government finds it necessary for the common benefit, advantage, and safety of the nation, for the security of our liberties, property, religion, and everything that is dear to us, that certain sums shall be yearly raised by taxes, duties, &c., and paid into the public treasury, thence to be dispensed by government for those purposes, ought not every *honest man* freely and willingly to pay his just proportion of this necessary expense? Can he possibly preserve a right to that character, if by fraud, stratagem, or contrivance, he avoids that payment in whole or in part?

What should we think of a companion who, having supped with his friends at a tavern, and partaken equally of the joys of the evening with the rest of us, would nevertheless contrive by some artifice to shift his share of the reckoning upon others, in order to go off scot-free? If a man who practised this would, when detected, be deemed and called a scoundrel, what ought he to be called who can enjoy all the inestimable benefits of public society, and yet, by smuggling or dealing with smugglers, contrive to evade paying his just share of the expense, as settled by his own representatives in parliament, and wrongfully throw it upon his honest and, perhaps, much poorer neighbours? He will, perhaps, be ready to tell me that he does not wrong his neighbours; he scorns the imputation; he only cheats the king a little, who is very able to bear it. This, however, is a mistake. The public treasure is the treasure of the nation, to be applied to national purposes. And when a duty is laid for a particular public and necessary purpose, if, through smuggling, that duty falls short of raising the sum required, and other duties must therefore be laid to make up the deficiency, all the additional sum laid by the new duties and paid by other people, though it should amount to no more than a halfpenny or a farthing per head, is so much actually picked out of the pockets of those other people by the smugglers and their abettors and encouragers. Are they, then, any better or other than pickpockets? and what mean, low, rascally pickpockets must those be that can pick pockets for halfpence and for farthings?

I would not, however, be supposed to allow, in what I have just said, that cheating the king is a less offence against honesty than cheating the public. The king and the public, in this case, are different names for the same thing; but if we consider the king distinctly it will not lessen the crime: it is no justification of a robbery, that the person robbed was rich and able to bear it. The king has as much right to justice as the meanest of his subjects; and as he is truly the common *father* of his people, those that rob him fall under the Scripture we pronounced against the son *that robbeth his father and saith it is no sin*.

Mean as this practice is, do we not daily see people of character and fortune engaged in it for trifling advantages to themselves? Is any lady ashamed to request of a gentleman of her acquaintance, that, when he returns from abroad, he would smuggle her home a piece of silk or lace from France or Flanders? Is any gentleman ashamed to undertake and execute the commission? Not in the least. They will talk of it freely, even before others whose pockets they are thus contriving to pick by this piece of knavery.

Among other branches of the revenue, that of the post office is, by a late law, appropriated to the discharge of our public debt, to defray the expenses of the state. None but members of parliament and a few public officers have now a right to avoid, by a frank, the payment of postage. When any letter, not written by them or on their business, is franked by any of them, it is a hurt to the revenue, an injury which they must now take the pains to conceal by writing the whole superscription themselves. And yet such is our insensibility to justice in this particular, that nothing is more common than to see, even in a reputable company, a *very honest* gentleman or lady declare his or her intention to cheat the nation of threepence by a frank, and, without blushing, apply to one of the very legislators themselves, with a modest request that he would be pleased to become an accomplice in the crime and assist in the perpetration.

There are those who, by these practices, take a great deal in a year out of the public purse, and put the money into their own private pockets. If, passing through a room where public treasure is deposited, a man takes the opportunity of clandestinely pocketing and carrying off a guinea, is he not truly and properly a thief? And if another evades paying into the treasury a guinea he ought to pay in, and applies it to his own use, when he knows it belongs to the public as much as that which has been paid in, what difference is there in the nature of the crime or the baseness of committing it?

## REMARKS CONCERNING THE SAVAGES OF NORTH AMERICA.

Savages we call them, because their manners differ from ours, which we think the perfection of civility; they think the same of theirs.

Perhaps, if we could examine the manners of different nations with impartiality, we should find no people so rude as to be without any rules of politeness, nor any so polite as not to have some remains of rudeness.

The Indian men, when young, are hunters and warriors; when old, counsellors; for all their government is by the council or advice of the sages. There is no force, there are no prisons, no officers to compel obedience or inflict punishment. Hence they generally study oratory, the best speaker having the most influence. The Indian women till the ground, dress the food, nurse and bring up the children, and preserve and hand down to posterity the memory of public transactions. These employments of men and women are accounted natural and honourable. Having few artificial wants, they have abundance of leisure for improvement by conversation. Our laborious manner of life, compared with theirs, they esteem slavish and base; and the learning on which we value ourselves, they regard as frivolous and useless. An instance of this occurred at the treaty of Lancaster, in Pennsylvania, anno 1744, between the government of Virginia and the Six Nations. After the principal business was settled, the commissioners from Virginia acquainted the Indians, by a speech, that there was at Williamsburgh a college, with a fund for educating Indian youth; and that, if the chiefs of the Six Nations would send down half a dozen of their sons to that college, the government would take care that they should be well provided for, and instructed in all the learning of the white people. It is one of the Indian rules of politeness not to answer a public proposition the same day that it is made; they think it would be treating it as a light matter, and that they show it respect by taking time to consider it, as of a matter important. They therefore deferred their answer till the day following, when their speaker began by expressing their deep sense of the kindness of the Virginia government in making them that offer; "for we know," says he, "that you highly esteem the kind of learning taught in those colleges, and that the maintenance of our young men, while with you, would be very expensive to you. We are convinced, therefore, that you mean to do us good by your proposal; and we thank you heartily. But you, who are wise, must know that different nations have different conceptions of things; and you will therefore not take it amiss if our ideas of this kind of education happen not to be the same with yours. We have had some experience of it: several of our young people were formerly brought up at the colleges of the northern provinces; they were instructed in all your sciences; but when they came back to us, they were bad runners, ignorant of every means of living in the woods, unable to bear either cold or hunger, knew neither how to build a cabin, take a deer, nor kill an enemy, spoke our language imperfectly, were therefore neither fit for hunters, warriors, nor counsellors; they were totally good for nothing. We are, however, not the less obliged by your kind offer, though we decline accepting it; and, to show our grateful sense of it, if the gentlemen of Virginia will send us a dozen of their sons, we will take great care of their education, instruct them in all we know, and make *men* of them."

Having frequent occasions to hold public councils, they have acquired great order and decency in conducting them. The old men sit in the foremost ranks, the warriors in the next, and the women and children in the hindmost. The business of the women is to take exact notice of what passes, imprint it in their memories, for they have no writing, and communicate it to their children. They are the records of the council, and they preserve the tradition of the stipulations in treaties a hundred years back; which, when we compare with our writings, we always find exact. He that would speak, rises. The rest observe a profound silence. When he has finished and sits down, they leave him five or six minutes to recollect, that, if he has omitted anything he intended to say, or has anything to add, he may rise again and deliver it. To interrupt another, even in common conversation, is reckoned highly indecent. How different this is from the conduct of a polite British House of Commons, where scarce a day passes without some confusion that makes the speaker hoarse in calling *to order*; and how different from the mode of conversation in many polite companies of Europe, where, if you do not deliver your sentence with great rapidity, you are cut off in the middle of it by the impatient loquacity of those you converse with, and never suffered to finish it!

The politeness of these savages in conversation is indeed carried to excess, since it does not permit them to contradict or deny the truth of what is asserted in their presence. By this means they indeed avoid disputes, but then it becomes difficult to know their minds, or what impression you make upon them. The missionaries who have attempted to convert them to Christianity all complain of this as one of the great difficulties of their mission. The

Indians hear with patience the truths of the gospel explained to them, and give their usual tokens of assent and approbation: you would think they were convinced. No such matter. It is mere civility.

A Swedish minister, having assembled the chiefs of the Susquehanna Indians, made a sermon to them, acquainting them with the principal historical facts on which our religion is founded; such as the fall of our first parents by eating an apple; the coming of Christ to repair the mischief; his miracles and sufferings, &c. When he had finished, an Indian orator stood up to thank him. "What you have told us," says he, "is all very good. We are much obliged by your kindness in coming so far to tell us those things which you have heard from your mothers. In return, I will tell you some of those we have heard from ours.

"In the beginning, our fathers had only the flesh of animals to subsist on, and if their hunting was unsuccessful, they were starving. Two of our young hunters, having killed a deer, made a fire in the woods to broil some parts of it. When they were about to satisfy their hunger, they beheld a beautiful young woman descend from the clouds, and seat herself on that hill which you see yonder among the Blue Mountains. They said to each other, it is a spirit that perhaps has smelt our broiling venison, and wishes to eat of it: let us offer some to her. They presented her with the tongue: she was pleased with the taste of it, and said, Your kindness shall be rewarded; come to this place after thirteen moons, and you shall find something that will be of great benefit in nourishing you and your children to the latest generations. They did so, and, to their surprise, found plants they had never seen before, but which, from that ancient time, have been constantly cultivated among us, to our great advantage. Where her right hand had touched the ground, they found maize; where her left hand had touched it, they found kidney-beans; and where she had sat on it, they found tobacco." The good missionary, disgusted with this idle tale, said, "What I delivered to you were sacred truths, but what you tell me is mere fable, fiction, and falsehood." The Indian, offended, replied, "My brother, it seems your friends have not done you justice in your education; they have not well instructed you in the rules of common civility. You saw that we, who understand and practise those rules, believed all your stories; why do you refuse to believe ours?"

When any of them come into our towns, our people are apt to crowd around them, gaze upon them, and incommode them where they desire to be private; this they esteem great rudeness, and the effect of the want of instruction in the rules of civility and good manners. "We have," say they "as much curiosity as you; and when you come into our towns, we wish for opportunities of looking at you; but for this purpose, we hide ourselves behind bushes, where you are to pass, and never intrude ourselves into your company."

Their manner of entering one another's villages has likewise its rules. It is reckoned uncivil in travelling strangers to enter a village abruptly, without giving notice of their approach. Therefore, as soon as they arrive within hearing, they stop and halloo, remaining there till invited to enter. Two old men usually come out to them and lead them in. There is in every village a vacant dwelling called the strangers' house. Here they are placed, while the old men go round from hut to hut, acquainting the inhabitants that strangers are arrived, who are probably hungry and weary; and every one sends them what he can spare of victuals, and skins to repose on. When the strangers are refreshed, pipes and tobacco are brought, and then, but not before, conversation begins, with inquiries who they are, whither bound, what news, &c., and it usually ends with offers of service if the strangers have occasion for guides, or any necessaries for continuing their journey; and nothing is exacted for the entertainment.

## ON FREEDOM OF SPEECH AND THE PRESS.

Freedom of speech is a principal pillar of a free government: when this support is taken away, the constitution of a free society is dissolved, and tyranny is erected on its ruins. Republics and limited monarchies derive their strength and vigour from a popular examination into the actions of the magistrates; this privilege, in all ages, has been, and always will be, abused. The best of men could not escape the censure and envy of the times they lived in. Yet this evil is not so great as it may appear at first sight. A magistrate who sincerely aims at the good of society will always have the inclinations of a great majority on his side, and an impartial posterity will not fail to render him justice.

Those abuses of the freedom of speech are the exercises of liberty. They ought to be repressed; but to whom dare we commit the care of doing it? An evil magistrate, intrusted with power to *punish for words*, would be armed with a weapon the most destructive and terrible. Under pretence of pruning off the exuberant branches, he would be apt to destroy the tree.

It is certain that he who robs another of his moral reputation, more richly merits a gibbet than if he had plundered him of his purse on the highway. *Augustus Cæsar*, under the specious pretext of preserving the character of the Romans from defamation, introduced the law whereby libelling was involved in the penalties of treason against the state. This law established his tyranny; and for one mischief which it prevented, ten thousand evils, horrible and afflicting, sprung up in its place. Thenceforward every person's life and fortune depended on the vile breath of informers. The construction of words being arbitrary, and left to the decision of the judges, no man could write or open his mouth without being in danger of forfeiting his head.

One was put to death for inserting in his history the praises of Brutus. Another for styling Cassius the last of the Romans. Caligula valued himself for being a notable dancer; and to deny that he excelled in that manly accomplishment was high treason. This emperor raised his horse, the name of which was *Incitatus*, to the dignity of consul; and though history is silent, I do not question but it was a capital crime to show the least contempt for that high officer of state! Suppose, then, any one had called the prime minister a *stupid animal*, the emperor's council might argue that the malice of the libel was the more aggravated by its being true, and, consequently, more likely to excite the *family of this illustrious magistrate* to a breach of the peace or to acts of revenge. Such a prosecution would to us appear ridiculous; yet, if we may rely upon tradition, there have been formerly proconsuls in America, though of more malicious dispositions, hardly superior in understanding to the consul *Incitatus*, and who would have thought themselves libelled to be called by their *proper names*.

*Nero* piqued himself on his fine voice and skill in music: no doubt a laudable ambition! He performed in public, and carried the prize of excellence. It was afterward resolved by all the judges as good law, that whosoever would *insinuate* the least doubt of Nero's pre-eminence in the *noble art of fiddling* ought to be deemed a traitor to the state.

By the help of inferences and innuendoes, treasons multiplied in a prodigious manner. Grief was treason: a lady of noble birth was put to death for bewailing the death of her *murdered son*: silence was declared an *overt act* to prove the treasonable purposes of the heart: looks were construed into treason: a serene, open aspect was an evidence that the person was pleased with the calamities that befel the emperor: a severe, thoughtful countenance was urged against the man that wore it as a proof of his plotting against the state: *dreams* were often made capital offences. A new species of informers went about Rome, insinuating themselves into all companies to fish out their dreams, which the priests (oh nefarious wickedness!) interpreted into high treason. The Romans were so terrified by this strange method of juridical and penal process, that, far from discovering their dreams, they durst not own that they slept. In this terrible situation, when every one had so much cause to fear, even *fear* itself was made a crime. Caligula, when he put his brother to death, gave it as a reason to the Senate that the youth was afraid of being murdered. To be eminent in any virtue, either civil or military, was the greatest crime a man could be guilty of. *O virtutes certissemum exitium.*[4]

These were some of the effects of the Roman law against libelling: those of the British kings that aimed at despotic power or the oppression of the subject, continually encouraged prosecutions for words.

Henry VII., a prince mighty in politics, procured that act to be passed whereby the jurisdiction of the Star Chamber was confirmed and extended. Afterward Empson and Dudley, two voracious dogs of prey, under the protection of this high court, exercised the most merciless acts of oppression. The subjects were terrified from uttering their griefs while they saw the thunder of the Star Chamber pointed at their heads. This caution, however, could not prevent several dangerous tumults and insurrections; for when the tongues of the people are restrained, they commonly discharge their resentments by a more dangerous organ, and break out into open acts of violence.

During the reign of Henry VIII., a high-spirited monarch! every light expression which happened to displease him was construed by his supple judges into a libel, and sometimes extended to high treason. When Queen Mary, of cruel memory, ascended the throne, the Parliament, in order to raise a *fence* against the violent prosecutions for words, which had rendered the lives, liberties, and properties of all men precarious, and, perhaps, dreading the furious persecuting spirit of this princess, passed an act whereby it was declared, "That if a libeller doth go so high as to libel against king or queen by denunciation, the judges shall lay no greater fine on him than one hundred pounds, with two months' imprisonment, and no corporeal punishment: neither was this sentence to be passed on him except the accusation was fully proved by two witnesses, who were to produce a certificate of their good demeanour for the credit of their report."

This act was confirmed by another, in the seventh year of the reign of Queen Elizabeth; only the penalties were heightened to two hundred pounds and three months' imprisonment. Notwithstanding she rarely punished invectives, though the malice of the papists was indefatigable in blackening the brightest characters with the most impudent falsehoods, she was often heard to applaud that rescript of *Theodosius*. If any person spoke ill of the emperor through a foolish rashness and inadvertence, it is to be despised; if out of madness, it deserves pity; if from malice and aversion, it calls for mercy.

Her successor, King James I., was a prince of a quite different genius and disposition; he used to say, that while he had the power of making judges and bishops, *he could have what law and gospel he pleased.* Accordingly, he filled those places with such as prostituted their professions to his notions of prerogative. Among this number, and I hope it is no discredit to the profession of the law, its great oracle, *Sir Edward Coke*, appears. The Star Chamber, which in the time of Elizabeth had gained a good repute, became an intolerable grievance in the reign of this *learned monarch*.

But it did not arrive at its meridian altitude till Charles I. began to wield the sceptre. As he had formed a design to lay aside parliaments and subvert the popular part of the constitution, he very well knew that the form of government could not be altered without laying a restraint on freedom of speech and the liberty of the press: therefore he issued his royal mandate, under the great seal of England, whereby he commanded his subjects, under pain of his displeasure, not to prescribe to him any time for parliaments. Lord Clarendon, upon this occasion, is pleased to write, "That all men took themselves to be prohibited, under the penalty of censure (the censure of the Star Chamber), which few men cared to incur, so much as to speak of parliaments, or so much as to mention that parliaments were again to be called."

The king's ministers, to let the nation see they were absolutely determined to suppress all freedom of speech, caused a prosecution to be carried on by the attorney general against three members of the House of Commons, for words spoken in that house, Anno 1628. The members pleaded to the information, that expressions in parliament ought only to be examined and punished there. This notwithstanding, *they were all three condemned as disturbers of the state*; one of these gentlemen, Sir John Eliot, was fined two thousand pounds, and sentenced to lie in prison till it was paid. His lady was denied admittance to him, even during his sickness; consequently, his punishment comprehended an additional sentence of divorce. This patriot, having endured many years imprisonment, sunk under the oppression, and died in prison: this was such a wound to the authority and rights of Parliament that, even after the restoration, the judgment was revered by Parliament.

That Englishmen of all ranks might be effectually intimidated from publishing their thoughts on any subject, except on the side of the court, his majesty's ministers caused an information, for several libels, to be exhibited in the Star Chamber against Messrs. *Prynn*, *Burton*, and *Bastwick*. They were each of them fined five thousand pounds, and adjudged to lose their ears on the pillory, to be branded on the cheeks with hot irons, and to suffer perpetual imprisonment! Thus these three gentlemen, each of worth and quality in their several professions, viz., divinity, law, and physic, were, for no other offence than writing on controverted points of church government, exposed on public scaffolds, and stigmatized and mutilated as common signal rogues or the most ordinary malefactors.

Such corporeal punishments, inflicted with all the circumstances of cruelty and infamy, bound down all other gentlemen under a servile fear of like treatment; so that, for several years, no one durst publicly speak or write in defence of the liberties of the people; which the king's ministers, his privy council, and his judges, had trampled under their feet. The spirit of the administration looked hideous and dreadful; the hate and resentment which the people conceived against it, for a long time lay smothered in their breasts, where those passions festered and grew venomous, and at last discharged themselves by an armed and vindictive hand.

King Charles II. aimed at the subversion of the government, but concealed his designs under a deep hypocrisy: a method which his predecessor, in the beginning of his reign, scorned to make use of. The father, who affected a high and rigid gravity, discountenanced all barefaced immorality. The son, of a gay, luxurious disposition, openly encouraged it: thus their inclinations being different, the restraint laid on some authors, and the encouragement given to others, were managed after a different manner.

In this reign a licenser was appointed for the stage and the press; no plays were encouraged but what had a tendency to debase the minds of the people. The original design of comedy was perverted; it appeared in all the shocking circumstances of immodest *double entendre*, obscure description, and lewd representation. Religion was sneered out of countenance, and public spirit ridiculed as an awkward oldfashioned virtue; the fine gentleman of the comedy, though embroidered over with wit, was a consummate debauchee; and a fine lady, though set off with a brilliant imagination, was an impudent coquette. Satire, which in the hands of *Horace*, *Juvenal*, and *Boileau*, was pointed with a generous resentment against vice, now became the declared foe of virtue and innocence. As the city of London, in all ages, as well as the time we are now speaking of, was remarkable for its opposition to arbitrary power, the poets levelled all their artillery against the metropolis, in order to bring the citizens into contempt: an alderman was never introduced on the theatre but under the complicated character of a sneaking, canting hypocrite, a miser, and a cuckold; while the court-wits, with impunity, libelled the most valuable part of the nation. Other writers, of a different stamp, with great learning and gravity, endeavoured to prove to the English people that slavery was *jure divino*.[5] Thus the stage and the press, under the direction of a licenser, became battering engines against religion, virtue, and liberty. Those who had courage enough to write in their defence, were stigmatized as schismatics, and punished as disturbers of the government.

But when the embargo on wit was taken off, *Sir Richard Steel* and *Mr.*

*Addison* soon rescued the stage from the load of impurity it laboured under with an inimitable address, they strongly recommended to our imitation the most amiable, rational manly characters; and this with so much success that I cannot suppose there is any reader to-day conversant in the writings of those gentlemen, that can taste with any tolerable relish the comedies of the once admired *Shadwell*. Vice was obliged to retire and give place to virtue: this will always be the consequence when truth has fair play: falsehood only dreads the attack, and cries out for auxiliaries: the truth never fears the encounter: she scorns the aid of the secular arm, and triumphs by her natural strength.

But, to resume the description of the reign of Charles II., the doctrine of servitude was chiefly managed by *Sir Roger Lestrange*. He had great advantages in the argument, being licenser for the press, and might have carried all before him without contradiction, if writings on the other side of the question had not been printed by stealth. The authors, whenever found, were prosecuted as seditious libellers; on all these occasions the king's counsel, particularly *Sawyer* and *Finch*, appeared most obsequious to accomplish the ends of the court.

During this *blessed* management, the king had entered into a secret league with France to render himself absolute and enslave his subjects. This fact was discovered to the world by Dr. *Jonathan Swift*, to whom *Sir William Temple* had intrusted the publication of his works.

*Sidney*, the sworn foe of tyranny, was a gentleman of noble family, of sublime understanding and exalted courage. The ministry were resolved to remove so great an obstacle out of the way of their designs. He was prosecuted for high treason. The overt act charged in the indictment was a libel found in his private study. Mr. Finch, the king's own solicitor-general, urged with great vehemence to this effect, "that the *imagining* the death of the king is *treason*, even while that imagination remains concealed in the mind, though the law cannot punish such secret treasonable thoughts till it arrives at the knowledge of them by some overt act. That the matter of the libel composed by Sidney was an *imagining how to compass the death of King Charles II.*; and the writing of it was an overt act of treason, for that to write was to act. (*Scribere est agere.*)" It seems that the king's counsel in this reign had not received the same directions as Queen Elizabeth had given hers; she told them they were to look upon themselves as not retained so much (*pro domina regina*, as *pro domina veritate*) for the power of the queen as for the power of truth.

Mr. Sidney made a strong and legal defence. He insisted that all the words in the book contained no more than general speculations on the principles of government, free for any man to write down; especially since the same are written in the parliament rolls and in the statute laws.

He argued on the injustice of applying by innuendoes, general assertions concerning principles of government, as overt acts to prove the writer was compassing the death of the king; for then no man could write of things done even by our ancestors, in defence of the constitution and freedom of England, without exposing himself to capital danger.

He denied that *scribere est agere*, but allowed that writing and publishing is to act (*Scribere et publicare est agere*), and therefore he urged that, as his book had never been published nor imparted to any person, it could not be an overt act, within the statutes of treasons, even admitting that it contained treasonable positions; that, on the contrary, it was a *covert fact*, locked up in his private study, as much concealed from the knowledge of any man as if it were locked up in the author's mind. This was the substance of Mr. Sidney's defence: but neither law, nor reason, nor eloquence, nor innocence ever availed where *Jefferies* sat as judge. Without troubling himself with any part of the defence, he declared in a rage, that Sidney's *known principles* were a *sufficient* proof of his intention to compass the death of the king.

A packed jury therefore found him guilty of high treason: great applications were made for his pardon. He was executed as a traitor.

This case is a pregnant instance of the danger that attends a law for punishing words, and of the little security the most valuable men have for their lives, in that society where a judge, by remote inferences and distant innuendoes, may construe the most innocent expressions into capital crimes. *Sidney*, the British *Brutus*, the warm, the steady friend of *liberty*; who, from an intrinsic love to mankind, left them that invaluable legacy, his immortal discourses on government, was for these very discourses murdered by the hands of lawless power. * * * *

Upon the whole, to suppress inquiries into the administration is good policy in an arbitrary government; but a free constitution and freedom of speech have such reciprocal dependance on each other, that they cannot subsist without consisting together.

The following extracts of a letter, signed Columella, and addressed to the editors of the British Repository for select Papers on Agriculture, Arts, and Manufactures (see vol. i.), will prepare those who read it for the following paper:

"Gentlemen,—There is now publishing in France a periodical work, called Ephemeridis du Citoyen,[6] in which several points, interesting to those concerned in agriculture, are from time to time discussed by some able hands. In looking over one of the volumes of this work a few days ago, I found a little piece written by one of our countrymen, and which our vigilant neighbours had taken from the London Chronicle in 1766. The author is a gentleman well known to every man of letters in Europe, and perhaps there is none in this age to whom mankind in general are more indebted.

"That this piece may not be lost to our own country, I beg you will give it a place in your Repository: it was written in favour of the farmers, when they suffered so much abuse in our public papers, and were also plundered by the mob in many places."

[4] Oh virtue! the most certain ruin.
[5] **By divine right.**
[6] Citizen's Journal.

*To Messieurs the Public.*

## ON THE PRICE OF CORN, AND THE MANAGEMENT OF THE POOR.

I am one of that class of people that feeds you all, and at present abused by you all; in short, I am a *farmer*.

By your newspapers we are told that God had sent a very short harvest to some other countries of Europe. I thought this might be in favour of Old England, and that now we should get a good price for our grain, which would bring millions among us, and make us flow in money: that, to be sure, is scarce enough.

But the wisdom of government forbade the exportation.

Well, says I, then we must be content with the market price at home.

No, say my lords the mob, you sha'n't have that. Bring your corn to market if you dare; we'll sell it for you for less money, or take it for nothing.

Being thus attacked by both ends *of the constitution*, the head and tail *of government*, what am I to do?

Must I keep my corn in the barn, to feed and increase the breed of rats? Be it so; they cannot be less thankful than those I have been used to feed.

Are we farmers the only people to be grudged the profits of our honest labour? And why? One of the late scribblers against us gives a bill of fare of the provisions at my daughter's wedding, and proclaims to all the world that we had the insolence to eat beef and pudding! Has he not read the precept in the good book, *thou shall not muzzle the mouth of the ox that treadeth out the corn*; or does he think us less worthy of good living than our oxen?

Oh, but the manufacturers! the manufacturers! they are to be favoured, and they must have bread at a cheap rate!

Hark ye, Mr. Oaf: The farmers live splendidly, you say. And, pray, would you have them hoard the money they get? Their fine clothes and furniture, do they make themselves or for one another, and so keep the money among them? Or do they employ these your darling manufacturers, and so scatter it again all over the nation?

The wool would produce me a better price if it were suffered to go to foreign markets; but that, Messieurs the Public, your laws will not permit. It must be kept all at home, that our *dear* manufacturers may have it the cheaper. And then, having yourselves thus lessened our encouragement for raising sheep, you curse us for the scarcity of mutton!

I have heard my grandfather say, that the farmers submitted to the prohibition on the exportation of wool, being made to expect and believe that, when the manufacturer bought his wool cheaper, they should also have their cloth cheaper. But the deuse a bit. It has been growing dearer and dearer from that day to this. How so? Why, truly, the cloth is exported: and that keeps up the price.

Now if it be a good principle that the exportation of a commodity is to be restrained, that so our people at home may have it the cheaper, stick to that principle, and go thorough stitch with it. Prohibit the exportation of your cloth, your leather and shoes, your ironware, and your manufactures of all sorts, to make them all cheaper at home. And cheap enough they will be, I will warrant you, till people leave off making them.

Some folks seem to think they ought never to be easy till England becomes another Lubberland, where it is fancied the streets are paved with penny-rolls, the houses tiled with pancakes, and chickens, ready roasted, cry, Come eat me.

I say, when you are sure you have got a good principle, stick to it and carry it through. I hear it is said, that though it was *necessary and right* for the ministry to advise a prohibition of the exportation of corn, yet it was *contrary to law*; and also, that though it was *contrary to law* for the mob to obstruct wagons, yet it was *necessary and right*. Just the same thing to a tittle. Now they tell me an act of indemnity ought to pass in favour of the ministry, to secure them from the consequences of having acted illegally. If so, pass another in favour of the mob. Others say, some of the mob ought to be hanged, by way of example. If so—but to say no more than I have said before, *when you are sure that you have a good principle, go through with it.*

You say poor labourers cannot afford to buy bread at a high price, unless they had higher wages. Possibly. But how shall we farmers be able to afford our labourers higher wages, if you will not allow us to get, when we might have it, a higher price for our corn?

By all that I can learn, we should at least have had a guinea a quarter more if the exportation had been allowed. And this money England would have got from foreigners.

But, it seems, we farmers must take so much less that the poor may have it so much cheaper.

This operates, then, as a tax for the maintenance of the poor. A very good thing, you will say. But I ask, why a partial tax? why laid on us farmers only? If it be a good thing, pray, Messieurs the Public, take your share of it, by indemnifying us a little out of your public treasury. In doing a good thing there is both honour and pleasure; you are welcome to your share of both.

For my own part, I am not so well satisfied of the goodness of this thing. I am for doing good to the poor, but I differ in opinion about the means. I think the best way of doing good to the poor is not making them easy *in* poverty, but leading or driving them *out* of it. In my youth I travelled much, and I observed in different countries that the more public provisions were made for the poor, the less they provided for themselves, and, of course, became poorer. And, on the contrary, the less was done for them, the more they did for themselves, and became richer. There is no country in the world where so many provisions are established for them; so many hospitals to receive them when they are sick or lame, founded and maintained by voluntary charities; so many almshouses for the aged of both sexes, together with a solemn general law made by the rich to subject their estates to a heavy tax for the support of the poor. Under all these obligations, are our poor modest, humble, and thankful? And do they use their best endeavours to maintain themselves, and lighten our shoulders of this burden! On the contrary, I affirm that there is no country in the world in which the poor are more idle, dissolute, drunken, and insolent.[7] The day you passed that act you took away from before their eyes the greatest of all inducements to industry, frugality, and sobriety, by giving them a dependance on somewhat else than a careful accumulation during youth and health, for support in age or sickness. In short, you offered a premium for the encouragement of idleness, and you should not now wonder that it has had its effect in the increase of poverty. Repeal this law, and you will soon see a change in their manners; *Saint Monday* and *Saint Tuesday* will soon cease to be holydays. Six *days shalt thou labour*, though one of the old commandments, long treated as out of date, will again be looked upon as a respectable precept; industry will increase, and with it plenty among the lower people; their circumstances will mend, and more will be done for their happiness by inuring them to provide for themselves, than could be done by dividing all your estates among them.

Excuse me, Messieurs the Public, if upon this *interesting* subject I put you to the trouble of reading a little of *my* nonsense; I am sure I have lately read a great deal of *yours*, and therefore, from you (at least from those of you who are writers) I deserve a little indulgence. I am yours, &c.

ARATOR.

[7] England in 1766

## SINGULAR CUSTOM AMONG THE AMERICANS, ENTITLED WHITEWASHING.

DEAR SIR,

My wish is to give you some account of the people of these new states; but I am far from being qualified for the purpose, having as yet seen but little more than the cities of New-York and Philadelphia. I have discovered but few national singularities among them. Their customs and manners are nearly the same with those of England, which they have long been used to copy. For, previous to the revolution, the Americans were from their infancy taught to look up to the English as patterns of perfection in all things. I have observed, however, one custom, which, for aught I know, is peculiar to this country. An account of it will serve to fill up the remainder of this sheet, and may afford you some amusement.

When a young couple are about to enter into the matrimonial state, a never-failing article in the marriage treaty is, that the lady shall have and enjoy the free and unmolested exercise of the rights of *whitewashing*, with all its ceremonials, privileges, and appurtenances. A young woman would forego the most advantageous connexion, and even disappoint the warmest wish of her heart, rather than resign the invaluable right. You would wonder what this privilege of *whitewashing* is: I will endeavour to give you some idea of the ceremony, as I have seen it performed.

There is no season of the year in which the lady may not claim her privilege, if she pleases; but the latter end of May is most generally fixed upon for the purpose. The attentive husband may judge by certain prognostics when the storm is nigh at hand. When the lady is unusually fretful, finds fault with the servants, is discontented with the children, and complains much of the filthiness of everything about her, these are signs which ought not to be neglected; yet they are not decisive, as they sometimes come on and go off again without producing any farther effect. But if, when the husband rises in the morning, he should observe in the yard a wheelbarrow with a quantity of lime in it, or should see certain buckets with lime dissolved in water, there is then no time to be lost; he immediately locks up the apartment or closet where his papers or his private property is kept, and, putting the key in his pocket, betakes himself to flight, for a husband, however beloved, becomes a perfect nuisance during the season of female rage; his authority is superseded, his commission is suspended, and the very scullion who cleans the brasses in the kitchen becomes of more consideration and importance than him. He has nothing for it but to abdicate, and run from an evil which he can neither prevent nor mollify.

The husband gone, the ceremony begins. The walls are in a few minutes stripped of their furniture: paintings, prints, and looking-glasses lie in a huddled heap about the floors; the curtains are torn from the testers, the beds crammed into the windows; chairs and tables, bedsteads and cradles, crowd the yard; and the garden fence bends beneath the weight of carpets, blankets, cloth cloaks, old coats, and ragged breeches. *Here* may be seen the lumber of the kitchen, forming a dark and confused mass: for the foreground of the picture, grid irons and frying-pans, rusty shovels and broken tongs, spits and pots, joint-stools, and the fractured remains of rush-bottomed chairs. *There* a closet has disgorged its bowels, cracked tumblers, broken wineglasses, vials of forgotten physic, papers of unknown powders, seeds, and dried herbs, handfuls of old corks, tops of teapots, and stoppers of departed decanters; from the raghole in the garret to the rathole in the cellar, no place escapes unrummaged. It would seem as if the day of general doom was come, and the utensils of the house were dragged forth to judgment. In this tempest the words of Lear naturally present themselves, and might, with some alteration, be made strictly applicable:

> "Let the great gods,
> That keep this dreadful pother o'er our heads,
> Find out their enemies now. Tremble, thou wretch,
> That hast within thee undivulged crimes
> Unwhipp'd of justice!
>
> "Close pent-up guilt,
> Raise your concealing continents, and ask
> These dreadful summoners grace!"

This ceremony completed and the house thoroughly evacuated, the next operation is to smear the walls and ceilings of every room and closet with brushes dipped in a solution of lime, called *white wash*; to pour buckets of water over every floor, and scratch all the partitions and wainscots with rough brushes wet with soapsuds and dipped in stonecutter's sand. The windows by no means escape the general deluge. A servant scrambles out upon the penthouse, at the risk of her neck, and with a mug in her hand and a bucket within reach, she dashes away innumerable gallons of water against the glass panes, to the great annoyance of the passengers in the street.

I have been told that an action at law was once brought against one of these water nymphs, by a person who had a new suit of clothes spoiled by this operation; but, after long argument, it was determined by the whole court that the action would not lie, inasmuch as the defendant was in the exercise of a legal right, and not answerable for the consequences: and so the poor gentleman was doubly nonsuited, for he lost not only his suit of clothes, but his suit at law.

These smearings and scratchings, washings and dashings, being duly performed, the next ceremonial is to cleanse and replace the distracted furniture. You may have seen a house-raising or a ship-launch, when all the hands within reach are collected together: recollect, if you can, the hurry, bustle, confusion, and noise of such a scene, and you will have some idea of this cleaning match. The misfortune is, that the sole object is to make things clean; it matters not how many useful, ornamental, or valuable articles are mutilated or suffer death under the operation; a mahogany chair and carved frame undergo the same discipline; they are to be made *clean* at all events, but their preservation is not worthy of attention. For instance, a fine large engraving is laid flat on the floor, smaller prints are piled upon it, and the superincumbent weight cracks the glasses of the lower tier: but this is of no consequence. A valuable picture is placed leaning against the sharp corner of a table, others are made to lean against that, until the pressure of the whole forces the corner of the table through the canvass of the first. The frame and glass of a fine print are to be *cleaned*; the spirit and oil used on this occasion are suffered to leak through and spoil the engraving; no matter, if the glass is clean and the frame shine, it is sufficient; the rest is not worthy of consideration. An able arithmetician has made an accurate calculation, founded on long experience, and has discovered that the losses and destructions incident to two whitewashings are equal to one removal, and three removals equal to one fire.

The cleaning frolic over, matters begin to resume their pristine appearance. The storm abates, and all would be well again; but it is impossible that so great a convulsion in so small a community should not produce some farther effects. For two or three weeks after the operation, the family are usually afflicted with sore throats or sore eyes, occasioned by the caustic quality of the lime, or with severe colds from the exhalations of wet floors or damp walls.

I know a gentleman who was fond of accounting for everything in a philosophical way. He considers this, which I have called a custom, as a real periodical disease, peculiar to the climate. His train of reasoning is ingenious and whimsical, but I am not at leisure to give you a detail. The result was, that he found the distemper to be incurable; but, after much study, he conceived he had discovered a method to divert the evil he could not subdue. For this purpose he caused a small building, about twelve feet square, to be erected in his garden, and furnished with some ordinary chairs and tables, and a few prints of the cheapest sort were hung against the walls. His hope was, that when the whitewashing phrensy seized the females of his family, they might repair to this apartment, and scrub, and smear, and scour to their heart's content, and so spend the violence of the disease in this outpost, while he enjoyed himself in quiet at headquarters. But the experiment did not answer his expectation; it was impossible it should, since a principal part of the gratification consists in the lady's having an uncontrolled right to torment her husband at least once a year, and to turn him out of doors, and take the reins of government into her own hands.

There is a much better contrivance than this of the philosopher, which is, to cover the walls of the house with paper; this is generally done, and though it cannot abolish, it at least shortens the period of female dominion. The paper is decorated with flowers of various fancies, and made so ornamental, that the women have admitted the fashion without perceiving the design.

There is also another alleviation of the husband's distress; he generally has the privilege of a small room or closet for his books and papers, the key of which he is allowed to keep. This is considered as a privileged place, and stands like the land of Goshen amid the plagues of Egypt. But then he must be extremely cautious, and ever on his guard. For should he inadvertently go abroad and leave the key in his door, the housemaid, who is always on the watch for such an opportunity, immediately enters in triumph with buckets, brooms, and brushes; takes possession of the premises, and forthwith puts all his books and papers *to rights*, to his utter confusion and sometimes serious detriment. For instance:

A gentleman was sued by the executors of a tradesman, on a charge found against him in the deceased's books to the amount of £30. The defendant was strongly impressed with an idea that he had discharged the debt and taken a receipt; but, as the transaction was of long standing, he knew not where to find the receipt. The suit went on in course, and the time approached when judgment would be obtained against him. He then sat seriously down to examine a large bundle of old papers, which he had untied and displayed on a table for that purpose. In the midst of his search he was suddenly called away on business of importance; he forgot to lock the door of his room. The housemaid, who had been long looking out for such an opportunity, immediately entered with the usual implements, and with great alacrity fell to cleaning the room and putting things to *rights*. The first object that struck her eye was the confused situation of the papers on the table; these were, without delay, bundled together like so many dirty knives and forks; but, in the action, a small piece of paper fell unnoticed on the floor, which happened to be the very receipt in question: as it had no very respectable appearance it was soon after swept out with the common dirt of the room, and carried in a rubbish-pan into the yard. The tradesman had neglected to enter the credit in his book; the defendant could find nothing to obviate the charge, and so judgment went against him for the debt and costs. A fortnight after the whole was settled and the money paid, one of the children found the receipt among the rubbish in the yard.

There is also another custom peculiar to the city of Philadelphia, and nearly allied to the former. I mean that of washing the pavement before the doors every Saturday evening. I at first took this to be a regulation of the police, but, on a farther inquiry, find it is a religious rite preparatory to the Sabbath, and is, I believe, the only religious rite in which the numerous sectaries of this city perfectly agree. The ceremony begins about sunset, and continues till about ten or eleven at night. It is very difficult for a stranger to walk the streets on those evenings; he runs a continual risk of having a bucket of dirty water thrown against his legs; but a Philadelphian born is so much accustomed to the danger that he avoids it with surprising dexterity. It is from this circumstance that a Philadelphian may be known anywhere by his gait. The streets of New-York are paved with rough stones; these, indeed, are not washed, but the dirt is so thoroughly swept from before the doors that the stones stand up sharp and prominent, to the great inconvenience of those who are not accustomed to so rough a path. But habit reconciles everything. It is diverting enough to see a Philadelphian at New-York; he walks the streets with as much painful caution as if his toes were covered with corns, or his feet lamed with the gout: while a New-Yorker, as little approving the plain masonry of Philadelphia, shuffles along the pavement like a parrot on a mahogany table.

It must be acknowledged that the ablutions I have mentioned are attended with no small inconvenience; but the women would not be induced, from any consideration, to resign their privilege. Notwithstanding this, I can give you the strongest assurances that the women of America make the most faithful wives and the most attentive mothers in the world; and I am sure you will join me in opinion, that if a married man is made miserable only *one* week in a whole year, he will have no great cause to complain of the matrimonial bond.

I am, &c.

## ON THE CRIMINAL LAWS AND THE PRACTICE OF PRIVATEERING.

*Letter to Benjamin Vaughan, Esq.*

March 14, 1785.

MY DEAR FRIEND

Among the pamphlets you lately sent me was one entitled *Thoughts on Executive Justice*. In return for that, I send you a French one on the same subject, *Observations concernant l'Exécution de l'Article II. de la Déclaration sur le Vol*. They are both addressed to the judges, but written, as you will see, in a very different spirit. The English author is for hanging *all* thieves. The Frenchman is for proportioning punishments to offences.

If we really believe, as we profess to believe, that the law of Moses was the law of God, the dictate of Divine wisdom, infinitely superior to human, on what principle do we ordain death as the punishment of an offence which, according to that law, was only to be punished by a restitution of fourfold? To put a man to death for an offence which does not deserve death, is it not a murder? And as the French writer says, *Doit-on punir un délit contre la société par un crime contre la nature?*[8]

Superfluous property is the creature of society. Simple and mild laws were sufficient to guard the property that was merely necessary. The savage's bow, his hatchet, and his coat of skins, were sufficiently secured, without law, by the fear of personal resentment and retaliation. When, by virtue of the first laws, part of the society accumulated wealth and grew powerful, they enacted others more severe, and would protect their property at the expense of humanity. This was abusing their power and commencing a tyranny. If a savage, before he entered into society, had been told, "Your neighbour, by this means, may become owner of a hundred deer; but if your brother, or your son, or yourself, having no deer of your own, and being hungry, should kill one, an infamous death must be the consequence," he would probably have preferred his liberty, and his common right of killing any deer, to all the advantages of society that might be proposed to him.

That it is better a hundred guilty persons should escape than that one innocent person should suffer, is a maxim that has been long and generally approved;

never, that I know of, controverted. Even the sanguinary author of the *Thoughts* agrees to it, adding well, "that the very thought of *injured* innocence, and much more that of *suffering* innocence, must awaken all our tenderest and most compassionate feelings, and, at the same time, raise our highest indignation against the instruments of it. But," he adds, "there is no danger of *either* from a strict adherence to the laws." Really! is it then impossible to make an unjust law? and if the law itself be unjust, may it not be the very "instrument" which ought "to raise the author's and everybody's highest indignation?" I see in the last newspapers from London that a woman is capitally convicted at the Old Bailey for privately stealing out of a shop some gauze, value fourteen shillings and threepence. Is there any proportion between the injury done by a theft, value fourteen shillings and threepence, and the punishment of a human creature, by death, on a gibbet? Might not that woman, by her labour, have made the reparation ordained by God in paying fourfold? Is not all punishment inflicted beyond the merit of the offence, so much punishment of innocence? In this light, how vast is the annual quantity of not only *injured*, but *suffering* innocence, in almost all the civilized states of Europe!

But it seems to have been thought that this kind of innocence may be punished by way of *preventing crimes*. I have read, indeed, of a cruel Turk in Barbary, who, whenever he bought a new Christian slave, ordered him immediately to be hung up by the legs, and to receive a hundred blows of a cudgel on the soles of his feet, that the severe sense of punishment and fear of incurring it thereafter might prevent the faults that should merit it. Our author himself would hardly approve entirely of this Turk's conduct in the government of slaves; and yet he appears to recommend something like it for the government of English subjects, when he applauds the reply of Judge Burnet to the convict horsestealer; who, being asked what he had to say why judgment of death should not pass against him, and answering that it was hard to hang a man for *only* stealing a horse, was told by the judge, "Man, thou art not to be hanged *only* for stealing a horse, but that horses may not be stolen." The man's answer, if candidly examined, will, I imagine, appear reasonable, as being founded on the eternal principle of justice and equity, that punishments should be proportioned to offences; and the judge's reply brutal and unreasonable, though the writer "wishes all judges to carry it with them whenever they go the circuit, and to bear it in their minds, as containing a wise reason for all the penal statutes which they are called upon to put in execution. It at once illustrates," says he, "the true grounds and reasons of all capital punishments whatsoever, namely, that every man's property, as well as his life, may be held sacred and inviolate." Is there, then, no difference in value between property and life? If I think it right that the crime of murder should be punished with death, not only as an equal punishment of the crime, but to prevent other murders, does it follow that I must approve of inflicting the same punishment for a little invasion on my property by theft? If I am not myself so barbarous, so bloody-minded and revengeful, as to kill a fellow-creature for stealing from me fourteen shillings and threepence, how can I approve of a law that does it? Montesquieu, who was himself a judge, endeavours to impress other maxims. He must have known what humane judges feel on such occasions, and what the effects of those feelings; and, so far from thinking that severe and excessive punishments prevent crimes, he asserts, as quoted by our French writer, that

"L'atrocité des loix en empêche l'exécution.

"Lorsque la peine est sans mesure, on est souvent obligé de lui préférer l'impunité.

"La cause de tous les relâchemens vient de l'impunité des crimes, et non de la modération des peines."[9]

It is said by those who know Europe generally that there are more thefts committed and punished annually in England than in all the other nations put together. If this be so, there must be a cause or causes for such depravity in our common people. May not one be the deficiency of justice and morality in our national government, manifested in our oppressive conduct to subjects, and unjust wars on our neighbours? View the long-persisted-in, unjust, monopolizing treatment of Ireland, at length acknowledged! View the plundering government exercised by our merchants in the Indies; the confiscating war made upon the American colonies; and, to say nothing of those upon France and Spain, view the late war upon Holland, which was seen by impartial Europe in no other light than that of a war of rapine and pillage; the hopes of an immense and easy prey being its only apparent, and probably its true and real motive and encouragement. Justice is as strictly due between neighbour nations as between neighbour citizens. A highwayman is as much a robber when he plunders in a gang as when single; and a nation that makes an unjust war is only a great gang. After employing your people in robbing the Dutch, it is strange that, being put out of that employ by peace, they still continue robbing, and rob one another? *Piraterie*, as the French call it, or privateering, is the universal bent of the English nation, at home and abroad, wherever settled. No less than seven hundred privateers were, it is said, commissioned in the last war! These were fitted out by merchants, to prey upon other merchants who had never done them any injury. Is there probably any one of those privateering merchants of London, who were so ready to rob the merchants of Amsterdam, that would not as easily plunder another London merchant of the next street, if he could do it with the same impunity? The avidity, the *alieni appetens*[10] is the same; it is the fear of the gallows that makes the difference. How, then, can a nation, which among the honestest of its people has so many thieves by inclination, and whose government encouraged and commissioned no less than seven hundred gangs of robbers; how can such a nation have the face to condemn the crime in individuals, and hang up twenty of them in a morning! It naturally puts one in mind of a Newgate anecdote. One of the prisoners complained that in the night somebody had taken his buckles out of his shoes. "What the devil!" says another, "have we then *thieves* among us? It must not be suffered. Let us search out the rogue and pump him to death."

There is, however, one late instance of an English merchant who will not profit by such ill-gotten gain. He was, it seems, part owner of a ship, which the other owners thought fit to employ as a letter of marque, which took a number of French prizes. The booty being shared, he has now an agent here inquiring, by an advertisement in the Gazette, for those who have suffered the loss, in order to make them, as far as in him lies, restitution. This conscientious man is a Quaker. The Scotch Presbyterians were formerly as tender; for there is still extant an ordinance of the town-council of Edinburgh, made soon after the Reformation, "forbidding the purchase of prize goods, under pain of losing the freedom of the burgh for ever, with other punishment at the will of the magistrate; the practice of making prizes being contrary to good conscience, and the rule of treating Christian brethren as we would wish to be treated; and such goods *are not to be sold by any Godly man within this burgh.*" The race of these Godly men in Scotland are probably extinct, or their principles abandoned, since, as far as that nation had a hand in promoting the war against the colonies, prizes and confiscations are believed to have been a considerable motive.

It has been for some time a generally received opinion, that a military man is not to inquire whether a war be just or unjust; he is to execute his orders. All princes who are disposed to become tyrants must probably approve of this opinion, and be willing to establish it; but is it not a dangerous one? since, on that principle, if the tyrant commands his army to attack and destroy not only an unoffending neighbour nation, but even his own subjects, the army is bound to obey. A negro slave in our colonies, being commanded by his master to rob and murder a neighbour, or do any other immoral act, may refuse, and the magistrate will protect him in his refusal. The slavery, then, of a soldier is worse than that of a negro! A conscientious officer, if not restrained by the apprehension of its being imputed to another cause, may indeed resign rather than be employed in an unjust war; but the private men are slaves for life; and they are, perhaps, incapable of judging for themselves. We can only lament their fate, and still more that of a sailor, who is often dragged by force from his honest occupation, and compelled to imbrue his hands in perhaps innocent blood. But methinks it well behooves merchants (men more enlightened by their education, and perfectly free from any such force or obligation) to consider well of the justice of a war, before they voluntarily engage a gang of ruffians to attack their fellow-merchants of a neighbouring nation, to plunder them of their property, and perhaps ruin them and their families if they yield it, or to wound, maim, and murder them, if they endeavour to defend it. Yet these things are done by Christian merchants, whether a war be just or unjust; and it can hardly be just on both sides. They are done by English and American merchants, who nevertheless complain of private theft, and hang by dozens the thieves they have taught by their own example.

It is high time, for the sake of humanity, that a stop were put to this enormity. The United States of America, though better situated than any European nation to make profit by privateering (most of the trade of Europe with the West Indies passing before their doors), are, as far as in them lies, endeavouring to abolish the practice, by offering, in all their treaties with other powers, an article, engaging solemnly that, in case of future war, no privateer shall be commissioned on either side; and that unarmed merchant ships on both sides shall pursue their voyages unmolested.[11] This will be a happy improvement of the law of nations. The humane and the just cannot but wish general success to the proposition.

With unchangeable esteem and affection,

I am, my dear friend,<br>Ever yours.

[8] Ought we to punish a crime against society by a crime against nature?

[9] The extreme severity of the laws prevents their execution. Where the punishment is excessive, it is frequently necessary to prefer impunity.

It is the exemption from punishment, and not its moderation which is the cause of crime.

[10] Coveting what is the property of another.

[11] This offer having been accepted by the late king of Prussia, a treaty of amity and commerce was concluded between that monarch and the United States, containing the following humane, philanthropic article, in the formation of which Dr. Franklin, as one of the American plenipotentiaries, was principally concerned, viz.,

"Art. XXIII. If war should arise between the two contracting parties, the merchants of either country then residing in the other shall be allowed to remain nine months to collect their debts and settle their affairs, and may depart freely, carrying off all their effects without molestation or hinderance; and all women and children, scholars of every faculty, cultivators of the earth, artisans, manufacturers, and fishermen, unarmed and inhabiting unfortified towns, villages, and places, and, in general, all others whose occupations are for the common subsistence and benefit of mankind, shall be allowed to continue their respective employments, and shall not be molested in their persons, nor shall their houses or goods be burned or otherwise destroyed, nor their fields wasted by the armed force of the enemy into whose power, by the events of war, they may happen to fall; but if anything is necessary to be taken from them for the use of such armed force, the same shall be paid for at a reasonable price. And all merchant and trading vessels employed in exchanging the products of different places, and thereby rendering the necessaries, conveniences, and comforts of human life more easy to be obtained, and more general, shall be allowed to pass free and unmolested; and neither of the contracting powers shall grant or issue any commission to any private armed vessels, empowering them to take or destroy such trading vessels or interrupt such commerce."

## LETTER FROM ANTHONY AFTERWIT.

MR. GAZETTEER,

I am an honest tradesman, who never meant harm to anybody. My affairs went on smoothly while a bachelor; but of late I have met with some difficulties, of which I take the freedom to give you an account.

About the time I first addressed my present spouse, her father gave out in speeches that, if she married a man he liked, he would give with her two hundred pounds in cash on the day of marriage. He never said so much to me, it is true; but he always received me very kindly at his house, and openly countenanced my courtship. I formed several fine schemes what to do with this same two hundred pounds, and in some measure neglected my business on that account; but, unluckily, it came to pass, that, when the old gentleman saw I was pretty well engaged, and that the match was too far gone to be easily broke off, he, without any reason given, grew very angry, forbid me the house, and told his daughter that if she married me he would not give her a farthing. However (as he thought), we were not to be disappointed in that manner, but, having stole a wedding, I took her home to my house, where we were not quite in so poor a condition as the couple described in the Scotch song, who had

> "Neither pot nor pan,
> But four bare legs together,"

for I had a house tolerably well furnished for a poor man before. No thanks to Dad, who, I understand, was very much pleased with his politic management; and I have since learned that there are other old curmudgeons (so called) besides him, who have this trick to marry their daughters, and yet keep what they might well spare till they can keep it no longer. But this by way of digression; a word to the wise is enough.

I soon saw that with care and industry we might live tolerably easy and in credit with our neighbours; but my wife had a strong inclination to be a gentlewoman. In consequence of this, my oldfashioned looking-glass was one day broke, as she said, *no one could tell which way*. However, since we could not be without a glass in the room, "My dear," saith she, "we may as well buy a large fashionable one, that Mr. Such-a-one has to sell. It will cost but little more than a common glass, and will look much handsomer and more creditable." Accordingly, the glass was bought and hung against the wall; but in a week's time I was made sensible, by little and little, that *the table was by no means suitable to such a glass*; and, a more proper table being procured, some time after, my spouse, who was an excellent contriver, informed me where we might have very handsome chairs *in the way*; and thus, by degrees, I found all my old furniture stowed up in the garret, and everything below altered for the better.

Had we stopped here, it might have done well enough. But my wife being entertained with tea by the good woman she visited, we could do no less than the like when they visited us; so we got a teatable, with all its appurtenances of China and silver. Then my spouse unfortunately overworked herself in washing the house, so that we could no longer without a maid. Besides this, it happened frequently that when I came home at one, the dinner was but just put in the pot, and *my dear thought really it had been but eleven*. At other times, when I came at the same hour, *she wondered I would stay so long, for dinner was ready about one, and had waited for me these two hours*. These irregularities, occasioned by mistaking the time, convinced me that it was absolutely necessary *to buy a clock*, which my spouse observed was *a great ornament to the room*. And lastly, to my grief, she was troubled with some ailment or other, and *nothing did her so much good as riding, and these hackney-horses were such wretched ugly creatures that*—I bought a very fine pacing mare, which cost twenty pounds; and hereabouts affairs have stood for about a twelvemonth past.

I could see all along that this did not at all suit with my circumstances, but had not resolution enough to help it, till lately, receiving a very severe dun, which mentioned the next court, I began in earnest to project relief. Last Monday, my dear went over the river to see a relation and stay a fortnight, because she could not bear the heat of the town air. In the interim I have taken my turn to make alterations; namely, I have turned away the maid, bag and baggage (for what should we do with a maid, who, besides our boy, have none but ourselves?) I have sold the pacing mare, and bought a good milch-cow with three pounds of the money. I have disposed of the table, and put a good spinning-wheel in its place, which, methinks, looks very pretty; nine empty canisters I have stuffed with flax, and with some of the money of the tea-furniture I have bought a set of knitting-needles, for, to tell you the truth, *I begin to want stockings*. The fine clock I have transformed into an hourglass, by which I have gained a good round sum; and one of the pieces of the old looking-glass, squared and framed, supplies the place of the great one, which I have conveyed into a closet, where it may possibly remain some years. In short, the face of things is quite changed, and methinks you would smile to see my hourglass hanging in the place of the clock. What a great ornament it is to the room! I have paid my debts, and find money in my pocket. I expect my dear home next Friday, and, as your paper is taken at the house where she is, I hope the reading of this will prepare her mind for the above surprising revolutions. If she can conform herself to this new manner of living, we shall be the happiest couple, perhaps, in the province, and, by the blessing of God, may soon be in thriving circumstances. I have reserved the great glass, because I know her heart is set upon it; I will allow her, when she comes in, to be taken suddenly ill with *the headache, the stomach-ache, fainting-fits,* or whatever other disorder she may think more proper, and she may retire to bed as soon as she pleases. But if I should not find her in perfect health, both of body and mind, the next morning, away goes the aforesaid great glass, with several other trinkets I have no occasion for, to the vendue, that very day; which is the irrevocable resolution

    Of, sir, her loving husband and
        Your very humble servant,

Anthony Afterwit.

P.S.—I would be glad to know how you approve my conduct.

*Answer.*—I don't love to concern myself in affairs between man and wife.

# LETTERS.

"*Mrs. Abiah Franklin.*

"Philadelphia, April (date uncertain).

"Honoured Mother,

"We received your kind letter of the 2d instant, by which we are glad to hear you still enjoy such a measure of health, notwithstanding your great age. We read your writings very easily. I never met with a word in your letter but what I could easily understand, for, though the hand is not always the best, the sense makes everything plain. My leg, which you inquire after, is now quite well. I shall keep these servants: but the man not in my own house. I have hired him out to the man that takes care of my Dutch printing-office, who agrees to keep him in victuals and clothes, and to pay me a dollar a week for his work. The wife, since that affair, behaves exceeding well: but we conclude to sell them both the first good opportunity, for we do not like negro servants. We got again about half what we lost.

"As to your grandchildren, Will is now 19 years of age, a tall, proper youth, and much of a beau. He acquired a habit of idleness on the expedition, but begins, of late, to apply himself to business, and, I hope, will become an industrious man. He imagined his father had got enough for him; but I have assured him that I intend to spend what little I have myself, if it please God that I live long enough, and he can see, by my going on, that I mean to be as good as my word.

"Sally grows a fine girl, and is extremely industrious with her needle, and delights in her work. She is of a most affectionate temper, and perfectly dutiful and obliging to her parents and to all. Perhaps I flatter myself too much, but I have hope that she will prove an ingenious, sensible, notable, and worthy woman, like her aunt Jenny; she goes now to the dancing school.

"For my own part, at present, I pass my time agreeably enough; I enjoy (through mercy) a tolerable share of health. I read a great deal, ride a little, do a little business for myself (now and then for others), retire when I can, and go into company when I please so; the years roll round, and the last will come, when I would rather have it said *he lived usefully* than *he died rich.*

"Cousins Josiah and Sally are well, and I believe will do well, for they are an industrious, loving young couple; but they want a little more stock to go on smoothly with their business.

"My love to brother and sister Mecom and their children, and to all my relations in general. I am your dutiful son,

"B. FRANKLIN."

---

"*Miss Jane Franklin.*[12]

"Philadelphia, January 6, 1726-7.

"DEAR SISTER,

"I am highly pleased with the account Captain Freeman gives me of you. I always judged by your behaviour when a child, that you would make a good, agreeable woman, and you know you were ever my peculiar favourite. I have been thinking what would be a suitable present for me to make, and for you to receive, as I hear you are grown a celebrated beauty. I had almost determined on a teatable; but when I considered that the character of a good housewife was far preferable to that of being only a pretty gentlewoman, I concluded to send you a *spinning-wheel*, which I hope you will accept as a small token of my sincere love and affection.

"Sister, farewell, and remember that modesty as it makes the most homely virgin amiable and charming, so the want of it infallibly renders the most perfect beauty disagreeable and odious. But when that brightest of female virtues shines among other perfections of body and mind in the same person, it makes the woman more lovely than an angel. Excuse this freedom, and use the same with me. I am, dear Jenny, your loving brother,

"B. FRANKLIN."

[12] His sister married Mr. Edward Mecom, July 27, 1727.

*To the same.*

Philadelphia, July 28, 1743.

"Dearest Sister Jenny,

"I took your admonition very kindly, and was far from being offended at you for it. If I say anything about it to you, 'tis only to rectify some wrong opinions you seem to have entertained of me; and this I do only because they give you some uneasiness, which I am unwilling to be the cause of. You express yourself as if you thought I was against worshipping of God, and doubt that good works would merit heaven; which are both fancies of your own, I think, without foundation. I am so far from thinking that God is not to be worshipped, that I have composed and wrote a whole book of devotions for my own use, and I imagine there are few, if any, in the world so weak as to imagine that the little good we can do here can merit so vast a reward hereafter.

"There are some things in your New-England doctrine and worship which I do not agree with: but I do not therefore condemn them, or desire to shake your belief or practice of them. We may dislike things that are nevertheless right in themselves: I would only have you make me the same allowance, and have a better opinion both of morality and your brother. Read the pages of Mr. Edwards's late book, entitled, 'Some Thoughts concerning the present Revival of Religion in New-England,' from 367 to 375; and when you judge of others, if you can perceive the fruit to be good, don't terrify yourself that the tree may be evil; but be assured it is not so, for you know who has said, 'Men do not gather grapes off thorns, and figs off thistles.' I have not time to add, but that I shall always be your affectionate brother,

"B. Franklin.

"P.S.—It was not kind in you, when your sister commenced good works, to suppose she intended it a reproach to you. 'Twas very far from her thoughts."

*"To Mr. George Whitefield.*

"Philadelphia, June 6, 1753.

"SIR,

"I received your kind letter of the 2d instant, and am glad to hear that you increase in strength; I hope you will continue mending till you recover your former health and firmness. Let me know whether you still use the cold bath, and what effect it has.

"As to the kindness you mention, I wish it could have been of more service to you. But if it had, the only thanks I should desire is, that you would always be equally ready to serve any other person that may need your assistance, and so let good offices go round; for mankind are all of a family.

"For my own part, when I am employed in serving others, I do not look upon myself as conferring favours, but as paying debts. In my travels and since my settlement, I have received much kindness from men to whom I shall never have an opportunity of making the least direct return, and numberless mercies from God, who is infinitely above being benefited by our services. Those kindnesses from men I can therefore only return on their fellow-men, and I can only show my gratitude for these mercies from God by a readiness to help his other children and my brethren. For I do not think that thanks and compliments, though repeated weekly, can discharge our real obligations to each other, and much less those to our Creator. You will see in this my notion of good works, that I am far from expecting to merit heaven by them. By heaven we understand a state of happiness infinite in degree and eternal in duration: I can do nothing to deserve such rewards. He that, for giving a draught of water to a thirsty person, should expect to be paid with a good plantation, would be modest in his demands compared with those who think they deserve heaven for the little good they do on earth. Even the mixed, imperfect pleasures we enjoy in this world are rather from God's goodness than our merit: how much more such happiness of heaven! For my part, I have not the vanity to think I deserve it, the folly to expect it, nor the ambition to desire it; but content myself in submitting to the will and disposal of that God who made me, who has hitherto preserved and blessed me, and in whose fatherly goodness I may well confide, that he will never make me miserable, and that even the afflictions I may at any time suffer shall tend to my benefit.
\* \* \* \*

"I wish you health and happiness.

"B. FRANKLIN."

"*To Mrs. D. Franklin.*

"Guadenhathen, January 25, 1756.

"My dear Child,

"This day week we arrived here; I wrote to you the same day, and once since. We all continue well, thanks be to God. We have been hindered with bad weather, yet our fort is in a good defensible condition, and we have every day more convenient living. Two more are to be built, one on each side of this, at about fifteen miles' distance. I hope both will be done in a week or ten days, and then I purpose to bend my course homeward.

"We have enjoyed your roast beef, and this day began on the roast veal; all agree that they are both the best that ever were of the kind. Your citizens, that have their dinners hot and hot, know nothing of good eating; we find it in much greater perfection when the kitchen is fourscore miles from the dining-room.

"The apples are extremely welcome, and do bravely to eat after our salt pork; the minced pies are not yet come to hand, but suppose we shall find them among the things expected up from Bethlehem on Tuesday; the capillaire is excellent, but none of us having taken cold as yet, we have only tasted it.

"As to our lodging, 'tis on deal feather beds, in warm blankets, and much more comfortable than when we lodged at our inn the first night after we left home; for the woman being about to put very damp sheets on the bed, we desired her to air them first; half an hour afterward she told us the bed was ready and the sheets *well aired*. I got into bed, but jumped out immediately, finding them as cold as death, and partly frozen. She had *aired* them indeed, but it was out upon the *hedge*. I was forced to wrap myself up in my greatcoat and woollen trousers; everything else about the bed was shockingly dirty.

"As I hope in a little time to be with you and my family, and chat things over, I now only add that I am, dear Debby, your affectionate husband,

"B. Franklin."

---

"*To the same.*

"Easton, Saturday morning, November 13, 1756.

"My Dear Child,

"I wrote to you a few days since by a special messenger, and enclosed letters for all our wives and sweethearts, expecting to hear from you by his return, and to have the northern newspapers and English letters per the packet; but he is just now returned without a scrap for poor us. So I had a good mind not to write to you by this opportunity; but I never can be ill-natured enough, even when there is the most occasion. The messenger says he left the letters at your house, and saw you afterward at Mr. Dentie's, and told you when he would go, and that he lodged at Honey's, next door to you, and yet you did not write; so let Goody Smith give one more just judgment, and say what should be done to you; I think I won't tell you that we are well, nor that we expect to return about the middle of the week, nor will I send you a word of news; that's poz. My duty to mother, love to the children, and to Miss Betsey and Gracey, &c., &c.

"B. FRANKLIN.

"P.S.—I have *scratched out the loving words*, being written in haste by mistake, *when I forgot . was angry.*"

---

"Mrs. Jane Mecom, Boston.
New-York, April 19, 1757.

"DEAR SISTER,

"I wrote a few lines to you yesterday, but omitted to answer yours relating to sister Dowse. *As having their own way* is one of the greatest comforts of life to old people, I think their friends should endeavour to accommodate them in that as well as anything else. When they have long lived in a house, it becomes natural to them; they are almost as closely connected with it as the tortoise with his shell: they die if you tear them out of it. Old folks and old trees, if you remove them, 'tis ten to one that you kill them, so let our good old sister be no more importuned on that head: we are growing old fast ourselves, and shall expect the same kind of indulgences; if we give them, we shall have a right to receive them in our turn.

"And as to her few fine things, I think she is in the right not to sell them, and for the reason she gives, that they will fetch but little, when that little is spent, they would be of no farther use to her; but perhaps the expectation of possessing them at her death may make that person tender and careful of her, and helpful to her to the amount of ten times their value. If so, they are put to the best use they possibly can be.

"I hope you visit sister as often as your affairs will permit, and afford her what assistance and comfort you can in her present situation. *Old age, infirmities*, and *poverty* joined, are afflictions enough. The *neglect* and *slights* of friends and near relations should never be added; people in her circumstances are apt to suspect this sometimes without cause, *appearances* should therefore be attended to in our conduct towards them as well as *relatives*. I write by this post to cousin William, to continue his care which I doubt not he will do.

"We expect to sail in about a week, so that I can hardly hear from you again on this side the water; but let me have a line from you now and then while I am in London; I expect to stay there at least a twelvemonth. Direct your letters to be left for me at the Pennsylvania Coffee-house, in Birchin Lane, London.

"B. Franklin.

"P.S., April 25.—We are still here, and perhaps may be here a week longer. Once more adieu, my dear sister."

---

*To the same.*

"Woodbridge, East New-Jersey, May 21, 1757.

"Dear Sister,

"I received your kind letter of the 9th instant, in which you acquainted me with some of your late troubles. These are troublesome times to us all; but perhaps you have heard more than you should. I am glad to hear that Peter is at a place where he has full employ. A trade is a valuable thing; but unless a habit of industry be acquired with it, it turns out of little use; if he gets THAT in his new place, it will be a happy exchange, and the occasion not an unfortunate one.

"It is very agreeable to me to hear so good an account of your other children: in such a number, to have no bad ones is a great happiness.

"The horse sold very low indeed. If I wanted one to-morrow, knowing his goodness, old as he is, I should freely give more than twice the money for him; but you did the best you could, and I will take of Benny no more than he produced.

"I don't doubt but Benny will do very well when he gets to work: but I fear his things from England may be so long a coming as to occasion the loss of the rent. Would it not be better for you to move into the house? Perhaps not, if he is near being married. I know nothing of that affair but what you write me, except that I think Miss Betsey a very agreeable, sweet-tempered, good girl, who has had a housewifery education, and will make, to a good husband, a very good wife. Your sister and I have a great esteem for her, and if she will be kind enough to accept of our nephew, we think it will be his own fault if he is not as happy as the married state can make him. The family is a respectable one, but whether there be any fortune I know not; and as you do not inquire about this particular, I suppose you think with me, that where everything else desirable is to be met with, that is not very material. If she does not bring a fortune she will have to make one. Industry, frugality, and prudent economy in a wife, are to a tradesman, in their effects, a fortune; and a fortune sufficient for Benjamin, if his expectations are reasonable. We can only add, that if the young lady and her friends are willing, we give our consent heartily and our blessing. My love to brother and the children concludes with me.

B. FRANKLIN."

To the same.

"New-York, May 30, 1757

"DEAR SISTER,

"I have before me yours of the 9th and 16th instant. I am glad you have resolved to visit sister Dowse oftener; it will be a great comfort to her to find she is not neglected by you, and your example may, perhaps, be followed by some other of her relations.

"As Neddy is yet a young man, I hope he may get over the disorder he complains of, and in time wear it out. My love to him and his wife and the rest of your children. It gives me pleasure to hear that Eben is likely to get into business at his trade. If he will be industrious and frugal, 'tis ten to one but he gets rich, for he seems to have spirit and activity.

"I am glad that Peter is acquainted with the crown soap business, so as to make what is good of the kind. I hope he will always take care to make it faithfully, never slight manufacture, or attempt to deceive by appearances. Then he may boldly put his name and mark, and in a little time it will acquire as good a character as that made by his late uncle, or any other person whatever. I believe his aunt at Philadelphia can help him to sell a good deal of it; and I doubt not of her doing everything in her power to promote his interest in that way. Let a box be sent to her (but not unless it be right good), and she will immediately return the ready money for it. It was beginning once to be in vogue in Philadelphia, but brother John sent me one box, an ordinary sort, which checked its progress. I would not have him put the Franklin arms on it; but the soapboiler's arms he has a right to use, if he thinks fit. The other would look too much like an attempt to counterfeit. In his advertisements he may value himself on serving his time with the original maker, but put his own mark or device on the papers, or anything he may be advised as proper; only on the soap, as it is called by the name of crown soap, it seems necessary to use a stamp of that sort, and perhaps no soapboiler in the king's dominions has a better right to the crown than himself.

"Nobody has wrote a syllable to me concerning his making use of the hammer, or made the least complaint of him or you. I am sorry, however, he took it without leave. It was irregular, and if you had not approved of his doing it I should have thought it indiscreet. *Leave*, they say, is *light*, and it seems to me a piece of respect that was due to his aunt to ask it, and I can scarce think she would have refused him the favour.

"I am glad to hear Jamey is so good and diligent a workman; if he ever sets up at the goldsmith's business, he must remember that there is one accomplishment without which he cannot possibly thrive in that trade (i. e., *to be perfectly honest*). It is a business that, though ever so uprightly managed, is always liable to suspicion; and if a man is once detected in the smallest fraud it soon becomes public, and every one is put upon their guard against him; no one will venture to try his hands, or trust him to make up their plate; so at once he is ruined. I hope my nephew will therefore establish a character as an *honest* and faithful as well as *skilful* workman, and then he need not fear employment.

"And now, as to what you propose for Benny, I believe he may be, as you say, well enough qualified for it; and when he appears to be settled, if a vacancy should happen, it is very probable he may be thought of to supply it; but it is a rule with me not to remove any officer that behaves well, keeps regular accounts, and pays duly; and I think the rule is founded on reason and justice. I have not shown any backwardness to assist Benny, where it could be done without injuring another. But if my friends require of me to gratify not only their inclinations, but their resentments, they expect too much of me. Above all things, I dislike family quarrels; and when they happen among my relations, nothing gives me more pain. If I were to set myself up as a judge of those subsisting between you and brother's widow and children, how unqualified must I be, at this distance, to determine rightly, especially having heard but one side. They always treated me with friendly and affectionate regard; you have done the same. What can I say between you but that I wish you were reconciled, and that I will love that side best that is most ready to forgive and oblige the other. You will be angry with me here for putting you and them too much upon a footing, but I shall nevertheless be

"B. Franklin."

---

"*Miss Stevenson, Wanstead.*

"Craven-street, May 16, 1760.

"I send my good girl the books I mentioned to her last night. I beg her to accept of them as a small mark of my esteem and friendship. They are written in the familiar, easy manner for which the French are so remarkable; and afford a good deal of philosophic and practical knowledge, unembarassed with the dry mathematics used by more exact reasoners, but which is apt to discourage young beginners.

"I would advise you to read with a pen in your hand, and enter in a little book short hints of what you find that is curious or that may be useful; for this will be the best method of imprinting such particulars in your memory, where they will be ready either for practice on some future occasion if they are matters of utility, or at least to adorn and improve your conversation if they are rather points of curiosity. And as many of the terms of science are such as you cannot have met with in your common reading, and may, therefore, be unacquainted with, I think it would be well for you to have a good dictionary at hand, to consult immediately when you meet with a word you do not comprehend the precise meaning of. This may at first seem troublesome and interrupting; but it is a trouble that will daily diminish, as you will daily find less and less occasion for your dictionary, as you become more acquainted with the terms; and in the mean time you will read with more satisfaction, because with more understanding. When any point occurs in which you would be glad to have farther information than your book affords you, I beg you would not in the least apprehend that I should think it a trouble to receive and answer your questions. It will be a pleasure, and no trouble. For though I may not be able, out of my own little stock of knowledge, to afford you what you require, I can easily direct you to the books where it may most readily be found.

"Adieu, and believe me ever, my dear friend,

"B. Franklin."

*"Lord Kames.*

"Portsmouth, August 17, 1761.

"My dear Lord,

"I am now waiting here only for a wind to waft me to America, but cannot leave this happy island and my friends in it without extreme regret, though I am going to a country and a people that I love. I am going from the Old World to the New, and I fancy I feel like those who are leaving this world for the next; grief at the parting; fear of the passage; hope of the future: these different passions all affect their minds at once, and these have *tendered* me down exceedingly. It is usual for the dying to beg forgiveness of their surviving friends if they have ever offended them. Can you, my lord, forgive my long silence, and my not acknowledging till now the favour you did me in sending me your excellent book? Can you make some allowance for a fault in others which you have never experienced in yourself; for the bad habit of postponing from day to day what one every day resolves to do to-morrow? A habit that grows upon us with years, and whose only excuse is we know not how to mend it. If you are disposed to favour me, you will also consider how much one's mind is taken up and distracted by the many little affairs one has to settle, before the undertaking such a voyage, after so long a residence in a country; and how little, in such a situation, one's mind is fitted for serious and attentive reading, which, with regard to the *Elements of Criticism*, I intended before I should write. I can now only confess and endeavour to amend. In packing up my books, I have reserved yours to read on the passage. I hope I shall therefore be able to write to you upon it soon after my arrival. At present I can only return my thanks, and say that the parts I have read gave me both pleasure and instruction; that I am convinced of your position, new as it was to me, that a good taste in the arts contributes to the improvement of morals; and that I have had the satisfaction of hearing the work universally commended by those who have read it.

"And now, my dear sir, accept my sincere thanks for the kindness you have shown me, and my best wishes of happiness to you and yours. Wherever I am, I shall esteem the friendship you honour me with as one of the felicities of my life; I shall endeavour to cultivate it by a more punctual correspondence; and I hope frequently to hear of your welfare and prosperity.

B. Franklin."

*To the same.*[13]

London, April 11, 1767.

"MY DEAR LORD,

I received your obliging favour of January the 19th. You have kindly relieved me from the pain I had long been under. You are goodness itself. I ought to have answered yours of December 25, 1765. I never received a letter that contained sentiments more suitable to my own. It found me under much agitation of mind on the very important subject it treated. It fortified me greatly in the judgment I was inclined to form (though contrary to the general vogue) on the then delicate and critical situation of affairs between Great Britain and the colonies, and on that weighty point, their *union*. You guessed aright in supposing that I would not be a *mute in that play*. I was extremely busy, attending members of both houses, informing, explaining, consulting, disputing, in a continual hurry from morning to night, till the affair was happily ended. During the course of its being called before the House of Commons I spoke my mind pretty freely. Enclosed I send you the imperfect account that was taken of that examination; you will there see how entirely we agree, except in a point of fact, of which you could not but be misinformed; the papers at that time being full of mistaken assertions, that the colonies had been the cause of the war, and had ungratefully refused to bear any part of the expense of it. I send it you now, because I apprehend some late accidents are likely to revive the contest between the two countries. I fear it will be a mischievous one. It becomes a matter of great importance, that clear ideas should be formed on solid principles, both in Britain and America, of the true political relation between them, and the mutual duties belonging to that relation. Till this is done they will be often jarring. I know none whose knowledge, sagacity, and impartiality qualify him so thoroughly for such a service as yours do you. I wish, therefore, you would consider it. You may thereby be the happy instrument of great good to the nation, and of preventing much mischief and bloodshed. I am fully persuaded with you, that a *consolidating union*, by a fair and equal representation of all the parts of this empire in Parliament, is the only firm basis on which its political grandeur and prosperity can be founded. Ireland once wished it, but now rejects it. The time has been when the colonies might have been pleased with it, they are now *indifferent* about it, and if it is much longer delayed, they too will *refuse* it. But the pride of this people cannot bear the thought of it, and therefore it will be delayed. Every man in England seems to consider himself as a piece of a sovereign over America; seems to jostle himself into the throne with the king, and talks of *our subjects in the colonies*. The Parliament cannot well and wisely make laws suited to the colonies, without being properly and truly informed of their circumstances, abilities, temper, &c. This it cannot be without representatives from thence; and yet it is fond of this power, and averse to the only means of acquiring the necessary knowledge for exercising it, which is desiring to be *omnipotent* without being *omniscient*.

"I have mentioned that the contest is likely to be revived. It is on this occasion: in the same session with the stamp-act, an act was passed to regulate the quartering of soldiers in America: when the bill was first brought in, it contained a clause empowering the officers to quarter their soldiers in private houses; this we warmly opposed, and got it omitted. The bill passed, however, with a clause that empty houses, barns, &c., should be hired for them; and that the respective provinces where they were should pay the expense, and furnish firing, bedding, drink, and some other articles to the soldiers, *gratis*. There is no way for any province to do this but by the Assembly's making a law to raise the money. Pennsylvania Assembly has made such a law; New-York Assembly has refused to do it; and now all the talk here is, of sending a force to compel them.

"The reasons given by the Assembly to the governor for the refusal are, that they understand the act to mean the furnishing such things to soldiers only while on their march through the country, and not to great bodies of soldiers, to be fixed, as at present, in the province; the burden in the latter case being greater than the inhabitants can bear; that it would put it in the power of the captain-general to oppress the province at pleasure, &c. But there is supposed to be another reason at bottom, which they intimate, though they do not plainly express it, to wit, that it is of the nature of an *internal tax* laid on them by Parliament, which has no right so to do. Their refusal is here called *rebellion*, and punishment is thought of.

"Now, waving that point of right, and supposing the legislatures in America subordinate to the legislatures of Great Britain, one might conceive, I think, a power in the superior legislature to forbid the inferior legislatures making particular laws; but to enjoin it to make a particular law, contrary to its own judgment, seems improper; an assembly or parliament not being an *executive* officer of government, whose duty it is, in law-making, to obey orders, but a *deliberative* body, who are to consider what comes before them, its propriety, practicability, or possibility, and to determine accordingly; the very nature of a parliament seems to be destroyed by supposing it may be bound and compelled by a law of a superior parliament to make a law contrary to its own judgment.

"Indeed, the act of Parliament in question has not, as in other acts, when a duty is enjoined, directed a penalty on neglect or refusal, and a mode of recovering that penalty. It seems, therefore, to the people in America as a requisition, which they are at liberty to comply with or not, as it may suit or not suit the different circumstances of the different provinces. Pennsylvania has, therefore, voluntarily complied. New-York, as I said before, has refused. The ministry that made the act, and all their adherents, call for vengeance. The present ministry are perplexed, and the measures they will finally take on the occasion are yet unknown. But sure I am that if *force* is used great mischief will ensue, the affections of the people of America to this country will be alienated, your commerce will be diminished, and a total separation of interests be the final consequence.

"It is a common but mistaken notion here, that the colonies were planted at the expense of Parliament, and that, therefore, the Parliament has a right to tax them, &c. The truth is, they were planted at the expense of private adventurers, who went over there to settle, with leave of the king, given by charter. On receiving this leave and those charters, the adventurers voluntarily engaged to remain the king's subjects, though in a foreign country; a country which had not been conquered by either king or parliament, but was possessed by a free people.

"When our planters arrived, they purchased the lands of the natives, without putting king or parliament to any expense. Parliament had no hand in their settlement, was never so much as consulted about their constitution, and took no kind of notice of them till many years after they were established. I except only the two modern colonies, or, rather, attempts to make colonies (for they succeed but poorly, and, as yet, hardly deserve the name of colonies), I mean Georgia and Nova Scotia, which have hitherto been little better than parliamentary jobs. Thus all the colonies acknowledge the king as their sovereign; his governors there represent his person: laws are made by their assemblies or little parliaments, with the governor's assent, subject still to the king's pleasure to affirm or annul them. Suits arising in the colonies, and between colony and colony, are determined by the king in council. In this view they seem so many separate little states, subject to the same prince. The sovereignty of the king is therefore easily understood. But nothing is more common here than to talk of the *sovereignty* of PARLIAMENT, and the sovereignty of this nation over the colonies; a kind of sovereignty, the idea of which is not so clear, nor does it clearly appear on what foundation it is established. On the other hand, it seems necessary, for the common good of the empire, that a power be lodged somewhere to regulate its general commerce; this can be placed nowhere so properly as in the Parliament of Great Britain; and, therefore, though that power has in some instances been executed with great partiality to Britain and prejudice to the colonies, they have nevertheless always submitted to it. Custom-houses are established in all of them, by virtue of laws made here, and the duties instantly paid, except by a few smugglers, such as are here and in all countries; but internal taxes laid on them by Parliament are still, and ever will be, objected to for the reason that you will see in the mentioned examination.

"Upon the whole, I have lived so great a part of my life in Britain, and have formed so many friendships in it, that I love it, and sincerely wish it prosperity; and, therefore, wish to see that union on which alone I think it can be secured and established. As to America, the advantages of such a union to her are not so apparent. She may suffer at present under the arbitrary power of this country; she may suffer for a while in a separation from it; but these are temporary evils which she will outgrow. Scotland and Ireland are differently circumstanced. Confined by the sea, they can scarcely increase in numbers, wealth, and strength, so as to overbalance England. But America, an immense territory, favoured by nature with all advantages of climate, soils, great navigable rivers, lakes, &c., must become a great country, populous and mighty; and will, in a less time than is generally conceived, be able to shake off any shackles that may be imposed upon her, and, perhaps, place them on the imposers. In the mean time, every act of oppression will sour their tempers, lessen greatly, if not annihilate, the profits of your commerce with them, and hasten their final revolt; for the seeds of liberty are universally found there, and nothing can eradicate them. And yet there remains among that people so much respect, veneration, and affection for Britain, that, if cultivated prudently, with a kind usage and tenderness for their privileges, they might be easily governed still for ages, without force or any considerable expense. But I do not see here a sufficient quantity of the wisdom that is necessary to produce such a conduct, and I lament the want of it.

"I borrowed at Millar's the new edition of your *Principles of Equity*, and have read with great pleasure the preliminary discourse on the principles of morality. I have never before met with anything so satisfactory on the subject. While reading it, I made a few remarks as I went along. They are not of much importance, but I send you the paper.

"I know the lady you mention (Mrs. Montague), having, when in England before, met her once or twice at Lord Bath's. I remember I then entertained the same opinion of her that you express. On the strength of your recommendation, I purpose soon to wait on her.

"This is unexpectedly grown a long letter. The visit to Scotland and the *Art of Virtue* we will talk of hereafter. It is now time to say that I am, with increasing esteem and affection,

"B. FRANKLIN."[14]

[13] Lord Kames had written to Dr. Franklin as early as 1765, when the first advices reached England of the disorders occasioned by the attempts to carry the stamp-act into execution; and he had written a second letter to him on the same subject in the beginning of 1767. This is a copy of Dr. Franklin's answer to these letters.

[14] This letter was intercepted by the British ministry; Dr. F. had preserved a copy of it, which was afterward transmitted to Lord Kames; but the wisdom that composed and conveyed it was thrown away upon the men at that time in power.

*"Lord Kames.*
"London, February 21, 1769.

"MY DEAR FRIEND,

"I received your excellent paper on the preferable use of oxen in agriculture, and have put it in the way of being communicated to the public here. I have observed in America that the farmers are more thriving in those parts of the country where horned cattle are used, than in those where the labour is done by horses. The latter are said to require twice the quantity of land to maintain them and, after all, are not good to eat—at least we don't think them so. Here is a waste of land that might afford subsistence for so many of the human species. Perhaps it was for this reason that the Hebrew lawgiver, having promised that the children of Israel should be as numerous as the sands of the sea, not only took care to secure the health of individuals by regulating their diet, that they might be better fitted for producing children, but also forbid their using horses, as those animals would lessen the quantity of subsistence for man. Thus we find, when they took any horses from their enemies, they destroyed them; and in the commandments, where the labour of the ox and ass is mentioned, and forbidden on the Sabbath, there is no mention of the horse, probably because they were to have none. And by the great armies suddenly raised in that small territory they inhabited, it appears to have been very full of people.[15]

"Food is *always* necessary to *all*, and much the greatest part of the labour of mankind is employed in raising provisions for the mouth. Is not this kind of labour, then, the fittest to be the standard by which to measure the values of all other labour, and, consequently, of all other things whose value depends on the labour of making or procuring them? may not even gold and silver be thus valued? If the labour of the farmer, in producing a bushel of wheat, be equal to the labour of the miner in producing an ounce of silver, will not the bushel of wheat just measure the value of the ounce of silver. The miner must eat; the farmer, indeed, can live without the ounce of silver, and so, perhaps, will have some advantage in settling the price. But these discussions I leave to you, as being more able to manage them: only, I will send you a little scrap I wrote some time since on the laws prohibiting foreign commodities.

"I congratulate you on your election as president of your Edinburgh Society. I think I formerly took notice to you in conversation, that I thought there had been some similarity in our fortunes and the circumstances of our lives. This is a fresh instance, for by letters just received I find that I was about the same time chosen President of our American Philosophical Society, established at Philadelphia.[16]

"I have sent by sea, to the care of Mr. Alexander a little box containing a few copies of the late edition of my books, for my friends in Scotland. One is directed for you, and one for your society, which I beg that you and they would accept as a small token of my respect.

"With the sincerest esteem and regard,

"B. FRANKLIN.

"P.S.—I am sorry my letter of 1767, concerning the American disputes, miscarried. I now send you a copy of it from my book. The examination mentioned in it you have probably seen. Things daily wear a worse aspect, and tend more and more to a breach and final separation."

[15] There is not in the Jewish law any express prohibition against the use of horses: it is only enjoined that the kings should not multiply the breed, or carry on trade with Egypt for the purchase of horses.—Deut. xvii., 16. Solomon was the first of the kings of Judah who disregarded this ordinance. He had 40,000 stalls of horses which he brought out of Egypt.—1 Kings iv., 26, and x., 28. From this time downward horses were in constant use in the Jewish armies. It is true that the country, from its rocky surface and unfertile soil, was extremely unfit for the maintenance of those animals.—*Note by Lord Kames.*

[16] The American Philosophical Society was instituted in 1769, and was formed by the union of two societies which had formerly subsisted at Philadelphia, whose views and objects were of a similar nature. Its members were classed in the following committees:

1. Geography, Mathematics, Natural Philosophy, and Astronomy.

2. Medicine and Anatomy.

3. Natural History and Chymistry.

4. Trade and Commerce.

5. Mechanics and Architecture.

6. Husbandry and American Improvements.

Several volumes have been published of the transactions of this American Society, in which are many papers by Dr. Franklin.—*Note by Lord Kames.*

"*John Alleyne.*

"Craven-street, August 9, 1768.

"DEAR JACK,

"You desire, you say, my impartial thoughts on the subject of an early marriage, by way of answer to the numberless objections that have been made by numerous persons to your own. You may remember, when you consulted me on the occasion, that I thought youth on both sides to be no objection. Indeed, from the marriages that have fallen under my observation, I am rather inclined to think that early ones stand the best chance of happiness. The temper and habits of the young are not yet become so stiff and uncomplying as when more advanced in life; they form more easily to each other, and hence many occasions of disgust are removed. And if youth has less of that prudence which is necessary to manage a family, yet the parents and elder friends of young married persons are generally at hand to afford their advice, which amply supplies that defect; and, by early marriage, youth is sooner formed to regular and useful life; and possibly some of those accidents or connexions, that might have injured the constitution or reputation, or both, are thereby happily prevented. Particular circumstances of particular persons may possibly, sometimes, make it prudent to delay entering into that state; but, in general, when nature has rendered our bodies fit for it, the presumption is in nature's favour, for she has not judged amiss in making us desire it. Late marriages are often attended, too, with this farther inconvenience, that there is not the same chance that the parents shall live to see their offspring educated. '*Late children*,' says the Spanish proverb, '*are early orphans.*' A melancholy reflection to those whose case it may be! With us in America marriages are generally in the morning of life; our children are therefore educated and settled in the world by noon; and thus, our business being done, we have an afternoon and evening of cheerful leisure to ourselves, such as our friend at present enjoys. By these early marriages we are blessed with more children; and from the mode among us, founded by nature, of every mother suckling and nursing her own child, more of them are raised. Thence the swift progress of population among us, unparalleled in Europe. In fine, I am glad you are married, and congratulate you most cordially upon it. You are now in the way of becoming a useful citizen; and you have escaped the unnatural state of celibacy for life—the fate of many here who never intended it, but who, having too long postponed the change of their condition, find at length that it is too late to think of it, and so live all their lives in a situation that greatly lessens a man's value. An odd volume of a set of books bears not the value of its proportion to the set: what think you of the odd half of a pair of scissors? it can't well cut anything; it may possibly serve to scrape a trencher.

"Pray make my compliments and best wishes acceptable to your bride. I am old and heavy, or I should, ere this, have presented them in person. I shall make but small use of the old man's privilege, that of giving advice to younger friends. Treat your wife always with respect; it will procure respect to you, not only from her, but from all that observe it. Never use a slighting expression to her, even in jest; for slights in jest, after frequent bandyings, are apt to end in angry earnest. Be studious in your profession, and you will be learned. Be industrious and frugal, and you will be rich. Be sober and temperate, and you will be healthy. Be in general virtuous, and you will be happy. At least, you will, by such conduct, stand the best chance for such consequences.

"I pray God to bless you both, being ever your affectionate friend,

"B. Franklin."

---

"*Governor Franklin.*

"London, Dec. 19, 1767.

"Dear Sir,

"The resolutions of the Boston people concerning trade make a great noise here. Parliament has not yet taken notice of them, but the newspapers are in full cry against America. Colonel Onslow told me at court last Sunday, that I could not conceive how much the friends of America were run upon and hurt by them, and how much the Grenvillians triumphed. I have just written a paper for next Thursday's Chronicle, to extenuate matters a little.

"Mentioning Colonel Onslow reminds me of something that passed at the beginning of this session in the house between him and Mr. Grenville. The latter had been raving against America, as traitorous, rebellious, &c., when the former, who has always been its firm friend, stood up and gravely said, that in reading the Roman history, he found it was a custom among that wise and magnanimous people, whenever the senate was informed of any discontent in the provinces, to send two or three of their body into the discontented provinces to inquire into the grievances complained of, and report to the senate, that mild measures might be used to remedy what was amiss before any severe steps were taken to enforce obedience. That this example he thought worthy our imitation in the present state of our colonies, for he did so far agree with the honourable gentleman that spoke just before him as to allow there were great discontents among them. He should therefore beg leave to move, that two or three members of Parliament be appointed to go over to New-England on this service. And that it might not be supposed he was for imposing burdens on others that he would not be willing to bear himself, he did at the same time declare his own willingness, if the house should think fit to appoint them, to go over thither *with that honourable gentleman.* Upon this there was a great laugh, which continued some time, and was rather increased by Mr. Grenville's asking, 'Will the gentleman engage that I shall be safe there? Can I be assured that I shall be allowed to come back again to make the report?' As soon as the laugh was so far subsided as that Mr. Onslow could be heard again, he added, 'I cannot absolutely engage for the honourable gentleman's safe return; but if he goes thither upon this service, I am strongly of opinion the *event* will contribute greatly to the future quiet of both countries.' On which the laugh was renewed and redoubled.

"If our people should follow the Boston example in entering into resolutions of frugality and industry, full as necessary for us as for them, I hope they will, among other things, give this reason, that 'tis to enable them more speedily and effectually to discharge their debts to Great Britain; this will soften a little, and, at the same time, appear honourable, and like ourselves. Yours, &c.,

"B. Franklin."

---

"*To Dr. Priestley.*

"Passy, June 7, 1782.

"Dear Sir,

"I received your kind letter of the 7th April, also one of the 3d of May. I have always great pleasure in hearing from you, in learning that you are well, and that you continue your experiments. I should rejoice much if I could once more recover the leisure to search with you into the works of nature; I mean the inanimate or moral part of them: the more I discovered of the former, the more I admired them; the more I know of the latter, the more I am disgusted with them. Men I find to be a sort of beings very badly constructed, as they are generally more easily provoked than reconciled, more disposed to do mischief to each other than to make reparation, much more easily deceived than undeceived, and having more pride and even pleasure in killing than in begetting one another. * * * In what light we are viewed by superior beings, may be gathered from a piece of late West India news, which, possibly, has not yet reached you. A young angel being sent down to this world on some business for the first time, had an old courier-spirit assigned him as a guide; they arrived over the seas of Martinico, in the middle of the long day of obstinate fight between the fleets of Rodney and De Grasse. When through the clouds of smoke he saw the fire of the guns, the decks covered with mangled limbs, and bodies dead or dying, the ships sinking, burning, or blown into the air, and the quantity of pain, misery, and destruction, the crews yet alive were thus with so much eagerness dealing round to one another, he turned angrily to his guide, and said, you blundering blockhead, you are ignorant of your business; you undertook to conduct me to the earth, and you have brought me into hell! No, sir, says the guide, I have made no mistake; this is really the earth, and these are men. Devils never treat one another in this cruel manner; they have more sense, and more of what men (vainly) call humanity.

"But to be serious, my dear old friend, I love you as much as ever, and I love all the honest souls that meet at the London Coffee-house. I only wonder how it happened that they and my other friends in England came to be such good creatures in the midst of so perverse a generation. I long to see them and you once more, and I labour for peace with more earnestness, that I may again be happy in your sweet society. * * *

"Yesterday the *Count du Nord*[17] was at the Academy of Sciences, when sundry experiments were exhibited for his entertainment; among them, one by M. Lavoisier, to show that the strongest fire we yet know is made in charcoal blown upon with dephlogisticated air. In a heat so produced, he melted platina presently, the fire being much more powerful than that of the strongest burning mirror. Adieu, and believe me ever, yours most affectionately,

B. Franklin."

*To the same.*

"London, September 19, 1772.

"Dear Sir,

"In the affair of so much importance to you, wherein you ask my advice, I cannot, for want of sufficient premises, counsel you *what* to determine; but, if you please, I will tell you *how*. When those difficult cases occur, they are difficult chiefly because, while we have them under consideration, all the reasons, *pro* and *con*, are not present to the mind at the same time; but sometimes one set present themselves, and at other times another, the first being out of sight. Hence the various purposes or inclinations that alternately prevail, and the uncertainty that perplexes us. To get over this, my way is, to divide half a sheet of paper by a line into two columns, writing over the one *pro* and over the other *con*: then, during three or four days' consideration, I put down under the different heads short hints of the different motives that at different times occur to me *for* or *against* the measure. When I have thus got them all together in one view, I endeavour to estimate their respective weights, and where I find two (one on each side), that seem equal, I strike them both out. If I find a reason *pro* equal to some *two* reasons *con* I strike out the *three*. If I judge some *two* reasons *con* equal to some *three* reasons *pro*, I strike out the *five*; and, thus proceeding, I find at length where the *balance* lies; and if, after a day or two of farther consideration, nothing new that is of importance occurs on either side, I come to a determination accordingly. And though the weight of reasons cannot be taken with the precision of algebraic quantities, yet, when each is thus considered separately and comparatively, and the whole lies before me, I think I can judge better, and am less liable to make a rash step; and, in fact, I have found great advantage from this kind of equation, in what may be called moral or *prudential algebra*.

"Wishing sincerely that you may determine for the best, I am ever, my dear friend, yours most affectionately,

B. Franklin."

"Mr. Mather, Boston.

"London, July, 4, 1773.

"REVEREND SIR,

"The remarks you have added on the late proceedings against America are very just and judicious; and I cannot see any impropriety in your making them, though a minister of the gospel. This kingdom is a good deal indebted for its liberties to the public spirit of its ancient clergy, who joined with the barons in obtaining Magna Charta, and joined heartily in forming the curses of excommunication against the infringers of it. There is no doubt but the claim of Parliament, of authority to make laws *binding on the colonies in all cases whatsoever*, includes an authority to change our religious constitution, and establish popery or Mohammedanism, if they please, in its stead; but, as you intimate, *power* does not infer *right*; and as the *right* is nothing and the *power* (by our increase) continually diminishing, the one will soon be as insignificant as the *other*. You seem only to have made a small mistake in supposing they modestly avoided to declare they had a right, the words of the act being, 'that they have, and of *right* ought to have, full power,' &c.

"Your suspicion that sundry others besides Governor Bernard 'had written hither their opinions and councils, encouraging the late measures to the prejudice of our country, which have been too much needed and followed,' is, I apprehend, but too well founded. You call them 'traitorous individuals,' whence I collect that you suppose them of our own country. There was among the twelve apostles one traitor, who betrayed with a kiss. It should be no wonder, therefore, if among so many thousand true patriots as New-England contains, there should be found even twelve Judases ready to betray their country for a few paltry pieces of silver. Their *ends*, as well as their views, ought to be similar. But all the oppressions evidently work for our good. Providence seems by every means intent on making us a great people. May our virtues, public and private, grow with us and be durable, that liberty, civil and religious, may be secured to our posterity, and to all from every part of the Old World that take refuge among us.

"With great esteem, and my best wishes for a long continuance of your usefulness, I am, reverend sir, your most obedient, humble servant,

"B. FRANKLIN."

"*Mr. Strahan.*

"Philadelphia, July 5, 1775.

"You are a member of Parliament, and one of that majority which has doomed my country to destruction. You have begun to burn our towns and murder our people. Look upon your hands! they are stained with the blood of your relations! You and I were long friends: you are now my enemy, and—I am yours,

B. FRANKLIN."

---

"Dr. Priestley.

"Philadelphia, October 3, 1775

"DEAR SIR,

"I am bound to sail to-morrow for the camp,[18] and, having but just heard of this opportunity, can only write a line to say that I am well and hearty. Tell our dear good friend, Dr. Price, who sometimes has his doubts and despondencies about our firmness, that America is determined and unanimous; a very few tories and placemen excepted, who will probably soon export themselves. Britain, at the expense of three millions, has killed one hundred and fifty Yankees this campaign, which is 20,000$l.$ a head; and at Bunker's Hill she gained a mile of ground, half of which she lost again by our taking post on Ploughed Hill. During the same time sixty thousand children have been born in America. From these *data* his mathematical head will easily calculate the time and expense necessary to kill us all and conquer our whole territory. My sincere repects to * *, and to the club of honest whigs at * *. Adieu.

"I am ever yours most affectionately,

"B. FRANKLIN."

[18] Dr. Franklin, Colonel Harrison, and Mr. Lynch, were at this time appointed by Congress (of which they were members) to confer on certain subjects with General Washington. The American army was then employed in blocking up General Howe in Boston; and it was during this visit that General Washington communicated the following memorable anecdote to Dr. Franklin, viz., "that there had been a time when his army had been so destitute of military stores as not to have powder enough in all its magazines to furnish more than five rounds per man for their small arms." Artillery were out of the question: they were fired now and then, only to show that they had them. Yet this secret was kept with so much address and good countenance from both armies, that General Washington was enabled effectually to continue the blockade.

---

"Mrs. Thompson, at Lisle.

Paris, February 8, 1777.

"You are too early, *hussy*, as well as too saucy, in calling me *rebel*; you should wait for the event, which will determine whether it is a *rebellion* or only a *revolution*. Here the ladies are more civil; they call us *les insurgens*, a character that usually pleases them; and methinks all other women who smart, or have smarted, under the tyranny of a bad husband, ought to be fixed in *revolution* principles, and act accordingly.

"In my way to Canada last spring, I saw dear Mrs. Barrow at New-York. Mr. Barrow had been from her two or three months, to keep Governor Tryon and other tories company on board the Asia, one of the king's ships which lay in the harbour; and in all that time that naughty man had not ventured once on shore to see her. Our troops were then pouring into the town, and she was packing up to leave it; fearing, as she had a large house, they would incommode her by quartering officers in it. As she appeared in great perplexity, scarce knowing where to go, I persuaded her to stay; and I went to the general officers then commanding there, and recommended her to their protection; which they promised and performed. On my return from Canada, where I was a piece of a governor (and, I think, a very good one) for a fortnight, and might have been so till this time if your wicked army, enemies to all good government, had not come and driven me out, I found her still in quiet possession of her house. I inquired how our people had behaved to her; she spoke in high terms of the respectful attention they had paid her, and the quiet and security they had procured her. I said I was glad of it, and that, if they had used her ill, I would have turned tory. Then, said she (with that pleasing gayety so natural to her), *I wish they had.* For you must know she is a *toryess* as well as you, and can as flippantly say *rebel*. I drank tea with her; we talked affectionately of you and our other friends the Wilkes, of whom she had received no late intelligence; what became of her since, I have not heard. The street she lived in was some months after chiefly burned down; but as the town was then, and ever since has been, in possession of the king's troops, I have had no opportunity of knowing whether she suffered any loss in the conflagration. I hope she did not, as if she did, I should wish I had not persuaded her to stay there. I am glad to learn from you, that that unhappy but deserving family, the W.'s, are getting into some business that may afford them subsistence. I pray that God will bless them, and that they may see happier days. Mr. Cheap's and Dr. H.'s good fortunes please me. Pray learn, if you have not already learned, like me, to be pleased with other people's pleasures, and happy with their happiness when none occur of your own; then, perhaps, you will not so soon be weary of the place you chance to be in, and so fond of rambling to get rid of your *ennui*. I fancy you have hit upon the right reason of your being weary of St. Omer's, viz., that you are out of temper, which is the effect of full living and idleness. A month in Bridewell, beating hemp, upon bread and water, would give you health and spirits, and subsequent cheerfulness and contentment with every other situation. I prescribe that regimen for you, my dear, in pure good-will, without a fee. And, let me tell you, if you do not get into temper, neither Brussels nor Lisle will suit you. I know nothing of the price of living in either of those places; but I am sure a single woman as you are might, with economy, upon two hundred pounds a year, maintain herself comfortably anywhere, and me into the bargain. Do not invite me in earnest, however, to come and live with you, for, being posted here, I ought not to comply, and I am not sure I should be able to refuse. Present my respects to Mrs. Payne and Mrs. Heathcoat; for, though I have not the honour of knowing them, yet as you say they are friends to the American cause, I am sure they must be women of good understanding. I know you wish you could see me, but as you can't, I will describe myself to you. Figure me in your mind as jolly as formerly, and as strong and hearty, only a few years older: very plainly dressed, wearing my thin gray straight hair, that peeps out under my only *coiffure*, a fine fur cap, which comes down my forhead almost to my spectacles. Think how this must appear among the powdered heads of Paris! I wish every lady and gentleman in France would only be so obliging as to follow my fashion, comb their own heads as I do mine, dismiss their *friseurs*, and pay me half the money they paid to them. You see the gentry might well afford this, and I could then enlist these friseurs, (who are at least 100,000), and with the money I would maintain them, make a visit with them to England, and dress the heads of your ministers and privy counsellors; which I conceive at present to be *un peu derangées*. Adieu! madcap, and believe me ever your affectionate friend and humble servant,

"B. FRANKLIN.

"P.S.—Don't be proud of this long letter. A fit of the gout, which has confined me five days, and made me refuse to see company, has given me little time to trifle; otherwise it would have been very short; visiters and business would have interrupted: and, perhaps, with Mrs. Barrow, you wish they had."

"*To Mr. Lith.*

"Passy, near Paris, April 6, 1777.

"SIR,

"I have just been honoured with a letter from you, dated the 26th past, in which you express yourself as astonished, and appear to be angry that you have no answer to a letter you wrote me of the 11th of December, which you are sure was delivered to me.

"In exculpation of myself, I assure you that I never received any letter from you of this date. And, indeed, being then but four days landed at Nantes, I think you could scarce have heard so soon of my being in Europe.

"But I received one from you of the 8th of January, which I own I did not answer. It may displease you if I give you the reason; but as it may be of use to you in your future correspondences, I will hazard that for a gentleman to whom I feel myself obliged, as an American, on account of his good-will to our cause.

"Whoever writes to a stranger should observe three points: 1. That what he proposes be practicable. 2. His propositions should be made in explicit terms, so as to be easily understood. 3. What he desires, should be in itself reasonable. Hereby he will give a favourable impression of his understanding, and create a desire of farther acquaintance. Now it happened that you were negligent in *all* these points: for, first, you desired to have means procured for you of taking a voyage to America '*avec sureté*,[19] which is not possible, as the dangers of the sea subsist always, and at present there is the additional danger of being taken by the English. Then you desire that this may be '*sans trop grandes dépenses*,'[20] which is not intelligible enough to be answered, because, not knowing your ability of bearing expenses, one cannot judge what may be *trop grandes*. Lastly, you desire letters of address to the Congress and to General Washington, which it is not reasonable to ask of one who knows no more of you than that your name is LITH, and that you live at BAYREUTH.

"In your last, you also express yourself in vague terms when you desire to be informed whether you may expect '*d'étre reçu d'une maniére cenvenable*'[21] in our troops. As it is impossible to know what your ideas are of the *maniére convenable*, how can one answer this? And then you demand whether I will support you by my authority in giving you letters of recommendation. I doubt not your being a man of merit, and, knowing it yourself, you may forget that it is not known to everybody; but reflect a moment, sir, and you will be convinced, that if I were to practise giving letters of recommendation to persons whose character I knew no more than I do of yours, my recommendations would soon be of no authority at all.

"I thank you, however, for your kind desire of being serviceable to my countrymen, and I wish, in return, that I could be of service to you in the scheme you have formed of going to America. But numbers of experienced officers here have offered to go over and join our army, and I could give them no encouragement, because I have no orders for that purpose, and I know it is extremely difficult to place them when they come there. I cannot but think, therefore, that it is best for you not to make so long, so expensive, and so hazardous a voyage, but to take the advice of your friends and *stay in Franconia*. I have the honour to be, sir, &c.,

"B. FRANKLIN."

[19] With safety.
[20] Without too great expense.
[21] To be received in a suitable manner.

---

*Answer to a letter from Brussels.*

"*Passy*, July 1, 1778.

"SIR,

"I received your letter dated at Brussels the 16th past.

"My vanity might possibly be flattered by your expressions of compliment to my understanding, if your proposals did not more clearly manifest a mean opinion of it.

"You conjure me, in the name of the omniscient and just God, before whom I must appear, and by my hopes of future fame, to consider if some expedient cannot be found to put a stop to the desolation of America, and prevent the miseries of a general war. As I am conscious of having taken every step in my power to prevent the breach, and no one to widen it, I can appear cheerfully before that God, fearing nothing from his justice in this particular, though I have much occasion for his mercy in many others. As to my future fame, I am content to rest it on my past and present conduct, without seeking an addition to it in the crooked, dark paths you propose to me, where I should most certainly lose it. This your solemn address would, therefore, have been more properly made to your sovereign and his venal parliament. He and they, who wickedly began and madly continue a war for the desolation of America, are accountable for the consequences.

"You endeavour to impress me with a bad opinion of French faith; but the instances of their friendly endeavours to serve a race of weak princes, who by their own imprudence defeated every attempt to promote their interest, weigh but little with me when I consider the steady friendship of France to the thirteen United States of Switzerland, which has now continued inviolate two hundred years. You tell me that she will certainly cheat us, and that she despises us already. I do not believe that she will cheat us, and I am not certain that she despises us: but I see clearly that you are endeavouring to cheat us by your conciliatory bills; that you actually despised our understandings when you flattered yourselves those artifices would succeed; and that not only France, but all Europe, yourselves included, most certainly and for ever, would despise us if we were weak enough to accept your insidious propositions.

"Our expectations of the future grandeur of America are not so magnificent, and, therefore, not so vain and visionary, as you represent them to be. The body of our people are not merchants, but humble husbandmen, who delight in the cultivation of their lands, which, from their fertility and the variety of our climates, are capable of furnishing all the necessaries of life without external commerce; and we have too much land to have the slightest temptation to extend our territory by conquest from peaceable neighbours, as well as too much justice to think of it. Our militia, you find by experience, are sufficient to defend our lands from invasion; and the commerce with us will be defended by all the nations who find an advantage in it. We therefore have not the occasion you imagine, of fleets or standing armies, but may leave those expensive machines to be maintained for the pomp of princes and the wealth of ancient states. We propose, if possible, to live in peace with all mankind; and, after you have been convinced, to your cost, that there is nothing to be got by attacking us, we have reason to hope that no other power will judge it prudent to quarrel with us, lest they divert us from our own quiet industry, and turn us into corsairs preying upon theirs. The weight, therefore, of an independent empire, which you seem certain of our inability to bear, will not be so great as you imagine. The expense of our civil government we have always borne, and can easily bear, because it is small. A virtuous and laborious people may be cheaply governed. Determining as we do to have no offices of profit, nor any sinecures or useless appointments, so common in ancient and corrupted states, we can govern ourselves a year for the sum you pay in a single department, or for what one jobbing contractor, by the favour of a minister, can cheat you out of in a single article.

"You think we flatter ourselves, and are deceived into an opinion that England *must* acknowledge our independence. We, on the other hand, think you flatter yourselves in imagining such an acknowledgment a vast boon which we strongly desire, and which you may gain some great advantage by granting or withholding. We have never asked it of you. We only tell you that you can have no treaty with us but as an independent state; and you may please yourselves and your children with the rattle of your right to govern us, as long as you have with that of your king being king of France, without giving us the least concern if you do not attempt to exercise it. That this pretended right is indisputable, as you say, we utterly deny. Your parliament never had a right to govern us, and your king has forfeited it by his bloody tyranny. But I thank you for letting me know a little of your mind, that even if the Parliament should acknowledge our independence, the act would not be binding to posterity, and that your nation would resume and prosecute the claim as soon as they found it convenient from the influence of your passions and your present malice against us. We suspected before that you would not be bound by your conciliatory acts longer than till they had served their purpose of inducing us to disband our forces; but we were not certain that you were knaves by principle, and that we ought not to have the least confidence in your offers, promises, or treaties, though confirmed by Parliament. I now indeed recollect my being informed, long since, when in England, that a certain very great personage, then young, studied much a certain book, entitled *Arcana imperii [Secrets of governing]*. I had the curiosity to procure the book and read it. There are sensible and good things in it, but some bad ones; for, if I remember right, a particular king is applauded for his politically exciting a rebellion among his subjects at a time when they had not strength to support it, that he might, in subduing them, take away their privileges which were troublesome to him: and a question is formally stated and discussed, *Whether a prince, to appease a revolt, makes promises of indemnity to the revolters, is obliged to fulfil those promises?* Honest and good men would say ay; but this politician says as you say, no. And he gives this pretty reason, that though it was right to make the promises, because otherwise the revolt would not be suppressed, yet it would be wrong to keep them, because revolters ought to be punished to deter future revolts. If these are the principles of your nation, no confidence can be placed in you; it is in vain to treat with you, and the wars can only end in being reduced to an utter inability of continuing them.

"One main drift of your letter seems to be to impress me with an idea of your own impartiality, by just censures of your ministers and measures, and to draw from me propositions of peace, or approbations of those you have enclosed me, which you intimate may by your means be conveyed to the king directly, without the intervention of those ministers. Would you have me give them to, or drop them for a stranger I may find next Monday in the Church of Notre Dame, to be known by a rose in his hat? You yourself, sir, are quite unknown to me; you have not trusted me with your right name. Our taking the least step towards a treaty with England, through you, might, if you are an enemy, be made use of to ruin us with our new and good friends. I may be indiscreet enough in many things, but certainly, if I were disposed to make propositions (which I cannot do, having none committed to me to make), I should never think of delivering them to the Lord knows who, to be carried the Lord knows where, to serve no one knows what purposes. Being at this time one of the most remarkable figures in Paris, even my appearance in the Church of Notre Dame, where I cannot have any conceivable business, and especially being seen to leave or drop any letter to any person there would be a matter of some speculation, and might, from the suspicions it must naturally give, have very mischievous consequences to our credit here. The very proposing of a correspondence so to be managed, in a manner not necessary where *fair dealing* is intended, gives just reason to suppose you intend the *contrary*. Besides, as your court has sent commissioners to treat with the Congress, with all the powers that would be given them by the crown under the act of Parliament, what *good purpose* can be served by privately obtaining propositions from us? Before those commissioners went, we might have treated in virtue of our general powers (with the knowledge, advice, and approbation of our friends), upon any propositions made to us. But, under the present circumstances, for us to make propositions while a treaty is supposed to be actually on foot with the Congress, would be extremely improper, highly presumptuous with regard to our honourable constituents, and answer no good end whatever.

"I write this letter to you, notwithstanding (which I think I can convey in a less mysterious manner; and guess it may come to your hands); I write it because I would let you know our sense of your procedure, which appears as insidious as that of your conciliatory bills. Your true way to obtain peace, if your ministers desire it, is to propose openly to the Congress fair and equal terms; and you may possibly come sooner to such a resolution, when you find that personal flatteries, general cajolings, and panegyrics on our *virtue* and *wisdom* are not likely to have the effect you seem to expect; the persuading us to act *basely* and *foolishly* in betraying our country and posterity into the hands of our most bitter enemies; giving up or selling of our arms and warlike stores, dismissing our ships of war and troops, and putting those enemies in possession of our forts and ports. This proposition of delivering ourselves, bound and gagged, ready for hanging, without even a right to complain, and without even a friend to be found afterward among all mankind, you would have us embrace on the faith of an act of Parliament! Good God! an act of your Parliament! This demonstrates that you do not yet know us, and that you fancy we do not know you: but it is not merely this flimsy faith that we are to act upon; you offer us *hope*, the hope of PLACES, PENSIONS, and PEERAGE. These, judging from yourselves, you think are motives irresistible. This offer to corrupt us, sir, is with me your credential, and convinces me that you are not a private volunteer in your application. It bears the stamp of British court intrigue, and the signature of your king. But think for a moment in what light it must be viewed in America. By places which cannot come among us, for you take care by a special article to keep them to yourselves. We must then pay the salaries in order to enrich ourselves with these places. But you will give us PENSIONS; probably to be paid, too, out of your expected American revenue; and which none of us can accept without deserving, and, perhaps, obtaining a *suspension*. PEERAGES! Alas! sir, our long observation of the vast servile majority of your peers, voting constantly for every measure proposed by a minister, however weak or wicked, leaves us small respect for them, and we consider it a sort of tar-and-feathered honour, or a mixture of foulness and folly; which every man among us who should accept from your king, would be obliged to renounce or exchange for that conferred by the mobs of their own country, or wear it with everlasting shame.

"B. Franklin."

---

"*Dr. Price, London.*

"Passy, February 6, 1780.

"Dear Sir,

"I received but very lately your kind favour of October 14. Dr. Ingenhausz, who brought it, having stayed long in Holland. I sent the enclosed directly to Mr. L. It gave me great pleasure to understand that you continue well. Your writings, after all the abuse you and they have met with, begin to make serious impressions on those who at first rejected the counsels you gave; and they will acquire new weight every day, and be in high esteem when the cavils against them are dead and forgotten. Please to present my affectionate respects to that honest, sensible, and intelligent society, who did me so long the honour of admitting me to share in their instructive conversations. I never think of the hours I so happily spent in that company, without regretting that they are never to be repeated; for I see no prospect of an end to this unhappy war in my time. Dr. Priestley, you tell me, continues his experiments with success. We make daily great improvements in *natural*—there is one I wish to see in *moral* philosophy; the discovery of a plan that would induce and oblige nations to settle their disputes without first cutting one another's throats. When will human reason be sufficiently improved to see the advantage of this? When will men be convinced that even successful wars at length become misfortunes to those who unjustly commenced them, and who triumphed blindly in their success, not seeing all its consequences. Your great comfort and mine in this war is, that we honestly and faithfully did everything in our power to prevent it. Adieu, and believe me ever, my dear friend, yours, &c.,

"B. Franklin."

"*Dr. Priestley.*

"Passy, February 8, 1780.

"Dear Sir,

"Your kind letter of September 27 came to hand but very lately, the bearer having stayed long in Holland.

"I always rejoice to hear of your being still employed in experimental researches into nature, and of the success you meet with. The rapid progress *true* science now makes, occasions my regretting sometimes that I was born so soon: it is impossible to imagine the height to which may be carried, in a thousand years, the power of man over matter; we may perhaps learn to deprive large masses of their gravity, and give them absolute levity for the sake of easy transport. Agriculture may diminish its labour and double its produce; all diseases may by sure means be prevented or cured (not excepting even that of old age), and our lives lengthened at pleasure even beyond the antediluvian standard. Oh! that moral science were in as fair a way of improvement; that men would cease to be wolves to one another; and that human beings would at length learn what they now improperly call humanity!

"I am glad that my little paper on the Aurora Borealis pleased. If it should occasion farther inquiry, and so produce a better hypothesis, it will not be wholly useless.

"B. Franklin."

[Enclosed in the foregoing letter; being an answer to a separate paper received from Dr. Priestley]

"I have considered the situation of that person very attentively; I think that, with a little help from the *Moral Algebra*, he might form a better judgment than any other person can form for him. But, since my opinion seems to be desired, I give it for continuing to the end of the term, under all the present disagreeable circumstances: the connexion will then die a natural death. No reason will be expected to be given for the separation, and, of course, no offence taken at reasons given; the friendship may still subsist, and, in some other way, be useful. The time diminishes daily, and is usefully employed. All human situations have their inconveniences; we *feel* those that we find in the present, and we neither *feel* nor *see* those that exist in another. Hence we make frequent and troublesome changes without amendment, and often for the worse. In my youth, I was passenger in a little sloop descending the river Delaware. There being no wind, we were obliged, when the ebb was spent, to cast anchor and wait for the next. The heat of the sun on the vessel was excessive, the company strangers to me, and not very agreeable. Near the river-side I saw what I took to be a pleasant green meadow, in the middle of which was a large shady tree, where it struck my fancy I could sit and read (having a book in my pocket), and pass the time agreeably till the tide turned; I therefore prevailed with the captain to put me ashore. Being landed, I found the greatest part of my meadow was really a marsh, in crossing which, to come at my tree, I was up to my knees in mire: and I had not placed myself under its shade five minutes before the moschetoes in swarms found me out, attacked my legs, hands, and face, and made my reading and my rest impossible; so that I returned to the beach, and called for the boat to come and take me on board again, where I was obliged to bear the heat I had strove to quit, and also the laugh of the company. Similar cases in the affairs of life have since frequently fallen under my observation.

"I have had thoughts of a college for him in America; I know no one who might be more useful to the public in the institution of youth. But there are possible unpleasantnesses in that situation: it cannot be obtained but by a too hazardous voyage at this time for a family: and the time for experiments would be all otherwise engaged.

"B. Franklin."

---

"To General Washington.

"Passy, March 5, 1780

"Sir,

"I received but lately the letter your excellency did me the honour of writing to me in recommendation of the Marquis de Lafayette. His modesty detained it long in his own hands. We became acquainted, however, from the time of his arrival at Paris; and his zeal for the honour of our country, his activity in our affairs here, and his firm attachment to our cause and to you, impressed me with the same regard and esteem for him that your excellency's letter would have done had it been immediately delivered to me.

"Should peace arrive after another campaign or two, and afford us a little leisure, I should be happy to see your excellency in Europe, and to accompany you, if my age and strength would permit, in visiting some of its most ancient and famous kingdoms. You would, on this side the sea, enjoy the great reputation you have acquired, pure and free from those little shades that the jealousy and envy of a man's countrymen and contemporaries are ever endeavouring to cast over living merit. Here you would know and enjoy what posterity will say of Washington. For a thousand leagues have nearly the same effect with a thousand years. The feeble voice of those grovelling passions cannot extend so far either in time or distance. At present I enjoy that pleasure for you, as I frequently hear the old generals of this martial country (who study the maps of America, and mark upon them all your operations) speak with sincere approbation and great applause of your conduct, and join in giving you the character of one of the greatest captains of the age.

"I must soon quit the scene, but you may live to see our country flourish, as it will amazingly and rapidly after the war is over. Like a field of young Indian corn, which long fair weather and sunshine had enfeebled and discoloured, and which in that weak state, by a thunder-gust of violent wind, hail, and rain, seemed to be threatened with absolute destruction; yet the storm being past, it recovers fresh verdure, shoots up with double vigour, and delights the eye not of its owner only, but of every observing traveller.

"The best wishes that can be formed for your health, honour, and happiness, ever attend you, from yours, &c.,

B. Franklin."

---

"To M. Court de Gebelin,[22] Paris.

"Passy, May 7, 1781.

"Dear Sir,

"I am glad the little book[23] proved acceptable. It does not appear to me intended for a grammar to teach the language. It is rather what we call in English a *spelling-book*, in which the only method observed is to arrange the words according to their number of syllables, placing those of one syllable together, and those of two syllables, and so on. And it is to be observed that *Sa ki ma*, for instance, is not three words, but one word of three syllables; and the reason that *hyphens* are not placed between the syllables is, that the printer had not enough of them.

"As the Indians had no letters, they had no orthography. The Delaware language being differently spelt from the Virginian, may not always arise from a difference in the languages; for strangers who learn the language of an Indian nation, finding no orthography, are at liberty, in writing the language, to use such compositions of letters as they think will best produce the sounds of the words. I have observed that our Europeans of different nations, who learn the same Indian language, form each his own orthography according to the usual sounds given to the letters in his own language. Thus the same words of the Mohock language written by an English, a French, and a German interpreter, often differ very much in the spelling; and without knowing the usual powers of the letters in the language of the interpreter, one cannot come at the pronunciation of the Indian words. The spelling-book in question was, I think, written by a German.

"You mention a Virginian Bible. Is it not the Bible of the Massachusetts language, translated by Elliot, and printed in New-England about the middle of the last century? I know this Bible, but have never heard of one in the Virginian language. Your observation of the similitude between many of the words and those of the ancient world, are indeed very curious.

"This inscription, which you find to be Phœnician, is, I think, near *Taunton* (not Jannston, as you write it). There is some account of it in the old Philosophical Transactions; I have never been at the place, but shall be glad to see your remarks on it.

"The compass appears to have been long known in China before it was known in Europe; unless we suppose it known to Homer, who makes the prince that lent ships to Ulysses boast that they had a *spirit* in them, by whose directions they could find their way in a cloudy day or the darkest night. If any Phœnicians arrived in America, I should rather think it was not by the accident of a storm, but in the course of their long and adventurous voyages; and that they coasted from Denmark and Norway, over to Greenland, and down southward by Newfoundland, Nova Scotia, &c., to New-England, as the Danes themselves certainly did some ages before Columbus.

"Our new American society will be happy in the correspondence you mention; and when it is possible for me, I shall be glad to attend the meetings of your society,[24] which I am sure must be very instructive.

"B. Franklin."

[22] Antoine Court de Gebelin, born at Nismes in 1725, became a minister of a Protestant communion in the Cevennes, then at Lausanne: he quitted the clerical function for literature, at Paris, where he acquired so great a reputation as an antiquary and philosopher that he was appointed to attend one of the museums. His reputation suffered by his zeal in favour of animal magnetism. He died at Paris, May 13, 1784. His great work is entitled, "Monde Primitif, analysé et comparé avec le Monde Moderne," 9 tom. 4to. The excellence of his character may be appreciated from the fact, that, on quitting Switzerland, he

voluntarily gave to his sister the principal part of his patrimony, reserving but little for himself, and relying for a maintenance upon the exercise of his talents.

[23] A Vocabulary of the Language of one of the Indian Tribes in North America.

[24] L'Academie des Inscriptions et Belles Letters.

---

*"To Francis Hopkinson, Philadelphia.*

*"Passy, September 13, 1781.*

"DEAR SIR,

"I have received your kind letter of July 17, with its duplicate, enclosing those for Messrs. Brandlight and Sons, which I have forwarded. I am sorry for the loss of the *squibs*. Everything of yours gives me pleasure.

"As to the friends and enemies you just mention, I have hitherto, thanks to God, had plenty of the former kind; they have been my treasure; and it has, perhaps, been of no disadvantage to me that I have had a few of the latter. They serve to put us upon correcting the faults we have, and avoiding those we are in danger of having. They counter-act the mischief flattery might do us, and their malicious attacks make our friends more zealous in serving us and promoting our interest. At present I do not know of more than two such enemies that I enjoy, viz., * * * and * * *. I deserved the enmity of the latter, because I might have avoided it by paying him a compliment, which I neglected. That to the former I owe to the people of France, who happened to respect me too much and him too little; which I could bear, and he could not. They are unhappy that they cannot make everybody hate me as much as they do; and I should be so if my friends did not love me much more than those gentlemen can possibly love one another.

"Enough of this subject. Let me know if you are in possession of my gimcrack instruments, and if you have made any new experiments. I lent, many years ago, a large glass globe, mounted, to Mr. Coombe, and an electric battery of bottles, which I remember; perhaps there were some other things. He may have had them so long as to think them his own. Pray ask him for them, and keep them for me, together with the rest.

"You have a new crop of prose writers. I see in your papers many of their fictitious names, but nobody tells me the real. You will oblige me by a little of your literary history. Adieu, my dear friend, and believe me ever, yours affectionately,

"B. FRANKLIN."

"*To Francis Hopkinson.*

"Paris, Dec 24, 1782.

"I thank you for your ingenious paper in favour of the trees. I own I now wish we had two rows of them in every one of our streets. The comfortable shelter they would afford us when walking from our burning summer suns, and the greater coolness of our walls and pavements, would, I conceive, in the improved health of the inhabitants, amply compensate the loss of a house now and then by fire, if such should be the consequence; but a tree is soon felled, and, as axes are near at hand in every neighbourhood, may be down before the engines arrive.

"You do well to avoid being concerned in the pieces of personal abuse, so scandalously common in our newspapers, that I am afraid to lend any of them here till I have examined and laid aside such as would disgrace us, and subject us among strangers to a reflection like that used by a gentleman in a coffee-house to two quarrellers, who, after a mutually free use of the words rogue, villain, rascal scoundrel, &c., seemed as if they would refer their dispute to him: 'I know nothing of you or your affairs,' said he; 'I only perceive *that you know one another.*'

"The conductor of a newspaper should, methinks, consider himself as in some degree the guardian of his country's reputation, and refuse to insert such writings as may hurt it. If people will print their abuses of one another, let them do it in little pamphlets, and distribute them where they think proper. It is absurd to trouble all the world with them, and unjust to subscribers in distant places, to stuff their paper with matter so unprofitable and so disagreeable. With sincere esteem and affection, I am, my dear friend, ever yours,

"B. FRANKLIN."

"*Samuel Huntingdon, President of Congress.*

"Passy, March 12, 1781.

SIR,

I had the honour of receiving, on the 13th of last month, your excellency's letter of the 1st of January, together with the instructions of November 28th and December 27th, a copy of those to Colonel Laurens, and the letter to the king. I immediately drew up a memorial, enforcing as strongly as I could the request contained in that letter, and directed by the instructions, and delivered the same with the letter, which were both well received. * * *

"I must now beg leave to say something relating to myself, a subject with which I have not often troubled the Congress. I have passed my seventy-fifth year, and I find that the long and severe fit of the gout which I had the last winter has shaken me exceedingly, and I am yet far from having recovered the bodily strength I before enjoyed. I do not know that my mental faculties are impaired. Perhaps I shall be the last to discover that; but I am sensible of great diminution in my activity, a quality I think particularly necessary in your minister at this court. I am afraid, therefore, that your affairs may some time or other suffer by my deficiency. I find also that the business is too heavy for me, and too confining. The constant attendance at home, which is necessary for receiving and accepting your bills of exchange (a matter foreign to my *ministerial functions*), to answer letters, and perform other parts of my employment, prevents my taking the air and exercise which my annual journeys formerly used to afford me, and which contributed much to the preservation of my health. There are many other little personal attentions which the infirmities of age render necessary to an old man's comfort, even in some degree to the continuance of his existence, and with which business often interferes. I have been engaged in public affairs, and enjoyed public confidence in some shape or other during the long term of fifty years, an honour sufficient to satisfy any reasonable ambition, and I have no other left but that of repose, which I hope the Congress will grant me by sending some person to supply my place.

"At the same time, I beg they may be assured that it is not any the least doubt of their success in the glorious cause, nor any disgust received in their service, that induces me to decline it, but purely and simply the reasons above mentioned; and as I cannot at present undergo the fatigues of a sea voyage (the last having been almost too much for me), and would not again expose myself to the hazard of capture and imprisonment in this time of war, I purpose to remain here at least till the peace; perhaps it may be for the remainder of my life; and if any knowledge or experience I have acquired here may be thought of use to my successor, I shall freely communicate it, and assist him with any influence I may be supposed to have or counsel that may be desired of me."

*"To the Bishop of St. Asaph.*[25]

"Passy, June 10, 1782.

"I received and read the letter from my dear and much respected friend with infinite pleasure. After so long a silence, and the long continuance of its unfortunate causes, a line from you was a prognostic of happier times approaching, when we may converse and communicate freely, without danger from the malevolence of men enraged by the ill-success of their distracted projects.

"I long with you for the return of peace, on the general principles of humanity. The hope of being able to pass a few more of my last days happily in the sweet conversations and company I once enjoyed at Twyford,[26] is a particular motive that adds strength to the general wish, and quickens my industry to procure that best of blessings. After much occasion to consider the folly and mischiefs of a state of warfare, and the little or no advantage obtained even by those nations who have conducted it with the most success, I have been apt to think that there has never been, nor ever will be, any such thing as a *good* war or a *bad* peace.

"You ask if I still relish my old studies? I relish them, but I cannot pursue them. My time is engrossed, unhappily, with other concerns. I requested from the Congress last year my discharge from this public station, that I might enjoy a little leisure in the evening of a long life of business; but it was refused me, and I have been obliged to drudge on a little longer.

"You are happy, as your years come on, in having that dear and most amiable family about you. Four daughters! how rich! I have but one, and she necessarily detained from me at a thousand leagues' distance. I feel the want of that tender care of me which might be expected from a daughter, and would give the world for one. Your shades are all placed in a row over my fireplace, so that I not only have you always in my mind, but constantly before my eyes.

"The cause of liberty and America has been greatly obliged to you. I hope you will live long to see that country flourish under its new constitution, which I am sure will give you great pleasure. Will you permit me to express another hope that, now your friends are in power, they will take the first opportunity of showing the sense they ought to have of your virtues and your merit?

"Please to make my best respects acceptable to Mrs. Shipley, and embrace for me tenderly all our dear children. With the utmost esteem, respect, and veneration, I am ever, my dear friend, yours most affectionately,

"B. FRANKLIN."

[25] Jonathan Shipley took his degrees at Christ Church, and in 1743 was made prebendary of Winchester. After travelling in 1745 with the Duke of Cumberland, he was promoted in 1749 to a canonry at Christ Church, became dean of Winchester in 1760, and 1769 bishop of St. Asaph. He was author of some elegant verses on the death of Queen Caroline, and published besides some poems and sermons, and died 1788. He was an ardent friend of American independence.

[26] The country residence of the bishop.

---

"*Miss Alexander.*

"Passy, June 27, 1782.

"I am not at all displeased that the thesis and dedication with which we were threatened are blown over, for I dislike much all sorts of mummery. The republic of letters has gained no reputation, whatever else it may have gained, by the commerce of dedications; I never made one, and never desired that one should be made to me. When I submitted to receive this, it was from the bad habit I have long had, of doing everything that ladies desire me to do: there is no refusing anything to Madame la Marck nor to you.

"I have been to pay my respects to that amiable lady, not merely because it was a compliment due to her, but because I love her: which induces me to excuse her not letting me in; the same reason I should have for excusing your faults, if you had any. I have not seen your papa since the receipt of your pleasing letter, so could arrange nothing with him respecting the carriage. During seven or eight days I shall be very busy; after that, you shall hear from me, and the carriage shall be at your service. How could you think of writing to me about chimneys and fires in such weather as this! Now is the time for the frugal lady you mention to save her wood, obtain *plus de chaleur*, and lay it up against winter, as people do ice against summer. Frugality is an enriching virtue, a virtue I never could acquire in myself, but I was once lucky enough to find it in a wife, who thereby became a fortune to me. Do you possess it? If you do, and I were twenty years younger, I would give your father one thousand guineas for you. I know you would be worth more to me as a *menagére*. I am covetous, and love good bargains. Adieu, my dear friend, and believe me ever yours most affectionately,

"B. Franklin."

---

"*Benjamin Vaughan.*

"Passy, July 10, 1782.

"By the original law of nations, war and extirpation was the punishment of injury. Humanizing by degrees, it admitted slavery instead of death. A farther step was the exchange of prisoners instead of slavery. Another, to respect more the property of private persons under conquest, and to be content with acquired dominion. Why should not the law of nations go on improving? Ages have intervened between its several steps; but, as knowledge of late increases rapidly, why should not those steps be quickened? Why should it not be agreed to as the future law of nations, that in any war hereafter the following descriptions of men should be undisturbed, have the protection of both sides, and be permitted to follow their employments in surety; viz.,

"1. Cultivators of the earth, because they labour for the subsistence of mankind.

"2. Fishermen, for the same reason.

"3. Merchants and traders in unarmed ships, who accommodate different nations by communicating and exchanging the necessaries and conveniences of life.

"4. Artists and mechanics, inhabiting and working in open towns.

"It is hardly necessary to add, that the hospitals of enemies should be unmolested; they ought to be assisted.

"In short, I would have nobody fought with but those who are paid for fighting. If obliged to take corn from the farmer, friend or enemy, I would pay him for it; the same for the fish or goods of the others.

"This once established, that encouragement to war which arises from a spirit of rapine would be taken away, and peace, therefore, more likely to continue and be lasting.

"B. Franklin."

---

"*Mrs. Hewson.*[27]

"Passy, January 27, 1783.

"The departure of my dearest friend,[28] which I learn from your last letter, greatly affects me. To meet with her once more in this life was one of the principal motives of my proposing to visit England again before my return to America. The last year carried off my friends Dr. Pringle and Dr. Fothergill, and Lord Kaimes and Lord Le Despencer; this has begun to take away the rest, and strikes the hardest. Thus the ties I had to that country, and, indeed, to the world in general, are loosened one by one, and I shall soon have no attachment left to make me unwilling to follow.

"I intended writing when I sent the eleven books, but lost the time in looking for the first. I wrote with that, and hope it came to hand. I therein asked your counsel about my coming to England: on reflection, I think I can, from my knowledge of your prudence, foresee what it will be; viz., not to come too soon, lest it should seem braving and insulting some who ought to be respected. I shall therefore omit that journey till I am near going to America, and then just step over to take leave of my friends, and spend a few days with you. I purpose bringing[29] Ben with me, and perhaps may leave him under your care.

"At length we are in peace, God be praised; and long, very long may it continue. All wars are follies, very expensive and very mischievous ones: when will mankind be convinced of this, and agree to settle their differences by arbitration? Were they to do it even by the cast of a die, it would be better than by fighting and destroying each other.

"Spring is coming on, when travelling will be delightful. Can you not, when your children are all at school, make a little party and take a trip hither? I have now a large house, delightfully situated, in which I could accommodate you and two or three friends; and I am but half an hour's drive from Paris.

"In looking forward, twenty five years seems a long period; but in looking back, how short! Could you imagine that 'tis now full a quarter of a century since we were first acquainted! it was in 1757. During the greatest part of the time I lived in the same house with my dear deceased friend your mother; of course you and I saw and conversed with each other much and often. It is to all our honours, that in all that time we never had among us the smallest misunderstanding. Our friendship has been all clear sunshine, without the least cloud in its hemisphere. Let me conclude by saying to you what I have had too frequent occasion to say to my other remaining old friends, *the fewer we become, the more let us love one another.*

"B. FRANKLIN."

[27] Widow of the eminent anatomist of that name, and formerly Miss Stevenson, to whom several of Dr. Franklin's letters on Philosophical subjects are addressed.

[28] Refers to Mrs. Hewson's mother.

[29] Benjamin Franklin Bache, a grandson of Dr. Franklin, by his daughter Sarah; he was the first editor of the AURORA at Philadelphia: died of yellow fever in September, 1798.

"*To David Hartley.*

"Passy, May 8, 1783.

"DEAR FRIEND,

"I send you enclosed the copies you desired of the papers I read to you yesterday.[30] I should be happy if I could see, before I die, the proposed improvement of the law of nations established. The miseries of mankind would be diminished by it, and the happiness of millions secured and promoted. If the practice of *privateering* could be profitable to any civilized nation, it might be so to us Americans, since we are so situated on the globe as that the rich commerce of Europe with the West Indies, consisting of manufactures, sugars, &c., is obliged to pass before our doors, which enables us to make short and cheap cruises, while our own commerce is in such bulky, low-priced articles, as that ten of our ships taken by you are not equal in value to one of yours, and you must come far from home at a great expense to look for them. I hope, therefore, that this proposition, if made by us, will appear in its true light, as having humanity only for its motive. I do not wish to see a new Barbary rising in America, and our long-extended coast occupied by piratical states. I fear lest our privateering success in the last two wars should already have given our people too strong a relish for that most mischievous kind of gaming, mixed blood; and if a stop is not now put to the practice, mankind may hereafter be more plagued with American corsairs than they have been and are with the Turkish. Try, my friend, what you can do in procuring for your nation the glory of being, though the greatest naval power, the first who voluntarily relinquished the advantage that power seems to give them, of plundering others, and thereby impeding the mutual communications among men of the gifts of God, and rendering miserable multitudes of merchants and their families, artisans, and cultivators of the earth, the most peaceable and innocent part of the human species.

B. FRANKLIN."

[30] See the Proposition about Privateering, annexed to letter to R. Oswald. January 14, 1783.

---

"*Dr. Percival.*

"Passy, July 17, 1784.

"DEAR SIR,

"I received yesterday, by Mr. White, your kind letter of May 11th, with the most agreeable present of your new book. I read it all before I slept, which is a proof of the good effects your happy manner has of drawing your reader on, by mixing little anecdotes and historical facts with your instructions. Be pleased to accept my grateful acknowledgments for the pleasure it has afforded me.

"It is astonishing that the murderous practice of duelling, which you so justly condemn, should continue so long in vogue. Formerly, when duels were used to determine lawsuits, from an opinion that Providence would in every instance favour truth and right with victory, they were excusable. At present they decide nothing. A man says something which another tells him is a lie. They fight; but, whichever is killed, the point in dispute remains unsettled. * * * How can such miserable sinners as we are entertain so much pride as to conceit that every offence against our imagined honour merits *death*? These petty princes, in their own opinion, would call that sovereign a tyrant who would put one of them to death for a little uncivil language, though pointed at his sacred person: yet every one of them makes himself judge in his own cause, condemns the offender without a jury, and undertakes himself to be the executioner.

"With sincere and great esteem, I have the honour to be, sir, your most obedient and humble servant,

B. FRANKLIN."

"*Sir Joseph Banks.*

"Passy, July 27, 1783.

"DEAR SIR,

"I received your very kind letter by Dr. Blagden, and esteem myself much honoured by your friendly remembrance. I have been too much and too closely engaged in public affairs since his being here to enjoy all the benefit of his conversation you were so good as to intend me. I hope soon to have more leisure, and to spend a part of it in those studies that are much more agreeable to me than political operations.

"I join with you most cordially in rejoicing at the return of peace. I hope it will be lasting, and that mankind will at length, as they call themselves reasonable creatures, have reason and sense enough to settle their differences without cutting throats: for, in my opinion, *there never was a good war nor a bad peace*. What vast additions to the conveniences and comforts of living might mankind have acquired, if the money spent in wars had been employed in works of public utility. What an extension of agriculture even to the tops of our mountains; what rivers rendered navigable, or joined by canals; what bridges, aqueducts, new roads, and other public works, edifices and improvements, rendering England a complete paradise, might not have been obtained, by spending those millions in doing good which in the last war have been spent in doing mischief; in bringing misery into thousands of families, and destroying the lives of so many thousands of working people, who might have performed the useful labour!

"I am pleased with the late astronomical discoveries made by our society. Furnished as all Europe now is with academies of science, with nice instruments and the spirit of experiment, the progress of human knowledge will be rapid, and discoveries made of which we have at present no conception. I begin to be almost sorry I was born so soon, since I cannot have the happiness of knowing what will be known one hundred years hence.

"I wish continued success to the labours of the Royal Society, and that you may long adorn their chair; being, with the highest esteem, dear sir, &c.

"B. Franklin."

"Dr. Blagden will acquaint you with the experiment of a vast globe sent up into the air, much talked of here, and which, if prosecuted, may furnish means of new knowledge."

"*Robert Morris, Esq.*

(Superintendent of Finances, United States.)

"Passy, Dec. 25, 1783.

"The remissness of our people in paying taxes is highly blameable, the unwillingness to pay them is still more so. I see in some resolutions of town meetings a remonstrance against giving Congress a power to take, as they call it, *the people's money* out of their pockets, though only to pay the interest and principal of debts duly contracted. They seem to mistake the point. Money justly due from the people is their creditor's money, and no longer the money of the people, who, if they withhold it, should be compelled to pay by some law. All property, indeed, except the savages' temporary cabin, his bow, his matchuat, and other little acquisitions absolutely necessary for his subsistence, seems to me to be the creature of public convention. Hence the public has the right of regulating descents, and all other conveyances of property, and even of limiting the quantity and the uses of it. All the property that is necessary to a man for the conservation of the individual and the propagation of the species, is his natural right, which none can justly deprive him of; but all property superfluous to such purposes is the property of the public, who, by their laws, have created it, and who may therefore, by other laws, dispose of it whenever the welfare of the public shall desire such disposition. He that does not like civil society on these terms, let him retire and live among savages. He can have no right to the benefits of society who will not pay his club towards the support of it.

"The Marquis de Lafayette, who loves to be employed in our affairs, and is often very useful, has lately had several conversations with the ministers and persons concerned in forming new regulations respecting the commerce between our two countries, which are not yet concluded. I thought it therefore, well to communicate to him a copy of your letter which contains so many sensible and just observations on that subject. He will make a proper use of them, and perhaps they may have more weight, as appearing to come from a Frenchman, than they would have if it were known that they were the observations of an American. I perfectly agree with all the sentiments you have expressed on this occasion.

"I am sorry, for the public's sake, that you are about to quit your office, but on personal considerations I shall congratulate you. For I cannot conceive of a more happy man than he who, having been long loaded with public cares, finds himself relieved from them, and enjoying private repose in the bosom of his friends and family.

"With sincere regard and attachment, I am ever, dear sir, yours, &c.,

B. FRANKLIN."

"To Dr. Mather, Boston.

"Passy, May 12, 1784.

"REV. SIR,

"I received your kind letter with your excellent advice to the people of the United States, which I read with great pleasure, and hope it will be duly regarded. Such writings, though they may be lightly passed over by many readers, yet if they make a deep impression on one active mind in a hundred, the effects may be considerable. Permit me to mention one little instance, which, though it relates to myself, will not be quite uninteresting to you. When I was a boy I met with a book entitled *Essays to do Good*, which I think was written by your father. It had been so little regarded by a former possessor, that several leaves of it were torn out: but the remainder gave me such a turn of thinking as to have an influence on my conduct through life; for I have always set a greater value on the character of a *doer of good*, than on any other kind of reputation; and if I have been, as you seem to think, a useful citizen, the public owes the advantage of it to that book. You mention your being in your 78th year: I am in my 79th; we are grown old together. It is now more than sixty years since I left Boston, but I remember well both your father and grandfather, having heard them both in the pulpit, and seen them in their houses. The last time I saw your father was in the beginning of 1724, when I visited him after my first trip to Pennsylvania. He received me in his library, and on my taking leave showed me a shorter way out of the house through a narrow passage, which crossed by a beam over head. We were still talking as I withdrew, he accompanying me behind, and I turning partly towards him, when he said hastily, *Stoop, stoop!* I did not understand him till I felt my head hit against the beam. He was a man that never missed any occasion of giving instruction, and upon this he said to me, *You are young, and have the world before you*; STOOP *as you go through it, and you will miss many hard thumps.* This advice, thus beat into my head, has frequently been of use to me; and I often think of it when I see pride mortified, and misfortunes brought upon people by their carrying their heads too high.

"I long much to see again my native place, and to lay my bones there. I left it in 1723; I visited it in 1733, 1743, 1753, and 1763. In 1773 I was in England; in 1775 I had a sight of it, but could not enter, it being in possession of the enemy. I did hope to have been there in 1783, but could not obtain my dismission from this employment here; and now I fear I shall never have that happiness. My best wishes, however, attend my dear country. *Esto perpetua.* It is now blessed with an excellent constitution; may it last for ever! * * *

"With great and sincere esteem, I have the honour to be, &c.,

B. FRANKLIN."

---

"*To William Strahan, M. P.*

"Passy, August 19, 1784.

"DEAR FRIEND,

"I received your kind letter of April 17. You will have the goodness to place my delay in answering to the account of indisposition and business, and excuse it. I have now that letter before me; and my grandson, whom you may formerly remember a little scholar at Mr. Elphinston's, purposing to set out in a day or two on a visit to his father in London, I sit down to scribble a little to you, first recommending him as a worthy young man to your civilities and counsels.

"You press me much to come to England. I am not without strong inducements to do so; the fund of knowledge you promise to communicate to me is, in addition to them, no small one. At present it is impracticable. But when my grandson returns, come with him. We will talk the matter over, and perhaps you may take me back with you. I have a bed at your service, and will try to make your residence, while you can stay with us, as agreeable to you, if possible, as I am sure it will be to me.

"You do not 'approve the annihilation of profitable places; for you do not see why a statesman who does his business well should not be paid for his labour as well as any other workman.' Agreed. But why more than any other workman? The less the salary the greater the honour. In so great a nation there are many rich enough to afford giving their time to the public; and there are, I make no doubt, many wise and able men who would take as much pleasure in governing for nothing, as they do in playing of chess for nothing. It would be one of the noblest amusements. That this opinion is not chimerical, the country I now live in affords a proof; its whole civil and criminal law administration being done for nothing, or, in some sense, for less than nothing, since the members of its judiciary parliaments buy their places, and do not make more than three per cent. for their money by their fees and emoluments, while the legal interest is five; so that, in fact, they give two per cent. to be allowed to govern, and all their time and trouble into the bargain. Thus *profit*, one motive for desiring place, being abolished, there remains only *ambition*; and that being in some degree balanced by *loss*, you may easily conceive that there will not be very violent factions and contentions for such places; nor much of the mischief to the country that attends your factions, which have often occasioned wars, and overloaded you with debts impayable.

"I allow you all the force of your joke upon the vagrancy of our Congress. They have a right to sit *where* they please, of which, perhaps, they have made too much use by shifting too often. But they have two other rights; those of sitting *when* they please and as *long* as they please, in which, methinks, they have the advantage of your Parliament; for they cannot be dissolved by the breath of a minister, or sent packing, as you were the other day, when it was your earnest desire to have remained longer together.

"You 'fairly acknowledge that the late war terminated quite contrary to your expectation.' Your expectation was ill-founded; for you would not believe your old friend, who told you repeatedly, that by those measures England would lose her colonies, as Epictetus warned in vain his master that he would break his leg. You believed rather the tales you heard of our poltroonery and impotence of body and mind. Do you not remember the story you told me of the Scotch sergeant who met with a party of forty American soldiers, and, though alone, disarmed them all and brought them in prisoners? a story almost as improbable as that of an Irishman, who pretended to have alone taken and brought in five of the enemy by *surrounding* them. And yet, my friend, sensible and judicious as you are, but partaking of the general infatuation, you seemed to believe it. The word *general* puts me in mind of a general, your General Clarke, who had the folly to say in my hearing, at Sir John Pringle's, that with a thousand British grenadiers he would undertake to go from one end of America to the other, and geld all the males, partly by force and partly by a little coaxing. It is plain he took us for a species of animals very little superior to brutes. The Parliament, too, believed the stories of another foolish general, I forget his name, that the Yankees never *felt bold*. Yankee was understood to be a sort of Yahoo, and the Parliament did not think the petitions of such creatures were fit to be received and read in so wise an assembly. What was the consequence of this monstrous pride and insolence? You first sent small armies to subdue us, believing them more than sufficient, but soon found yourselves obliged to send greater; these, whenever they ventured to penetrate our country beyond the protection of their ships, were ether repulsed and obliged to scamper out, or were surrounded, beaten, and taken prisoners. An American planter, who had never seen Europe, was chosen by us to command our troops, and continued during the whole war. This man sent home to you, one after another, five of your best generals baffled, their heads bare of laurels, disgraced even in the opinion of their employers. Your contempt of our understandings, in comparison with your own, appeared to be much better founded than that of our courage, if we may judge by this circumstance, that in whatever court of Europe a Yankee negotiator appeared, the wise British minister was routed, put in a passion, picked a quarrel with your friends, and was sent home with a flea in his ear. But, after all, my dear friend, do not imagine that I am vain enough to ascribe our success to any superiority in any of those points. I am too well acquainted with all the springs and levers of our machine not to see that our human means were unequal to our undertaking, and that, if it had not been for the justice of our cause, and the consequent interposition of Providence, in which we had faith, we must have been ruined. If I had ever before been an Atheist, I should now have been convinced of the being and government of a Deity! It is he that abases the proud and favours the humble. May we never forget his goodness to us, and may our future conduct manifest our gratitude!

"But let us leave these serious reflections and converse with our usual pleasantry. I remember your observing once to me, as we sat together in the House of Commons, that no two journeymen printers within your knowledge had met with such success in the world as ourselves. You were then at the head of your profession, and soon afterward became member of Parliament. I was an agent for a few provinces, and now act for them all. But we have risen by different modes. I, as a republican printer, always liked a form well *planed down*; being averse to those *overbearing* letters that hold their heads so *high* as to hinder their neighbours from appearing. You, as a monarchist, chose to work upon *crown* paper, and found it profitable; while I worked upon *pro patria* (often, indeed, called *foolscap*) with no less advantage. Both our *heaps hold out* very well, and we seem likely to make a pretty good *day's work* of it. With regard to public affairs (to continue in the same style), it seems to me that your *compositors* in your *chapel* do not *cast off their copy well*, nor perfectly understand *imposing*: their *forms*, too, are continually pestered by the *outs* and *doubles* that are not easy to be *corrected*. And I think they were wrong in laying aside some *faces*, and particularly certain *headpieces*, that would have been both useful and ornamental. But, courage! The business may still flourish with good management, and the master become as rich as any of the company. * *

"I am ever, my dear friend, yours most affectionately,

B. Franklin."

---

"*George Wheatley.*

"Passy, May 23, 1785.

"Dear old Friend,

"I sent you a few lines the other day with the medallion, when I should have written more, but was prevented by the coming in of a *bavard*, who worried me till evening. I bore with him, and now you are to bear with me: for I shall probably *bavarder* in answering your letter.

"I am not acquainted with the saying of Alphonsus, which you allude to as a sanctification of your rigidity in refusing to allow me the plea of old age as an excuse for my want of exactness in correspondence. What was that saying? You do not, it seems, feel any occasion for such an excuse, though you are, as you say, rising 75. But I am rising (perhaps more properly falling) 80, and I leave the excuse with you till you arrive at that age; perhaps you may then be more sensible of its validity, and see fit to use it for yourself.

"I must agree with you that the gout is bad, and that the stone is worse. I am happy in not having them both together, and I join in your prayer that you may live till you die without either. But I doubt the author of the epitaph you send me was a little mistaken, when he, speaking of the world, says that

"'He ne'er cared a pin
What they said or may say of the mortal within.'

"It is so natural to wish to be well spoken of, whether alive or dead, that I imagine he could not be quite exempt from that desire; and that at least he wished to be thought a wit, or he would not have given himself the trouble of writing so good an epitaph to leave behind him. Was it not as worthy of his care that the world should say he was an honest and a good man? I like better the concluding sentiment in the old song, called the *Old Man's Wish*, wherein, after wishing for a warm house in a country town, an easy horse, some good authors, ingenious and cheerful companions, a pudding on Sundays, with stout ale and a bottle of Burgundy, &c., &c., in separate stanzas, each ending with this burden,

"'May I govern my passons with absolute sway,
Grow wiser and better as my strength wears away,
Without gout or stone, by a gentle decay.'

He adds,

"'With a courage undaunted may I face my last day,
And when I am gone may the better sort say,
In the morning when sober, in the evening when
    mellow.
He's gone, and has not left behind him his fellow.
    For he governed his passions,' &c.

"But what signifies our wishing? Things happen, after all, as they will happen. I have sung that *wishing song* a thousand times when I was young, and now find at fourscore that the three contraries have befallen me, being subject to the gout and the stone, and not being yet master of all my passions. Like the proud girl in my country, who wished and resolved not to marry a parson, nor a Presbyterian, nor an Irishman, and at last found herself married to an Irish Presbyterian parson. You see I have some reason to wish that, in a future state, I may not only be *as well as I was*, but a little better. And I hope it: for I too, with your poet, *trust in God*. And when I observe that there is great frugality as well as wisdom in his works, since he has been evidently sparing both of labour and materials; for, by the various wonderful inventions of propagation, he has provided for the continual peopling his world with plants and animals, without being at the trouble of repeated new creations; and by the natural reduction of compound substances to their original elements, capable of being employed in new compositions, he has prevented the necessity of creating new matter; for that the earth, water, air, and perhaps fire, which, being compounded from wood, do, when the wood is dissolved, return, and again become air, earth, fire, and water: I say, that when I see nothing annihilated, and not even a drop of water wasted, I cannot suspect the annihilation of souls, or believe that he will suffer the daily waste of millions of minds ready made that now exist, and put himself to the continual trouble of making new ones. Thus, finding myself to exist in the world, I believe I shall, in some shape or other, always exist: and with all the inconveniences human life is liable to, I shall not object to a new edition of mine; hoping, however, that the errata of the last may be corrected. * * *

"B. Franklin."

---

"David Hartley.

"Passy, July 5, 1785.

"I cannot quit the coasts of Europe without taking leave of my ever dear friend Mr. Hartley. We were long fellow-labourers in the best of all works, the work of peace. I leave you still in the field, but, having finished my day's task, I am going home *to go to bed*. Wish me a good night's rest, as I do you a pleasant evening. Adieu! and believe me ever yours most affectionately,

"B. Franklin,<br>"In his 80th year"

---

"To the Bishop of St. Asaph.

"Philadelphia, Feb. 24, 1786.

"Dear Friend,

"I received lately your kind letter of November 27. My reception here was, as you have heard, very honourable indeed; but I was betrayed by it, and by some remains of ambition, from which I had imagined myself free, to accept of the chair of government for the State of Pennsylvania, when the proper thing for me was repose and a private life. I hope, however, to be able to bear the fatigue for one year, and then retire.

"I have much regretted our having so little opportunity for conversation when we last met.[31] You could have given me informations and counsels that I wanted, but we were scarce a minute together without being broken in upon. I am to thank you, however, for the pleasure I had, after our parting, in reading the new book[32] you gave me, which I think generally well written and likely to do good: though the reading time of most people is of late so taken up with newspapers and little periodical pamphlets, that few nowadays venture to attempt reading a quarto volume. I have admired to see that in the last century a folio, *Burton on Melancholy*, went through six editions in about forty years. We have, I believe, more readers now, but not of such large books.

"You seem desirous of knowing what progress we make here in improving our governments. We are, I think, in the right road of improvement, for we are making experiments. I do not oppose all that seem wrong, for the multitude are more effectually set right by experience, than kept from going wrong by reasoning with them. And I think we are daily more and more enlightened; so that I have no doubt of our obtaining, in a few years, as much public felicity as good government is capable of affording. * * * *

"As to my domestic circumstances, of which you kindly desire to hear something, they are at present as happy as I could wish them. I am surrounded by my offspring, a dutiful and affectionate daughter in my house, with six grandchildren, the eldest of which you have seen, who is now at college in the next street, finishing the learned part of his education; the others promising both for parts and good dispositions. What their conduct may be when they grow up and enter the important scenes of life, I shall not live to *see*, and I cannot *foresee*. I therefore enjoy among them the present hour, and leave the future to Providence.

"He that raises a large family does, indeed, while he lives to observe them, *stand*, as Watts says, *a broader mark for sorrow*; but then he stands a broader mark for pleasure too. When we launch our little fleet of barks into the ocean, bound to different ports, we hope for each a prosperous voyage; but contrary winds, hidden shoals, storms, and enemies, come in for a share in the disposition of events; and though these occasion a mixture of disappointment, yet, considering the risk where we can make no ensurance, we should think ourselves happy if some return with success. My son's son (Temple Franklin), whom you have also seen, having had a fine farm of 600 acres conveyed to him by his father when we were at Southampton, has dropped for the present his views of acting in the political line, and applies himself ardently to the study and practice of agriculture. This is much more agreeable to me, who esteem it the most useful, the most independent, and, therefore, the noblest of employments. His lands are on navigable water, communicating with the Delaware, and but about 16 miles from this city. He has associated to himself a very skilful English farmer, lately arrived here, who is to instruct him in the business, and partakes for a term of the profits; so that there is a great apparent probability of their success. You will kindly expect a word or two about myself. My health and spirits continue, thanks to God, as when you saw me. The only complaint I then had does not grow worse, and is tolerable. I still have enjoyment in the company of my friends; and, being easy in my circumstances, have many reasons to like living. But the course of nature must soon put a period to my present mode of existence. This I shall submit to with less regret, as having seen, during a long life, a good deal of this world, I feel a growing curiosity to be acquainted with some other; and can cheerfully, with filial confidence, resign my spirit to the conduct of that great and good Parent of mankind who created it, and who has so graciously protected and prospered me from my birth to the present hour. Wherever I am, I always hope to retain the pleasing remembrance of your friendship; being, with sincere and great esteem, my dear friend, yours most affectionately,

"B. FRANKLIN.

"We all join in respects to Mrs. Shipley."

[31] At Southampton, previous to Dr. Franklin's embarking for the United States.
[32] Paley's Moral Philosophy.

---

"*Mrs. Hewson, London.*

"Philadelphia, May 6, 1786.

"MY DEAR FRIEND,

"A long winter has passed, and I have not had the pleasure of a line from you, acquainting me with your and your childrens' welfare, since I left England. I suppose you have been in Yorkshire, out of the way and knowledge of opportunities, for I will not think you have forgotten me. To make me some amends, I received a few days past a large packet from Mr. Williams, dated September, 1776, near ten years since, containing three letters from you, one of December 12, 1775. This packet had been received by Mr. Bache after my departure for France, lay dormant among his papers during all my absence, and has just now broke out upon me *like words* that had been, as somebody says, *congealed in Northern air*. Therein I find all the pleasing little family history of your children; how William had began to spell, overcoming by strength of memory all the difficulty occasioned by the common wretched alphabet, while you were convinced of the utility of our new one. How Tom, genius-like, struck out new paths, and, relinquishing the old names of the letters, called U *bell* and P *bottle*. How Eliza began to grow jolly, that is, fat and handsome, resembling Aunt Rooke, whom I used to call *my lovely*. Together with all the *then* news of Lady Blunt's having produced at length a boy; of Dolly's being well, and of poor good Catharine's decease. Of your affairs with Muir and Atkinson, and of their contract for feeding the fish in the Channel. Of the Vinys, and their jaunt to Cambridge in the long carriages. Of Dolly's journey to Wales with Mr. Scot. Of the Wilkeses, the Pearces, Elphinston, &c., &c. Concluding with a kind promise that, as soon as the ministry and Congress agreed to make peace, I should have you with me in America. That peace has been some time made, but, alas! the promise is not yet fulfilled. And why is it not fulfilled?

"I have found my family here in health, good circumstances, and well respected by their fellow-citizens. The companions of my youth are indeed almost all departed, but I find an agreeable society among their children and grandchildren. I have public business enough to preserve me from *ennui*, and private amusement besides, in conversation, books, and my garden. Considering our well-furnished plentiful market as the best of gardens, I am turning mine, in the midst of which my house stands, into grassplats and gravel-walks, with trees and flowering shrubs. * * *

"Temple has turned his thoughts to agriculture, which he pursues ardently, being in possession of a fine farm that his father lately conveyed to him. Ben is finishing his studies at college, and continues to behave as well as when you knew him, so that I still think he will make you a good son. His younger brothers and sisters are also all promising, appearing to have good tempers and dispositions, as well as good constitutions. As to myself, I think my general health and spirits rather better than when you saw me, and the particular malady I then complained of continues tolerable. With sincere and very great esteem, I am ever, my dear friend, yours most affectionately,

"B. Franklin."

"*To M. Veillard.*
"Philadelphia, April 15, 1787

"My dear Friend,

"I am quite of your opinion, that our independence is not quite complete till we have discharged our public debt. This state is not behindhand in its proportion, and those who are in arrear are actually employed in contriving means to discharge their respective balances; but they are not all equally diligent in the business, nor equally successful; the whole will, however, be paid, I am persuaded, in a few years.

"The English have not yet delivered up the posts on our frontier agreeable to treaty; the pretence is, that our merchants here have not paid their debts. I was a little provoked when I first heard this, and I wrote some remarks upon it, which I send you: they have been written near a year, but I have not yet published them, being unwilling to encourage any of our people who may be able to pay in their neglect of that duty. The paper is therefore only for your amusement, and that of our excellent friend the Duke de la Rochefoucauld.

"As to my malady, concerning which you so kindly inquire, I have never had the least doubt of its being the stone, and I am sensible that it has increased; but, on the whole, it does not give me more pain than when at Passy. People who live long, who will drink of the cup of life to the very bottom, must expect to meet with some of the usual dregs; and when I reflect on the number of terrible maladies human nature is subject to, I think myself favoured in having to my share only the stone and gout.

"You were right in conjecturing that I wrote the remarks on the '*thoughts concerning executive justice.*' I have no copy of these remarks at hand, and forget how the saying was introduced, that it is better a thousand guilty persons should escape than one innocent suffer. Your criticisms thereon appear to be just, and I imagine you may have misapprehended my intention in mentioning it. I always thought with you, that the prejudice in Europe, which supposes a family dishonoured by the punishment of one of its members, was very absurd, it being, on the contrary, my opinion, that a rogue hanged out of a family does it more honour than ten that live in it.

B. FRANKLIN."

"*Mr. Jordain.*

"Philadelphia, May 18, 1787.

"DEAR SIR,

"I received your very kind letter of February 27, together with the cask of porter you have been so good as to send me. We have here at present what the French call *une assemblée des notables*, a convention composed of some of the principal people from the several states of our confederation. They did me the honour of dining with me last Wednesday, when the cask was broached, and its contents met with the most cordial reception and universal approbation. In short, the company agreed unanimously that it was the best porter they had ever tasted. Accept my thanks, a poor return, but all I can make at present.

"Your letter reminds me of many happy days we have passed together, and the dear friends with whom we passed them; some of whom, alas! have left us, and we must regret their loss, although our Hawkesworth[33] is become an adventurer in more happy regions; and our Stanley[34] gone, 'where only his own *harmony* can be exceeded.' You give me joy in telling me that you are 'on the pinnacle of *content*.' Without it no situation can be happy; with it, any. One means of becoming content with one's situation is the comparing it with a worse Thus, when I consider how many terrible diseases the human body is liable to, I comfort myself that only three incurable ones have fallen to my share, the gout, the stone, and old age; and that these have not yet deprived me of my natural cheerfulness, my delight in books, and enjoyment of social conversation.

"I am glad to hear that Mr. Fitzmaurice is married, and has an amiable lady and children. It is a better plan than that he once proposed, of getting Mrs. Wright to make him a waxwork wife to sit at the head of his table. For, after all, wedlock is the natural state of man. A bachelor is not a complete human being. He is like the odd half of a pair of scissors, which has not yet found its fellow, and, therefore, is not even half so useful as they might be together.

"I hardly know which to admire most, the wonderful discoveries made by Herschel, or the indefatigable ingenuity by which he has been enabled to make them. Let us hope, my friend, that, when free from these bodily embarrassments, we may roam together through some of the systems he has explored, conducted by some of our old companions already acquainted with them. Hawkesworth will enliven our progress with his cheerful, sensible converse, and Stanley accompany the music of the spheres.

"Mr. Watraaugh tells me, for I immediately inquired after her, that your daughter is alive and well. I remember her a most promising and beautiful child, and therefore do not wonder that she is grown, as he says, a fine woman.

"God bless her and you, my dear friend, and everything that pertains to you, is the sincere prayer of yours most affectionately,

"B. FRANKLIN,
"IN HIS 82D YEAR."

[33] John Hawkesworth, LL.D., author of the Adventurer, and compiler of the account of the Discoveries made in the South Seas by Captain Cook.

[34] John Stanley, an eminent musician and composer, though he became blind at the age of two years.

---

### *"To Miss Hubbard.*

"I condole with you. We have lost a most dear and valuable relation. But it is the will of God and nature that these mortal bodies be laid aside, when the soul is to enter into real life. This is rather an embryo state, a preparation for living. A man is not completely born until he be dead. Why, then, should we grieve that a new child is born among the immortals, a new member added to their happy society? We are spirits. That bodies should be lent us while they can afford us pleasure, to assist us in acquiring knowledge, or doing good to our fellow-creatures, is a kind and benevolent act of God. When they become unfit for these purposes, and afford us pain instead of pleasure, instead of an aid become an encumbrance, and answer none of the intentions for which they were given, it is equally kind and benevolent that a way is provided by which we may get rid of them. Death is that way. We ourselves, in some cases, prudently choose a partial death. A mangled, painful limb, which cannot be restored, we willingly cut off. He who plucks out a tooth, parts with it freely, since the pain goes with it; and he who quits the whole body, parts at once with all pains, and possibilities of pains and diseases it was liable to, or capable of making him suffer.

"Our friend and we were invited abroad on a party of pleasure which is to last for ever. His chair was ready first, and he is gone before us. We could not all conveniently start together; and why should you and I be grieved at this, since we are soon to follow, and know where to find him?

"Adieu,

B. FRANKLIN."

---

### *"To George Wheatley.*

"Philadelphia, May 18, 1787.

"I received duly my good old friend's letter of the 19th of February. I thank you much for your notes on banks; they are just and solid, as far as I can judge of them. Our bank here has met with great opposition, partly from envy, and partly from those who wish an emission of more paper money, which they think the bank influence prevents. But it has stood all attacks, and went on well, notwithstanding the Assembly repealed its charter. A new Assembly has restored it, and the management is so prudent that I have no doubt of its continuing to go on well: the dividend has never been less than six per cent., nor will that be augmented for some time, as the surplus profit is reserved to face accidents. The dividend of eleven per cent., which was once made, was from a circumstance scarce unavoidable. A new company was proposed, and prevented only by admitting a number of new partners. As many of the first set were averse to this and chose to withdraw, it was necessary to settle their accounts; so all were adjusted, the profits shared that had been accumulated, and the new and old proprietors jointly began on a new and equal footing. Their notes are always instantly paid on demand, and pass on all occasions as readily as silver, because they will produce silver.

"Your medallion is in good company; it is placed with those of Lord Chatham, Lord Camden. Marquis of Rockingham, Sir George Saville, and some others who honoured me with a show of friendly regard when in England. I believe I have thanked you for it, but I thank you again.

"I believe with you, that if our plenipo. is desirous of concluding a treaty of commerce, he may need patience. If I were in his place and not otherwise instructed, I should be apt to say 'take your own time, gentlemen.' If the treaty cannot be made as much to your advantage as ours, don't make it. I am sure the want of it is not more to our disadvantage than to yours. Let the merchants on both sides treat with one another. *Laissez les faire.*

"I have never considered attentively the Congress's scheme for coining, and I have it not now at hand, so that at present I can say nothing to it. The chief uses of coining seem to be the ascertaining the fineness of the metals, and saving the time that would otherwise be spent in weighing to ascertain the quantity. But the convenience of fixed values to pieces is so great as to force the currency of some whose stamp is worn off, that should have assured their fineness, and which are evidently not of half their due weight; the case at present with the sixpences in England, which, one with another, do not weigh threepence.

"You are now 78, and I am 82; you tread fast upon my heels; but, though you have more strength and spirit, you cannot come up with me until I stop, which must now be soon; for I am grown so old as to have buried most of the friends of my youth; and I now often hear persons whom I knew when children, called *old* Mr. Such-a-one, to distinguish them from their sons, now men grown and in business; so that, by living twelve years beyond David's period, I seem to have intruded myself into the company of posterity when I ought to have been abed and asleep. Yet, had I gone at seventy, it would have cut off twelve of the most active years of my life, employed, too, in matters of the greatest importance; but whether I have been doing good or mischief is for time to discover. I only know that I intended well, and I hope all will end well.

"Be so good as to present my affectionate respects to Dr. Riley. I am under great obligations to him, and shall write to him shortly. It will be a pleasure to him to know that my malady does not grow sensibly worse, and that is a great point; for it has always been so tolerable as not to prevent my enjoying the pleasures of society, and being cheerful in conversation; I owe this in a great measure to his good counsels.

"B. FRANKLIN."

---

"*B. Vaughan.*

"October 24, 1788.

"Having now finished my term in the presidentship, and resolving to engage no more in public affairs, I hope to be a better correspondent for the little time I have to live. I am recovering from a long-continued gout, and am diligently employed in writing the History of my Life, to the doing of which the persuasions contained in your letter of January 31, 1783, have not a little contributed. I am now in the year 1756, just before I was sent to England. To shorten the work, as well as for other reasons, I omit all facts and transactions that may not have a tendency to benefit the young reader, by showing him from my example, and my success in emerging from poverty, and acquiring some degree of wealth, power, and reputation, the advantages of certain modes of conduct which I observed, and of avoiding the errors which were prejudicial to me. If a writer can judge properly of his own work, I fancy, on reading over what is already done, that the book may be found entertaining and useful, more so than I expected when I began it. If my present state of health continues, I hope to finish it this winter: when done, you shall have a manuscript copy of it, that I may obtain from your judgment and friendship such remarks as may contribute to its improvement.

"The violence of our party debates about the new constitution seems much abated, indeed almost extinct, and we are getting fast into good order. I kept out of those disputes pretty well, having wrote only one piece, which I send you enclosed.

"I regret the immense quantity of misery brought upon mankind by this Turkish war; and I am afraid the King of Sweden may burn his fingers by attacking Russia. When will princes learn arithmetic enough to calculate, if they want pieces of one another's territory, how much cheaper it would be to buy them than to make war for them, even though they were to give a hundred years' purchase; but if glory cannot be valued, and, therefore, the wars for it cannot be subject to arithmetical calculation, so as to show their advantages or disadvantages, at least wars for trade, which have gain for their object, may be proper subjects for such computation; and a trading nation, as well as a single trader, ought to calculate the probabilities of profit and loss before engaging in any considerable adventure. This, however, nations seldom do, and we have had frequent instances of their spending more money in wars for acquiring or securing branches of commerce, than a hundred years' profit, or the full enjoyment of them can compensate. * *

"B. FRANKLIN."

---

"*To the President of Congress.*

"Philadelphia, Nov. 29, 1788.

"SIR,

"When I had the honour of being the minister of the United States at the court of France, Mr. Barclay arriving there, brought me the following resolution of Congress:

"'Resolved, That a commissioner be appointed by Congress with full power and authority to liquidate and *finally to settle* the accounts of all the servants of the United States who have been intrusted with the expenditure of public money in Europe, and to commence and prosecute such suits, causes, and actions as may be necessary for that purpose, or for the recovery of any property of the said United States in the hands of any person or persons whatsoever.

"'That the said commissioner be authorized to appoint one or more clerks, with such allowance as he may think reasonable.

"'That the said commissioner and clerks respectively take an oath, before some person duly authorized to administer an oath, faithfully to execute the trust reposed in them respectively.

"'Congress proceeded to the election of a commissioner, and ballots being taken, Mr. T. Barclay was elected.'

"In pursuance of this resolution, and as soon as Mr. Barclay was at leisure from more pressing business, I rendered to him all my accounts, which he examined and stated methodically. By his statements he found a balance due to me on the 4th May, 1785, of 7533 livres, 19 sols, 3 deniers, which I accordingly received of the Congress Bank; the difference between my statement and his being only seven sols, which by mistake I had overcharged, about threepence halfpenny sterling.

"At my request, however, the accounts were left open for the consideration of Congress, and not finally settled, there being some articles on which I desired their judgment, and having some equitable demands, as I thought them, for extra services, which he had not conceived himself empowered to allow, and therefore I did not put them in my account. He transmitted the accounts to Congress, and had advice of their being received. On my arrival at Philadelphia, one of the first things I did was to despatch my grandson, W. T. Franklin, to New-York, to obtain a final settlement of those accounts, he having long acted as my secretary, and, being well acquainted with the transactions, was able to give an explanation of the articles that might seem to require explaining, if any such there were. He returned without effecting the settlement, being told that it would not be made till the arrival of some documents expected from France. What those documents were I have not been informed, nor can I readily conceive, as all the vouchers existing there had been examined by Mr. Barclay. And I having been immediately after my arrival engaged in public business of this state, I waited in expectation of hearing from Congress, in case any part of my accounts had been objected to.

"It is now more than three years that those accounts have been before that honourable body, and to this day no notice of any such objection has been communicated to me. But reports have for some time past been circulated here, and propagated in newspapers, that I am greatly indebted to the United States for large sums that had been put into my hands, and that I avoid a settlement.

"This, together with the little time one of my age may expect to live, makes it necessary for me to request earnestly, which I hereby do, that the Congress would be pleased, without farther delay, to examine those accounts, and if they find therein any article or articles which they do not understand or approve, that they would cause me to be acquainted with the same, that I may have an opportunity of offering such explanations or reasons in support of them as may be in my power, and then that the account may be finally closed.

"I hope the Congress will soon be able to attend to this business for the satisfaction of the public, as well as in condescension to my request. In the mean time, if there be no impropriety in it, I would desire that this letter, together with another on the same subject, the copy of which is hereto annexed, be put upon their minutes.

"B. FRANKLIN."

"*Mrs. Green.*

"Philadelphia, March 2, 1789.

"DEAR FRIEND,

"Having now done with public affairs, which have hitherto taken up so much of my time, I shall endeavour to enjoy, during the small remainder of life that is left to me, some of the pleasures of conversing with my old friends by writing, since their distance prevents my hope of seeing them again.

"I received one of the bags of sweet corn you was so good as to send me a long time since, but the other never came to hand; even the letter mentioning it, though dated December 10, 1787, has been above a year on its way, for I received it but about two weeks since from Baltimore, in Maryland. The corn I did receive was excellent, and gave me great pleasure. Accept my hearty thanks.

"I am, as you suppose in the above-mentioned old letter, much pleased to hear that my young friend Ray is 'smart in the farming way,' and makes such substantial fences. I think agriculture the most honourable of all employments, being the most independent. The farmer has no need of popular favour, nor the favour of the great; the success of his crops depending only on the blessing of God upon his honest industry. I congratulate your good spouse, that he as well as myself is now free from public cares, and that he can bend his whole attention to his farming, which will afford him both profit and pleasure; a business which nobody knows better how to manage with advantage. I am too old to follow printing again myself, but, loving the business, I have brought up my grandson Benjamin to it, and have built and furnished a printing-house for him, which he now manages under my eye. I have great pleasure in the rest of my grandchildren, who are now in number eight, and all promising, the youngest only six months old, but shows signs of great good-nature. My friends here are numerous, and I enjoy as much of their conversation as I can reasonably wish; and I have as much health and cheerfulness as can well be expected at my age, now eighty-two. Hitherto this long life has been tolerably happy, so that, if I were allowed to live it over again, I should make no objection, only wishing for leave to do, what authors do in a second edition of their works, correct some of my errata. Among the felicities of my life I reckon your friendship, which I shall remember with pleasure as long as life lasts, being ever, my dear friend, yours most affectionately,

"B. FRANKLIN."

---

"*Dr. Price.*

"Philadelphia, May 31, 1789.

"MY VERY DEAR FRIEND,

"I lately received your kind letter, enclosing one from Miss Kitty Shipley, informing me of the good bishop's decease, which afflicted me greatly. My friends drop off one after another, when my age and infirmities prevent me making new ones, and if I still retain the necessary activity and ability, I hardly see among the existing generation where I could make them of equal goodness. So that, the longer I live, I must expect to be the more wretched. As we draw nearer the conclusion of life, nature furnishes us with more helps to wean us from it, among which one of the most powerful is the loss of such dear friends.

"I send you with this the two volumes of our Transactions, as I forget whether you had the first before. If you had, you will please to give this to the French ambassador, requesting his conveyance of it to the good Duke de la Rochefoucauld. My best wishes attend you, being ever, with sincere and great esteem, my dear friend, yours most affectionately,

B. FRANKLIN."

---

"*B. Vaughan.*

"Philadelphia, June 3, 1789.

"MY DEAREST FRIEND,

"I received your kind letter of March 4, and wish I may be able to complete what you so earnestly desire, the Memoirs of my Life. But of late I am so interrupted by extreme pain, which obliges me to have recourse to opium, that between the effects of both I have but little time in which I can write anything. My grandson, however, is copying what is done, which will be sent to you for your opinion, by the next vessel; and not merely for your opinion, but for your advice; for I find it a difficult task to speak decently and properly of one's own conduct; and I feel the want of a judicious friend to encourage me in scratching out.

"I have condoled sincerely with the bishop of St. Asaph's family. He was an excellent man. Losing our friends thus one by one is the tax we pay for long living; and it is indeed a heavy one!

"I have not seen the King of Prussia's posthumous works; what you mention makes me desirous to have them. Please to mention it to your brother William, and that I request he would add them to the books I have desired him to buy for me.

"Our new government is now in train, and seems to promise well. But events are in the hand of God! I am ever, my dear friend, yours most affectionately,

B. FRANKLIN."

---

"*Dr. Rush.*

"Philadelphia.
[Without date, but supposed to be in 1789.]

"MY DEAR FRIEND>,

"During our long acquaintance you have shown many instances of your regard for me, yet I must now desire you to add one more to the number, which is that if you publish your ingenious discourse on the *moral sense*, you will totally omit and suppress that extravagant encomium on your friend Franklin, which hurt me exceedingly in the unexpected hearing, and will mortify me beyond conception if it should appear from the press.

"Confiding in your compliance with this earnest request, I am ever, my dear friend, yours most affectionately,

B. FRANKLIN."

---

*To Miss Catharine Louisa Shipley.*

"Philadelphia, April 27, 1789.

"It is only a few days since the kind letter of my dear young friend, dated

December 24, came to my hands. I had before, in the public papers, met with the afflicting news that letter contained. That excellent man has then left us! his departure is a loss, not to his family and friends only, but to his nation and to the world: for he was intent on doing good, had wisdom to devise the means, and talents to promote them. His sermon before the Society for Propagating the Gospel, and "*his speech intended to be spoken*," are proofs of his ability as well as his humanity. Had his counsels in those pieces been attended to by the ministers, how much bloodshed might have been prevented, and how much expense and disgrace to the nation avoided!

"Your reflections on the constant calmness and composure attending his death are very sensible. Such instances seem to show that the good sometimes enjoy, in dying, a foretaste of the happy state they are about to enter.

"According to the course of years, I should have quitted this world long before him: I shall, however, not be long in following. I am now in my eighty-fourth year, and the last year has considerably enfeebled me, so that I hardly expect to remain another. You will then, my dear friend, consider this as probably the last line to be received from me, and as a taking leave.

"Present my best and most sincere respects to your good mother, and love to the rest of the family, to whom I wish all happiness; and believe me to be, while I *do* live, yours most affectionately,

"B. Franklin."

To * * *.

(Withoute date.)

"Dear Sir,

"I have read your manuscript with some attention. By the argument it contains against a particular Providence, though you allow a general Providence, you strike at the foundations of all religion. For without the belief of a Providence that takes cognizance of, guards and guides, and may favour particular persons, there is no motive to worship a Deity, to fear its displeasure, or to pray for its protection. I will not enter into any discussion of your principles, though you seem to desire it. At present I shall only give you my opinion, that though your reasonings are subtle, and may prevail with some readers, you will not succeed so as to change the general sentiments of mankind on that subject, and the consequence of printing this piece will be, a great deal of odium drawn upon yourself, mischief to you, and no benefit to others. He that spits against the wind, spits in his own face. But were you to succeed, do you imagine any good would be done by it? You yourself may find it easy to live a virtuous life without the assistance afforded by religion; you having a clear perception of the advantages of virtue and the disadvantages of vice, and possessing a strength of resolution sufficient to enable you to resist common temptations. But think how great a portion of mankind consists of weak and ignorant men and women, and of inexperienced, inconsiderate youth of both sexes, who have need of the motives of religion to restrain them from vice, to support their virtue, and retain them in the practice of it till it becomes *habitual*, which is the great point of its security. And perhaps you are indebted to her originally, that is, to your religious education, for the habits of virtue upon which you now justly value yourself. You might easily display your excellent talents of reasoning upon a less hazardous subject, and thereby obtain a rank with our most distinguished authors. For among us it is not necessary, as among the Hottentots, that a youth to be raised into the company of men should prove his manhood by beating his mother. I would advise you, therefore, not to attempt unchaining the tiger, but to burn this piece before it is seen by any other person, whereby you will save yourself a great deal of mortification from the enemies it may raise against you, and, perhaps, a great deal of regret and repentance. If men are so wicked *with religion*, what would they be if *without it*? I intend this letter itself as a *proof* of my friendship, and, therefore, add no *professions* to it; but subscribe simply yours,

B. Franklin."

*Copy of the last Letter written by Dr. Franklin.*

"Philadelphia, April 8, 1790.

"Sir,

"I received your letter of the 31st of last past relating to encroachments made on the eastern limits of the United States by settlers under the British government, pretending that it is the *western*, and not the *eastern* river of the Bay of Passamaquoddy which was designated by the name of St. Croix, in the treaty of peace with that nation; and requesting of me to communicate any facts which my memory or papers may enable me to recollect, and which may indicate the true river which the commissioners on both sides had in their view to establish as the boundary between the two nations.

"Your letter found me under a severe fit of my malady, which prevented my answering it sooner, or attending, indeed, to any kind of business. I now can assure you that I am perfectly clear in the remembrance that the map we used in tracing the boundary was brought to the treaty by the commissioners from England, and that it was the same that was published by *Mitchell* above twenty years before. Having a copy of that map by me in loose sheets, I send you that sheet which contains the Bay of Passamaquoddy, where you will see that part of the boundary traced. I remember, too, that in that part of the boundary we relied much on the opinion of Mr. Adams, who had been concerned in some former disputes concerning those territories. I think, therefore, that you may obtain still farther light from him.

"That the map we used was Mitchell's map, Congress were acquainted at the time, by letter to their secretary for foreign affairs, which I suppose may be found upon their files.

"I have the honour to be, with the greatest esteem and respect, sir, your most obedient and most humble servant,

"B. Franklin.

"To Thomas Jefferson, }
"Secretary of State of the United States."}

# PHILOSOPHICAL SUBJECTS.

*To the Abbé Soulavie.*[35]

*Theory of the Earth.*—Read in the American Philosophical Society, November 22, 1782.

Passy, September 22, 1782.

I return the papers with some corrections. I did not find coal mines under the calcareous rocks in Derbyshire. I only remarked, that at the lowest part of that rocky mountain which was in sight, there were oyster shells mixed in the stone; and part of the high county of Derby being probably as much above the level of the sea as the coal mines of Whitehaven were below it, seemed a proof that there had been a great *boulversement* in the surface of that island, some part of it having been depressed under the sea, and other parts, which had been under it, being raised above it. Such changes in the superficial parts of the globe seemed to me unlikely to happen if the earth were solid to the centre. I therefore imagined that the internal parts might be a fluid more dense, and of greater specific gravity than any of the solids we are acquainted with, which therefore might swim in or upon that fluid. Thus the surface of the globe would be a shell, capable of being broken or disordered by the violent movements of the fluid on which it rested. And as air has been compressed by art so as to be twice as dense as water, in which case, if such air and water could be contained in a strong glass vessel, the air would be seen to take the lowest place, and the water to float above and upon it; and as we know not yet the degree of density to which air may be compressed, and M. Amontons calculated that its density increasing as it approached the centre in the same proportion as above the surface, it would, at the depth of—— leagues, be heavier than gold; possibly the dense fluid occupying the internal parts of the globe might be air compressed. And as the force of expansion in dense air, when heated, is in proportion to its density, this central air might afford another agent to move the surface, as well as be of use in keeping alive the subterraneous fires; though, as you observe, the sudden rarefaction of water coming into contact without those fires, may also be an agent sufficiently strong for that purpose, when acting between the incumbent earth and the fluid on which it rests.

If one might indulge imagination in supposing how such a globe was formed, I should conceive, that all the elements in separate particles being originally mixed in confusion, and occupying a great space, they would (as soon as the almighty fiat ordained gravity, or the mutual attraction of certain parts and the mutual repulsion of others, to exist) all move to their common centre: that the air, being a fluid whose parts repel each other, though drawn to the common centre by their gravity, would be densest towards the centre, and rarer as more remote; consequently, all matters lighter than the central parts of that air and immersed in it, would recede from the centre, and rise till they arrived at that region of the air which was of the same specific gravity with themselves, where they would rest; while other matter, mixed with the lighter air, would descend, and the two, meeting, would form the shell of the first earth, leaving the upper atmosphere nearly clear. The original movement of the parts towards their common centre would naturally form a whirl there, which would continue upon the turning of the new-formed globe upon its axis, and the greatest diameter of the shell would be in its equator. If by any accident afterward the axis should be changed, the dense internal fluid, by altering its form, must burst the shell and throw all its substance into the confusion in which we find it. I will not trouble you at present with my fancies concerning the manner of forming the rest of our system. Superior beings smile at our theories, and at our presumption in making them. I will just mention, that your observations on the ferruginous nature of the lava which is thrown out from the depths of our volcanoes, gave me great pleasure. It has long been a supposition of mine, that the iron contained in the surface of the globe has made it capable of becoming, as it is, a great magnet; that the fluid of magnetism perhaps exists in all space; so that there is a magnetical north and south of the universe, as well as of this globe, and that, if it were possible for a man to fly from star to star, he might govern his course by the compass; that it was by the power of this general magnetism this globe became a particular magnet. In soft or hot iron the fluid of magnetism is naturally diffused equally; when within the influence of the magnet it is drawn to one end of the iron, made denser there and rarer at the other. While the iron continues soft and hot, it is only a temporary magnet; if it cools or grows hard in that situation, it becomes a permanent one, the magnetic fluid not easily resuming its equilibrium. Perhaps it may be owing to the permanent magnetism of this globe, which it had not at first, that its axis is at present kept parallel to itself, and not liable to the changes it formerly suffered, which occasioned the rupture of its shell, the submersions and emersions of its lands, and the confusion of its seasons. The present polar and equatorial diameters differing from each other near ten leagues, it is easy to conceive, in case some power should shift the axis gradually, and place it in the present equator, and make the new equator pass through the present poles, what a sinking of the waters would happen in the equatorial regions, and what a rising in the present polar regions; so that vast tracts would be discovered that now are under water, and others covered that are now dry, the water rising and sinking in the different extremes near five leagues. Such an operation as this possibly occasioned much of Europe, and, among the rest, this mountain of Passy on which I live, and which is composed of limestone, rock, and seashells, to be abandoned by the sea, and to change its ancient climate, which seems to have been a hot one. The globe being now become a perfect magnet, we are, perhaps, safe from any change of its axis. But we are still subject to the accidents on the surface, which are occasioned by a wave in the internal ponderous fluid; and such a wave is producible by the sudden violent explosion you mention, happening from the junction of water and fire under the earth, which not only lifts the incumbent earth that is over the explosion, but, impressing with the same force the fluid under it, creates a wave that may run a thousand leagues, lifting, and thereby shaking, successively, all the countries under which it passes. I know not whether I have expressed myself so clearly as not to get out of your sight in these reveries. If they occasion any new inquiries, and produce a better hypothesis, they will not be quite useless. You see I have given a loose to imagination; but I approve much more your method of philosophizing, which proceeds upon actual observation, makes a collection of facts, and concludes no farther than those facts will warrant. In my present circumstances, that mode of studying the nature of the globe is out of my power, and therefore I have permitted myself to wander a little in the wilds of fancy. With great esteem,

B. Franklin.

P.S.—I have heard that chymists can by their art decompose stone and wood, extracting a considerable quantity of water from the one and air from the other. It seems natural to conclude from this, that water and air were ingredients in their original composition; for men cannot make new matter of any kind. In the same manner, may we not suppose, that when we consume combustibles of all kinds, and produce heat or light, we do not create that heat or light, but decompose a substance which received it originally as a part of its composition? Heat may be thus considered as originally in a fluid state; but, attracted by organized bodies in their growth, becomes a part of the solid. Besides this, I can conceive, that in the first assemblage of the particles of which the earth is composed, each brought its portion of loose heat that had been connected with it, and the whole, when pressed together, produced the internal fire that still subsists.

[35] Occasioned by his sending me some notes he had taken of what I had said to him in conversation on the Theory of the Earth. I wrote it to set him right in some points wherein he had mistaken my meaning.—B. F.

*To Dr. John Pringle.*

## ON THE DIFFERENT STRATA OF THE EARTH.

Craven-street, Jan. 6, 1758.

I return you Mr. Mitchell's paper on the strata of the earth[36] with thanks. The reading of it, and the perusal of the draught that accompanies it, have reconciled me to those convulsions which all naturalists agree this globe has suffered. Had the different strata of clay, gravel, marble, coals, limestone, sand, minerals, &c., continued to lie level, one under the other, as they may be supposed to have done before those convulsions, we should have had the use only of a few of the uppermost of the strata, the others lying too deep and too difficult to be come at; but the shell of the earth being broke, and the fragments thrown into this oblique position, the disjointed ends of a great number of strata of different kinds are brought up to day, and a great variety of useful materials put into our power, which would otherwise have remained eternally concealed from us. So that what has been usually looked upon as a *ruin* suffered by this part of the universe, was, in reality, only a preparation, or means of rendering the earth more fit for use, more capable of being to mankind a convenient and comfortable habitation.

B. FRANKLIN.

[36] The paper of Mr. Mitchell, here referred to, was published afterward in the Philosophical Transactions of London.

*To Mr. Bowdoin.*

*Queries and Conjectures relating to Magnetism and the Theory of the Earth.*—Read in the American Philosophical Society January 15, 1790.

I received your favours by Messrs. Gore, Hilliard, and Lee, with whose conversation I was much pleased, and wished for more of it; but their stay with us was too short. Whenever you recommend any of your friends to me, you oblige me.

I want to know whether your Philosophical Society received the second volume of our Transactions. I sent it, but never heard of its arriving. If it miscarried, I will send another. Has your Society among its books the French work *Sur les Arts et les Metiers*? It is voluminous, well executed, and may be useful in our country. I have bequeathed it them in my will; but if they have it already, I will substitute something else.

Our ancient correspondence used to have something philosophical in it. As you are now free from public cares, and I expect to be so in a few months, why may we not resume that kind of correspondence? Our much regretted friend Winthrop once made me the compliment, that I was good at starting game for philosophers, let me try if I can start a little for you.

Has the question, how came the earth by its magnetism, ever been considered?

Is it likely that *iron ore* immediately existed when this globe was at first formed; or may it not rather be supposed a gradual production of time?

If the earth is at present magnetical, in virtue of the masses of iron ore contained in it, might not some ages pass before it had magnetic polarity?

Since iron ore may exist without that polarity, and, by being placed in certain circumstances, may obtain it from an external cause, is it not possible that the earth received its magnetism from some such cause?

In short, may not a magnetic power exist throughout our system, perhaps through all systems, so that if men could make a voyage in the starry regions, a compass might be of use? And may not such universal magnetism, with its uniform direction, be serviceable in keeping the diurnal revolution of a planet more steady to the same axis?

Lastly, as the poles of magnets may be changed by the presence of stronger magnets, might not, in ancient times, the near passing of some large comet, of greater magnetic power than this globe of ours, have been a means of changing its poles, and thereby wrecking and deranging its surface, placing in different regions the effect of centrifugal force, so as to raise the waters of the sea in some, while they were depressed in others?

Let me add another question or two, not relating indeed to magnetism, but, however, to the theory of the earth.

Is not the finding of great quantities of shells and bones of animals (natural to hot climates) in the cold ones of our present world, some proof that its poles have been changed? Is not the supposition that the poles have been changed, the easiest way of accounting for the deluge, by getting rid of the old difficulty how to dispose of its waters after it was over! Since, if the poles were again to be changed, and placed in the present equator, the sea would fall there about fifteen miles in height, and rise as much in the present polar regions; and the effect would be proportionable if the new poles were placed anywhere between the present and the equator.

Does not the apparent wreck of the surface of this globe, thrown up into long ridges of mountains, with strata in various positions, make it probable that its internal mass is a fluid, but a fluid so dense as to float the heaviest of our substances? Do we know the limit of condensation air is capable of?

Supposing it to grow denser *within* the surface in the same proportion nearly as it does *without*, at what depth may it be equal in density with gold?

Can we easily conceive how the strata of the earth could have been so deranged, if it had not been a mere shell supported by a heavier fluid? Would not such a supposed internal fluid globe be immediately sensible of a change in the situation of the earth's axis, alter its form, and thereby burst the shell and throw up parts of it above the rest? As if we would alter the position of the fluid contained in the shell of an egg, and place its longest diameter where the shortest now is, the shell must break; but would be much harder to break if the whole internal substance were as solid and as hard as the shell.

Might not a wave, by any means raised in this supposed internal ocean of extremely dense fluid, raise, in some degree as it passes, the present shell of incumbent earth, and break it in some places, as in earthquakes. And may not the progress of such wave, and the disorders it occasions among the solids of the shell, account for the rumbling sound being first heard at a distance, augmenting as it approaches, and gradually dying away as it proceeds? A circumstance observed by the inhabitants of South America, in their last great earthquake, that noise coming from a place some degrees north of Lima, and being traced by inquiry quite down to Buenos Ayres, proceeded regularly from north to south at the rate of____leagues per minute, as I was informed by a very ingenious Peruvian whom I met with at Paris.

B. Franklin.

*To M. Dubourg.*

ON THE NATURE OF SEACOAL.

I am persuaded, as well as you, that the seacoal has a vegetable origin, and that it has been formed near the surface of the earth; but, as preceding convulsions of nature had served to bring it very deep in many places, and covered it with many different strata, we are indebted to subsequent convulsions for having brought within our view the extremities of its veins, so as to lead us to penetrate the earth in search of it. I visited last summer a large coalmine at Whitehaven, in Cumberland; and in following the vein, and descending by degrees towards the sea, I penetrated below the ocean where the level of its surface was more than eight hundred fathoms above my head, and the miners assured me that their works extended some miles beyond the place where I then was, continually and gradually descending under the sea. The slate, which forms the roof of this coalmine, is impressed in many places with the figures of leaves and branches of fern, which undoubtedly grew at the surface when the slate was in the state of sand on the banks of the sea. Thus it appears that this vein of coal has suffered a prodigious settlement.

B. Franklin.

## CAUSES OF EARTHQUAKES.

The late earthquake felt here, and probably in all the neighbouring provinces, having made many people desirous to know what may be the natural cause of such violent concussions, we shall endeavour to gratify their curiosity by giving them the various opinions of the learned on that head.

Here naturalists are divided. Some ascribe them to water, others to fire, and others to air, and all of them with some appearance of reason. To conceive which, it is to be observed that the earth everywhere abounds in huge subterraneous caverns, veins, and canals, particularly about the roots of mountains; that of these cavities, veins, &c., some are full of water, whence are composed gulfs, abysses, springs, rivulets; and others full of exhalations; and that some parts of the earth are replete with nitre, sulphur, bitumen, vitriol, &c. This premised,

1. The earth itself may sometimes be the cause of its own shaking; when the roots or basis of some large mass being dissolved, or worn away by a fluid underneath, it sinks into the same, and, with its weight, occasions a tremour of the adjacent parts, produces a noise, and frequently an inundation of water.

2. The subterraneous waters may occasion earthquakes by their overflowing, cutting out new courses, &c. Add that the water, being heated and rarefied by the subterraneous fires, may emit fumes, blasts, &c., which, by their action either on the water or immediately on the earth itself, may occasion great succussions.

3. The air may be the cause of earthquakes; for the air being a collection of fumes and vapours raised from the earth and water, if it be pent up in too narrow viscera of the earth, the subterraneous or its own native heat rarefying and expanding it, the force wherewith it endeavours to escape may shake the earth; hence there arises divers species of earthquakes, according to the different position, quantity, &c., of the imprisoned *aura*.

Lastly, fire is a principal cause of earthquakes; both as it produces the aforesaid subterraneous *aura* or vapours, and as this *aura* or spirit, from the different matter and composition whereof arise sulphur, bitumen, and other inflammable matters, takes fire, either from other fire it meets withal, or from its collision against hard bodies, or its intermixture with other fluids; by which means, bursting out into a greater compass, the place becomes too narrow for it, so that, pressing against it on all sides, the adjoining parts are shaken, till, having made itself a passage, it spends itself in a volcano or burning mountain.

But to come nearer to the point. Dr. Lister is of opinion that the material cause of thunder, lightning, and earthquakes, is one and the same, viz., the inflammable breath of the pyrites, which is a substantial sulphur, and takes fire of itself.

The difference between these three terrible phenomena he takes only to consist in this: that the sulphur in the former is fired in the air, and in the latter under ground. Which is a notion Pliny had long before him: "*Quid enim,*" says he, "*aliud est in terrâ tremor, quam in nube tonitru?*" For wherein does the trembling of the earth differ from that occasioned by thunder in the clouds?

This he thinks abundantly indicated by the same sulphurous smell being found in anything burned with lightning, and in the waters, &c., cast up in earthquakes, and even in the air before and after them.

Add that they agree in the manner of the noise which is carried on, as in a train fired; the one, rolling and rattling through the air, takes fire as the vapours chance to drive; as the other, fired under ground in like manner, moves with a desultory noise.

Thunder, which is the effect of the trembling of the air, caused by the same vapours dispersed through it, has force enough to shake our houses; and why there may not be thunder and lightning under ground, in some vast repositories there, I see no reason; especially if we reflect that the matter which composes the noisy vapour above us is in much larger quantities under ground.

That the earth abounds in cavities everybody allows; and that these subterraneous cavities are, at certain times and in certain seasons, full of inflammable vapours, the damps in mines sufficiently witness, which, fired, do everything as in an earthquake, save in a lesser degree.

Add that the pyrites alone, of all the known minerals, yields this inflammable vapour, is highly probable; for that no mineral or ore whatsoever is sulphurous, but as it is wholly or in part a pyrites, and that there is but one species of brimstone which the pyrites naturally and only yields. The *sulphur vive*, or natural brimstone, which is found in and about the burning mountains, is certainly the effects of sublimation, and those great quantities of it said to be found about the skirts of volcanoes is only an argument of the long duration and vehemence of those fires. Possibly the pyrites of the volcanoes, or burning mountains, may be more sulphurous than ours; and, indeed, it is plain that some of ours in England are very lean, and hold but little sulphur; others again very much, which may be some reason why England is so little troubled with earthquakes, and Italy, and almost all round the Mediterranean Sea, so much; though another reason is, the paucity of pyrites in England.

Comparing our earthquakes, thunder, and lightning, with theirs, it is observed that there it lightens almost daily, especially in summer-time, here seldom; there thunder and lightning is of long duration, here it is soon over; there the earthquakes are frequent, long, and terrible, with many paroxysms in a day, and that for many days; here very short, a few minutes, and scarce perceptible. To this purpose the subterraneous caverns in England are small and few compared to the vast vaults in those parts of the world; which is evident from the sudden disappearance of whole mountains and islands.

Dr. Woodward gives us another theory of earthquakes. He endeavours to show that the subterraneous heat or fire (which is continually elevating water out of the abyss, to furnish the earth with rain, dew, springs, and rivers), being stopped in any part of the earth, and so diverted from its ordinary course by some accidental glut or obstruction in the pores or passages through which it used to ascend to the surface, becomes, by such means, preternaturally assembled in a greater quantity than usual into one place, and therefore causeth a great rarefaction and intumescence of the water of the abyss, putting it into great commotions and disorders, and at the same time making the like effort on the earth, which, being expanded upon the face of the abyss, occasions that agitation and concussion we call an earthquake.

This effort in some earthquakes, he observes, is so vehement, that it splits and tears the earth, making cracks and chasms in it some miles in length, which open at the instant of the shock, and close again in the intervals between them; nay, it is sometimes so violent that it forces the superincumbent strata, breaks them all throughout, and thereby perfectly undermines and ruins the foundation of them; so that, these failing, the whole tract, as soon as the shock is over, sinks down into the abyss, and is swallowed up by it, the water thereof immediately rising up and forming a lake in the place where the said tract before was. That this effort being made in all directions indifferently, the fire, dilating and expanding on all hands, and endeavouring to get room and make its way through all obstacles, falls as foul on the waters of the abyss beneath as on the earth above, forcing it forth, which way soever it can find vent or passage, as well through its ordinary exits, wells, springs, and the outlets of rivers, as through the chasms then newly opened, through the *camini* or spiracles of Ætna, or other neighbouring volcanoes, and those hiatuses at the bottom of the sea whereby the abyss below opens into it and communicates with it. That as the water resident in the abyss is, in all parts of it, stored with a considerable quantity of heat, and more especially in those where those extraordinary aggregations of this fire happen, so likewise is the water which is thus forced out of it, insomuch that, when thrown forth and mixed with the waters of wells, or springs of rivers and the sea, it renders them very sensibly hot.

He adds, that though the abyss be liable to those commotions in all parts, yet the effects are nowhere very remarkable except in those countries which are mountainous, and, consequently, stony or cavernous underneath; and especially where the disposition of the strata is such that those caverns open the abyss, and so freely admit and entertain the fire which, assembling therein, is the cause of the shock; it naturally steering its course that way where it finds the readiest reception, which is towards those caverns. Besides, that those parts of the earth which abound with strata of stone or marble, making the strongest opposition to this effort, are the most furiously shattered, and suffer much more by it than those which consist of gravel, sand, and the like laxer matter, which more easily give way, and make not so great resistance. But, above all, those countries which yield great store of sulphur and nitre are by far the most injured by earthquakes; those minerals constituting in the earth a kind of natural gunpowder, which, taking fire upon this assemblage and approach of it, occasions that murmuring noise, that subterraneous thunder, which is heard rumbling in the bowels of the earth during earthquakes, and by the assistance of its explosive power renders the shock much greater, so as sometimes to make miserable havoc and destruction.

And it is for this reason that Italy, Sicily, Anatolia, and some parts of Greece, have been so long and often alarmed and harassed by earthquakes; these countries being all mountainous and cavernous, abounding with stone and marble, and affording sulphur and nitre in great plenty.

Farther, that Ætna, Vesuvius, Hecla, and the other volcanoes, are only so many spiracles, serving for the discharge of this subterraneous fire, when it is thus preternaturally assembled. That where there happens to be such a structure and conformation of the interior part of the earth, as that the fire may pass freely, and without impediment, from the caverns wherein it assembles unto those spiracles, it then readily gets out, from time to time, without shaking or disturbing the earth; but where such communication is wanting, or passage not sufficiently large and open, so that it cannot come at the spiracles, it heaves up and shocks the earth with greater or lesser impetuosity, according to the quantity of fire thus assembled, till it has made its way to the mouth of the volcano. That, therefore, there are scarce any countries much annoyed by earthquakes but have one of these fiery vents, which are constantly in flames when any earthquake happens, as disgorging that fire which, while underneath, was the cause of the disaster. Lastly, that were it not for these *diverticula*, it would rage in the bowels of the earth much more furiously, and make greater havoc than it doth.

We have seen what fire and water may do, and that either of them are sufficient for all the phenomena of earthquakes; if they should both fail, we have a third agent scarce inferior to either of them; the reader must not be surprised when we tell him it is air.

Monsieur Amontons, in his Mémoires de l'Académie des Sciences, An. 1703, has an express discourse to prove, that on the foot of the new experiments of the weight and spring of the air, a moderate degree of heat may bring the air into a condition capable of causing earthquakes. It is shown that at the depth of 43,528 fathoms below the surface of the earth, air is only one fourth less heavy than mercury. Now this depth of 43,528 fathoms is only a seventy-fourth part of the semi-diameter of the earth. And the vast sphere beyond this depth, in diameter 6,451,538 fathoms, may probably be only filled with air, which will be here greatly condensed, and much heavier than the heaviest bodies we know in nature. But it is found by experiment that, the more air is compressed, the more does the same degree of heat increase its spring, and the more capable does it render it of a violent effect; and that, for instance, the degree of heat of boiling water increases the spring of the air above what it has in its natural state, in our climate, by a quantity equal to a third of the weight wherewith it is pressed. Whence we may conclude that a degree of heat, which on the surface of the earth will only have a moderate effect, may be capable of a very violent one below. And as we are assured that there are in nature degrees of heat much more considerable than boiling water, it is very possible there may be some whose violence, farther assisted by the exceeding weight of the air, may be more than sufficient to break and overturn this solid orb of 43,528 fathoms, whose weight, compared to that of the included air, would be but a trifle.

Chymistry furnishes us a method of making artificial earthquakes which shall have all the great effects of natural ones; which, as it may illustrate the process of nature in the production of these terrible phenomena under ground, we shall here add.

To twenty pounds of iron filings add as many of sulphur; mix, work, and temper the whole together with a little water, so as to form a mass half wet and half dry. This being buried three or four feet under ground, in six or seven hours time will have a prodigious effect; the earth will begin to tremble, crack, and smoke, and fire and flame burst through.

Such is the effect even of the two cold bodies in cold ground; there only wants a sufficient quantity of this mixture to produce a true Ætna. If it were supposed to burst out under the sea, it would produce a spout; and if it were in the clouds, the effect would be thunder and lightning.

An earthquake is defined to be a vehement shake or agitation of some considerable place, or part of the earth, from natural causes, attended with a huge noise like thunder, and frequently with an eruption of water, or fire, or smoke, or winds, &c.

They are the greatest and most formidable phenomena of nature. Aristotle and Pliny distinguish two kinds, with respect to the manner of the shake, viz., a tremour and a pulsation; the first being horizontal, in alternate vibrations, compared to the shaking of a person in an ague; the second perpendicular, up and down, their motion resembling that of boiling.

Agricola increases the number, and makes four kinds, which Albertus Magnus again reduces to three, viz., inclination, when the earth vibrates alternately from right to left, by which mountains have been sometimes brought to meet and clash against each other; pulsation, when it beats up and down, like an artery; and trembling, when it shakes and totters every way, like a flame.

The Philosophical Transactions furnish us with abundance of histories of earthquakes, particularly one at Oxford in 1665, by Dr. Wallis and Mr. Boyle. Another at the same place in 1683, by Mr. Pigot. Another in Sicily, in 1692-3, by Mr. Hartop, Father Alessandro Burgos, and Vin. Bonajutus, which last is one of the most terrible ones in all history.

It shook the whole island; and not only that, but Naples and Malta shared in the shock. It was of the second kind mentioned by Aristotle and Pliny, viz., a perpendicular pulsation or succussion. It was impossible, says the noble Bonajutus, for anybody in this country to keep on their legs on the dancing earth; nay, those that lay on the ground were tossed from side to side as on a rolling billow; high walls leaped from their foundations several paces.

The mischief it did is amazing; almost all the buildings in the countries were thrown down. Fifty-four cities and towns, besides an incredible number of villages, were either destroyed or greatly damaged. We shall only instance the fate of Catania, one of the most famous, ancient, and flourishing cities in the kingdom, the residence of several monarchs, and a university. "This once famous, now unhappy Catania," to use words of Father Burgos, "had the greatest share in the tragedy. Father Antonio Serovita, being on his way thither, and at the distance of a few miles, observed a black cloud, like night, hovering over the city, and there arose from the mouth of Mongibello great spires of flame, which spread all around. The sea, all of a sudden, began to roar and rise in billows, and there was a blow, as if all the artillery in the world had been at once discharged. The birds flew about astonished, the cattle in the fields ran crying, &c. His and his companion's horse stopped short, trembling; so that they were forced to alight. They were no sooner off but they were lifted from the ground above two palms. When, casting his eyes towards Catania, he with amazement saw nothing but a thick cloud of dust in the air. This was the scene of their calamity; for of the magnificent Catania there is not the least footstep to be seen." Bonajutus assures us, that of 18,914 inhabitants, 18,000 perished therein. The same author, from a computation of the inhabitants before and after the earthquake, in the several cities and towns, finds that near 60,000 perished out of 254,900.

Jamaica is remarkable for earthquakes. The inhabitants, Dr. Sloane informs us, expect one every year. The author gives the history of one in 1687; another horrible one, in 1692, is described by several anonymous authors. In two minutes' time it shook down and drowned nine tenths of the town of Port Royal. The houses sunk outright, thirty or forty fathoms deep. The earth, opening, swallowed up people, and they rose in other streets; some in the middle of the harbour, and yet were saved; though there were two thousand people lost, and one thousand acres of land sunk. All the houses were thrown down throughout the island. One Hopkins had his plantation removed half a mile from its place. Of all wells, from one fathom to six or seven, the water flew out at the top with a vehement motion. While the houses on the one side of the street were swallowed up, on the other they were thrown in heaps; and the sand in the street rose like waves in the sea, lifting up everybody that stood on it, and immediately dropping down into pits; and at the same instant, a flood of waters breaking in, rolled them over and over; some catching hold of beams and rafters, &c. Ships and sloops in the harbour were overset and lost; the Swan frigate particularly, by the motion of the sea and sinking of the wharf, was driven over the tops of many houses.

It was attended with a hollow rumbling noise like that of thunder. In less than a minute three quarters of the houses, and the ground they stood on, with the inhabitants, were all sunk quite under water, and the little part left behind was no better than a heap of rubbish. The shake was so violent that it threw people down on their knees or their faces, as they were running about for shelter. The ground heaved and swelled like a rolling sea, and several houses, still standing, were shuffled and moved some yards out of their places. A whole street is said to be twice as broad now as before; and in many places the earth would crack, and open, and shut, quick and fast, of which openings two or three hundred might be seen at a time; in some whereof the people were swallowed up, others the closing earth caught by the middle and pressed to death, in others the heads only appeared. The larger openings swallowed up houses; and out of some would issue whole rivers of waters, spouted up a great height into the air, and threatening a deluge to that part the earthquake spared. The whole was attended with stenches and offensive smells, the noise of falling mountains at a distance, &c., and the sky in a minute's time was turned dull and reddish, like a glowing oven. Yet, as great a sufferer as Port Royal was, more houses were left standing therein than on the whole island besides. Scarce a planting-house or sugar-work was left standing in all Jamaica. A great part of them were swallowed up, houses, people, trees, and all at one gape; in lieu of which afterward appeared great pools of water, which, when dried up, left nothing but sand, without any mark that ever tree or plant had been thereon.

Above twelve miles from the sea the earth gaped and spouted out, with a prodigious force, vast quantities of water into the air, yet the greatest violences were among the mountains and rocks; and it is a general opinion, that the nearer the mountains, the greater the shake, and that the cause thereof lay there. Most of the rivers were stopped up for twenty-four hours by the falling of the mountains, till, swelling up, they found themselves new tracts and channels, tearing up in their passage trees, &c. After the great shake, those people who escaped got on board ships in the harbour, where many continued above two months; the shakes all that time being so violent, and coming so thick, sometimes two or three in an hour, accompanied with frightful noises, like a ruffling wind, or a hollow, rumbling thunder, with brimstone blasts, that they durst not come ashore. The consequence of the earthquake was a general sickness, from the noisome vapours belched forth, which swept away above three thousand persons.

After the detail of these horrible convulsions, the reader will have but little curiosity left for the less considerable phenomena of the earthquake at Lima in 1687, described by Father Alvarez de Toledo, wherein above five thousand persons were destroyed; this being of the vibratory kind, so that the bells in the church rung of themselves; or that at Batavia in 1699, by Witsen; that in the north of England in 1703, by Mr. Thoresby; or, lastly, those in New-England in 1663 and 1670, by Dr. Mather.

*To David Rittenhouse.*

New and curious Theory of Light and Heat.—Read in the American Philosophical Society, November 20, 1788.

Universal space, as far as we know of it, seems to be filled with a subtile fluid, whose motion or vibration is called light.

This fluid may possibly be the same with that which, being attracted by, and entering into other more solid matter, dilutes the substance by separating the constituent particles, and so rendering some solids fluid, and maintaining the fluidity of others; of which fluid, when our bodies are totally deprived, they are said to be frozen; when they have a proper quantity, they are in health, and fit to perform all their functions; it is then called natural heat; when too much, it is called fever; and when forced into the body in too great a quantity from without, it gives pain, by separating and destroying the flesh, and is then called burning, and the fluid so entering and acting is called fire.

While organized bodies, animal or vegetable, are augmenting in growth, or are supplying their continual waste, is not this done by attracting and consolidating this fluid called fire, so as to form of it a part of their substance? And is it not a separation of the parts of such substance, which, dissolving its solid state, sets that subtile fluid at liberty, when it again makes its appearance as fire?

For the power of man relative to matter seems limited to the separating or mixing the various kinds of it, or changing its form and appearance by different compositions of it; but does not extend to the making or creating new matter, or annihilating the old. Thus, if fire be an original element or kind of matter, its quantity is fixed and permanent in the universe. We cannot destroy any part of it, or make addition to it; we can only separate it from that which confines it, and so set it at liberty; as when we put wood in a situation to be burned, or transfer it from one solid to another, as when we make lime by burning stone, a part of the fire dislodged in the fuel being left in the stone. May not this fluid, when at liberty, be capable of penetrating and entering into all bodies, organized or not, quitting easily in totality those not organized, and quitting easily in part those which are; the part assumed and fixed remaining till the body is dissolved?

Is it not this fluid which keeps asunder the particles of air, permitting them to approach, or separating them more in proportion as its quantity is diminished or augmented?

Is it not the greater gravity of the particles of air which forces the particles of this fluid to mount with the matters to which it is attached, as smoke or vapour?

Does it not seem to have a greater affinity with water, since it will quit a solid to unite with that fluid, and go off with it in vapour, leaving the solid cold to the touch, and the degree measurable by the thermometer?

The vapour rises attached to this fluid, but at a certain height they separate, and the vapour descends in rain, retaining but little of it, in snow or hail less. What becomes of that fluid? Does it rise above our atmosphere, and mix with the universal mass of the same kind?

Or does a spherical stratum of it, denser, as less mixed with air, attracted by this globe, and repelled or pushed up only to a certain height from its surface by the greater weight of air, remain there surrounding the globe, and proceeding with it round the sun?

In such case, as there may be a continuity of communication of this fluid through the air quite down to the earth, is it not by the vibrations given to it by the sun that light appears to us? And may it not be that every one of the infinitely small vibrations, striking common matter with a certain force, enters its substance, is held there by attraction, and augmented by succeeding vibrations till the matter has received as much as their force can drive into it?

Is it not thus that the surface of this globe is continually heated by such repeated vibrations in the day, and cooled by the escape of the heat when those vibrations are discontinued in the night, or intercepted and reflected by clouds?

Is it not thus that fire is amassed, and makes the greatest part of the substance of combustible bodies?

Perhaps, when this globe was first formed, and its original particles took their place at certain distances from the centre, in proportion to their greater or less gravity, the fluid fire, attracted towards that centre, might in great part be obliged, as lightest, to take place above the rest, and thus form the sphere of fire above supposed, which would afterward be continually diminishing by the substance it afforded to organized bodies, and the quantity restored to it again by the burning or other separating of the parts of those bodies?

Is not the natural heat of animals thus produced, by separating in digestion the parts of food, and setting their fire at liberty?

Is it not this sphere of fire which kindles the wandering globes that sometimes pass through it in our course round the sun, have their surface kindled by it, and burst when their included air is greatly rarefied by the heat on their burning surfaces?

May it not have been from such considerations that the ancient philosophers supposed a sphere of fire to exist above the air of our atmosphere?

B. FRANKLIN.

*Of Lightning; and the Methods now used in America for the securing Buildings and Persons from its mischievous Effects.*

Experiments made in electricity first gave philosophers a suspicion that the matter of lightning was the same with the electric matter. Experiments afterward made on lightning obtained from the clouds by pointed rods, received into bottles, and subjected to every trial, have since proved this suspicion to be perfectly well founded; and that, whatever properties we find in electricity, are also the properties of lightning.

This matter of lightning or of electricity is an extreme subtile fluid, penetrating other bodies, and subsisting in them, equally diffused.

When, by any operation of art or nature, there happens to be a greater proportion of this fluid in one body than in another, the body which has most will communicate to that which has least, till the proportion becomes equal; provided the distance between them be not too great; or, if it is too great, till there be proper conductors to convey it from one to the other.

If the communication be through the air without any conductor, a bright light is seen between the bodies, and a sound is heard. In our small experiments we call this light and sound the electric spark and snap; but in the great operations of nature the light is what we call *lightning*, and the sound (produced at the same time, though generally arriving later at our ears than the light does to our eyes) is, with its echoes, called *thunder*.

If the communication of this fluid is by a conductor, it may be without either light or sound, the subtile fluid passing in the substance of the conductor.

If the conductor be good and of sufficient bigness, the fluid passes through it without hurting it. If otherwise, it is damaged or destroyed.

All metals and water are good conductors. Other bodies may become conductors by having some quantity of water in them, as wood and other materials used in building; but, not having much water in them, they are not good conductors, and, therefore, are often damaged in the operation.

Glass, wax, silk, wool, hair, feathers, and even wood, perfectly dry, are non-conductors: that is, they resist instead of facilitating the passage of this subtile fluid.

When this fluid has an opportunity of passing through two conductors, one good and sufficient, as of metal, the other not so good, it passes in the best, and will follow it in any direction.

The distance at which a body charged with this fluid will discharge itself suddenly, striking through the air into another body that is not charged or not so highly charged, is different according to the quantity of the fluid, the dimensions and form of the bodies themselves, and the state of the air between them. This distance, whatever it happens to be, between any two bodies, is called the *striking distance*, as, till they come within that distance of each other, no stroke will be made.

The clouds have often more of this fluid, in proportion, than the earth; in which case, as soon as they come near enough (that is, within the striking distance) or meet with a conductor, the fluid quits them and strikes into the earth. A cloud fully charged with this fluid, if so high as to be beyond the striking distance from the earth, passes quietly without making noise or giving light, unless it meets with other clouds that have less.

Tall trees and lofty buildings, as the towers and spires of churches, become sometimes conductors between the clouds and the earth; but, not being good ones, that is, not conveying the fluid freely, they are often damaged.

Buildings that have their roofs covered with lead or other metal, the spouts of metal continued from the roof into the ground to carry off the water, are never hurt by lightning as, whenever it falls on such a building, it passes in the metals and not in the walls.

When other buildings happen to be within the striking distance from such clouds, the fluid passes in the walls, whether of wood, brick, or stone, quitting the walls only when it can find better conductors near them, as metal rods, bolts, and hinges of windows or doors, gilding on wainscot or frames of pictures, the silvering on the backs of looking-glasses, the wires for bells, and the bodies of animals, as containing watery fluids. And, in passing through the house, it follows the direction of these conductors, taking as many in its way as can assist it in its passage, whether in a straight or crooked line, leaping from one to the other, if not far distant from each other, only rending the wall in the spaces where these partial good conductors are too distant from each other.

An iron rod being placed on the outside of a building, from the highest part continued down into the moist earth in any direction, straight or crooked, following the form of the roof or parts of the building, will receive the lightning at the upper end, attracting it so as to prevent its striking any other part, and affording it a good conveyance into the earth, will prevent its damaging any part of the building.

A small quantity of metal is found able to conduct a great quantity of this fluid. A wire no bigger than a goosequill has been known to conduct (with safety to the building as far as the wire was continued) a quantity of lightning that did prodigious damage both above and below it; and probably larger rods are not necessary, though it is common in America to make them of half an inch, some of three quarters or an inch diameter.

The rod may be fastened to the wall, chimney &c., with staples of iron. The lightning will not leave the rod (a good conductor) through those staples. It would rather, if any were in the walls, pass out of it into the rod, to get more readily by that conductor into the earth.

If the building be very large and extensive, two or more rods may be placed at different parts, for greater security.

Small ragged parts of clouds, suspended in the air between the great body of clouds and the earth (like leaf gold in electrical experiments) often serve as partial conductors for the lightning, which proceeds from one of them to another, and by their help comes within the striking distance to the earth or a building. It therefore strikes through those conductors a building that would otherwise be out of the striking distance.

Long sharp points communicating with the earth, and presented to such parts of clouds, drawing silently from them the fluid they are charged with, they are then attracted to the cloud, and may leave the distance so great as to be beyond the reach of striking.

It is therefore that we elevate the upper end of the rod six or eight feet above the highest part of the building, tapering it gradually to a fine sharp point, which is gilt to prevent its rusting.

Thus the pointed rod either prevents the stroke from the cloud, or, if a stroke is made, conducts it to the earth with safety to the building.

The lower end of the rod should enter the earth so deep as to come at the moist part, perhaps two or three feet; and if bent when under the surface so as to go in a horizontal line six or eight feet from the wall, and then bent again downward three or four feet, it will prevent damage to any of the stones of the foundation.

A person apprehensive of danger from lightning, happening during the time of thunder to be in a house not so secured, will do well to avoid sitting near the chimney, near a looking-glass, or any gilt pictures or wainscot; the safest place is the middle of the room (so it be not under a metal lustre suspended by a chain), sitting on one chair and laying the feet up in another. It is still safer to bring two or three mattresses or beds into the middle of the room, and, folding them up double, place the chair upon them; for they not being so good conductors as the walls, the lightning will not choose an interrupted course through the air of the room and the bedding, when it can go through a continued better conductor, the wall. But where it can be had, a hammock or swinging bed, suspended by silk cords equally distant from the walls on every side, and from the ceiling and floor above and below, affords the safest situation a person can have in any room whatever; and what, indeed, may be deemed quite free from danger of any stroke by lightning.

B. FRANKLIN.

Paris, September, 1767.

---

*To Peter Collinson, London.*

ELECTRICAL KITE.

Philadelphia, October 16, 1752.

As frequent mention is made in public papers from Europe of the success of the Philadelphia experiment for drawing the electric fire from clouds by means of pointed rods of iron erected on high buildings, &c., it may be agreeable to the curious to be informed that the same experiment has succeeded in Philadelphia, though made in a different and more easy manner, which is as follows:

Make a small cross of two light strips of cedar, the arms so long as to reach to the four corners of a large thin silk handkerchief when extended; tie the corners of the handkerchief to the extremities of the cross, so you have the body of a kite, which, being properly accommodated with a tail, loop, and string, will rise in the air like those made of paper; but this, being of silk, is fitter to bear the wet and wind of a thunder-gust without tearing. To the top of the upright stick of the cross is to be fixed a very sharp-pointed wire, rising a foot or more above the wood. To the end of the twine next the hand is to be tied a silk riband, and where the silk and twine join, a key may be fastened. This kite is to be raised when a thunder-gust appears to be coming on, and the person who holds the string must stand within a door or window, or under some cover, so that the silk riband may not be wet; and care must be taken that the twine does not touch the frame of the door or window. As soon as any of the thunder-clouds come over the kite, the pointed wire will draw the electric fire from them, and the kite, with all the twine, will be electrified, and the loose filaments of the twine will stand out every way, and be attracted by an approaching finger. And when the rain has wetted the kite and twine, so that it can conduct the electric fire freely, you will find it stream out plentifully from the key on the approach of your knuckle. At this key the vial may be charged; and from electric fire thus obtained, spirits may be kindled, and all the other electric experiments be performed, which are usually done by the help of a rubbed glass globe or tube, and thereby the sameness of the electric matter with that of lightning completely demonstrated.

B. Franklin.

*Physical and Meteorological Observations, Conjectures, and Suppositions.—* Read at the Royal Society, June 3, 1756.

The particles of air are kept at a distance from each other by their mutual repulsion * * *

Whatever particles of other matter (not endued with that repellancy) are supported in air, must adhere to the particles of air, and be supported by them; for in the vacancies there is nothing they can rest on.

Air and water mutually attract each other. Hence water will dissolve in air, as salt in water.

The specific gravity of matter is not altered by dividing the matter, though the superfices be increased. Sixteen leaden bullets, of an ounce each, weigh as much in water as one of a pound, whose superfices is less.

Therefore the supporting of salt in water is not owing to its superfices being increased.

A lump of salt, though laid at rest at the bottom of a vessel of water, will dissolve therein, and its parts move every way, till equally diffused in the water; therefore there is a mutual attraction between water and salt. Every particle of water assumes as many of salt as can adhere to it; when more is added, it precipitates, and will not remain suspended.

Water, in the same manner, will dissolve in air, every particle of air assuming one or more particles of water. When too much is added, it precipitates in rain.

But there not being the same contiguity between the particles of air as of water, the solution of water in air is not carried on without a motion of the air so as to cause a fresh accession of dry particles.

Part of a fluid, having more of what it dissolves, will communicate to other parts that have less. Thus very salt water, coming in contact with fresh, communicates its saltness till all is equal, and the sooner if there is a little motion of the water. * * *

Air, suffering continual changes in the degrees of its heat, from various causes and circumstances, and, consequently, changes in its specific gravity, must therefore be in continual motion.

A small quantity of fire mixed with water (or degree of heat therein) so weakens the cohesion of its particles, that those on the surface easily quit it and adhere to the particles of air.

Air moderately heated will support a greater quantity of water invisibly than cold air; for its particles being by heat repelled to a greater distance from each other, thereby more easily keep the particles of water that are annexed to them from running into cohesions that would obstruct, refract, or reflect the light.

Hence, when we breathe in warm air, though the same quantity of moisture may be taken up from the lungs as when we breathe in cold air, yet that moisture is not so visible.

Water being extremely heated, *i. e.*, to the degree of boiling, its particles, in quitting it, so repel each other as to take up vastly more space than before and by that repellancy support themselves, expelling the air from the space they occupy. That degree of heat being lessened, they again mutually attract, and having no air particles mixed to adhere to, by which they might be supported and kept at a distance, they instantly fall, coalesce, and become water again.

The water commonly diffused in our atmosphere never receives such a degree of heat from the sun or other cause as water has when boiling; it is not, therefore, supported by such heat, but by adhering to air. * * *

A particle of air loaded with adhering water or any other matter, is heavier than before, and would descend.

The atmosphere supposed at rest, a loaded descending particle must act with a force on the particles it passes between or meets with sufficient to overcome, in some degree, their mutual repellancy, and push them nearer to each other.*

\* \*

Every particle of air, therefore, will bear any load inferior to the force of these repulsions.

Hence the support of fogs, mists, clouds.

Very warm air, clear, though supporting a very great quantity of moisture, will grow turbid and cloudy on the mixture of colder air, as foggy, turbid air will grow clear by warming.

Thus the sun, shining on a morning fog, dissipates it; clouds are seen to waste in a sunshiny day.

But cold condenses and renders visible the vapour: a tankard or decanter filled with cold water will condense the moisture of warm, clear air on its outside, where it becomes visible as dew, coalesces into drops, descends in little streams.

The sun heats the air of our atmosphere most near the surface of the earth; for there, besides the direct rays, there are many reflections. Moreover, the earth itself, being heated, communicates of its heat to the neighbouring air.

The higher regions, having only the direct rays of the sun passing through them, are comparatively very cold. Hence the cold air on the tops of mountains, and snow on some of them all the year, even in the torrid zone. Hence hail in summer.

If the atmosphere were, all of it (both above and below), always of the same temper as to cold or heat, then the upper air would always be *rarer* than the lower, because the pressure on it is less; consequently lighter, and, therefore, would keep its place.

But the upper air may be more condensed by cold than the lower air by pressure; the lower more expanded by heat than the upper for want of pressure. In such case the upper air will become the heavier, the lower lighter.

The lower region of air being heated and expanded, heaves up and supports for some time the colder, heavier air above, and will continue to support it while the equilibrium is kept. Thus water is supported in an inverted open glass, while the equilibrium is maintained by the equal pressure upward of the air below; but the equilibrium by any means breaking, the water descends on the heavier side, and the air rises into its place.

The lifted heavy cold air over a heated country becoming by any means unequally supported or unequal in its weight, the heaviest part descends first, and the rest follows impetuously. Hence gusts after heats, and hurricanes in hot climates. Hence the air of gusts and hurricanes is cold, though in hot climates and seasons; it coming from above.

The cold air descending from above, as it penetrates our warm region full of watery particles, condenses them, renders them visible, forms a cloud thick and dark, overcasting sometimes, at once, large and extensive; sometimes, when seen at a distance, small at first, gradually increasing; the cold edge or surface of the cloud condensing the vapours next it, which form smaller clouds that join it, increase its bulk, it descends with the wind and its acquired weight, draws nearer the earth, grows denser with continual additions of water, and discharges heavy showers.

Small black clouds thus appearing in a clear sky, in hot climates portend storms, and warn seamen to hand their sails.

The earth turning on its axis in about twenty-four hours, the equatorial parts must move about fifteen miles in each minute; in northern and southern latitudes this motion is gradually less to the poles, and there nothing.

If there was a general calm over the face of the globe, it must be by the air's moving in every part as fast as the earth or sea it covers. * * *

The air under the equator and between the tropics being constantly heated and rarefied by the sun, rises. Its place is supplied by air from northern and southern latitudes, which, coming from parts wherein the earth and air had less motion, and not suddenly acquiring the quicker motion of the equatorial earth, appears an east wind blowing westward; the earth moving from west to east, and slipping under the air.[37]

Thus, when we ride in a calm, it seems a wind against us: if we ride with the wind, and faster, even that will seem a small wind against us.

The air rarefied between the tropics, and rising, must flow in the higher region north and south. Before it rose it had acquired the greatest motion the earth's rotation could give it. It retains some degree of this motion, and descending in higher latitudes, where the earth's motion is less, will appear a westerly wind, yet tending towards the equatorial parts, to supply the vacancy occasioned by the air of the lower regions flowing thitherward.

Hence our general cold winds are about northwest, our summer cold gusts the same.

The air in sultry weather, though not cloudy, has a kind of haziness in it, which makes objects at a distance appear dull and indistinct. This haziness is occasioned by the great quantity of moisture equally diffused in that air. When, by the cold wind blowing down among it, it is condensed into clouds, and falls in rain, the air becomes purer and clearer. Hence, after gusts, distant objects appear distinct, their figures sharply terminated.

Extreme cold winds congeal the surface of the earth by carrying off its fire. Warm winds afterward blowing over that frozen surface will be chilled by it. Could that frozen surface be turned under, and warmer turned up from beneath it, those warm winds would not be chilled so much.

The surface of the earth is also sometimes much heated by the sun: and such heated surface, not being changed, heats the air that moves over it.

Seas, lakes, and great bodies of water, agitated by the winds, continually change surfaces; the cold surface in winter is turned under by the rolling of the waves, and a warmer turned up; in summer the warm is turned under, and colder turned up. Hence the more equal temper of seawater, and the air over it. Hence, in winter, winds from the sea seem warm, winds from the land cold. In summer the contrary.

Therefore the lakes northwest of us,[38] as they are not so much frozen, nor so apt to freeze as the earth, rather moderate than increase the coldness of our winter winds.

The air over the sea being warmer, and, therefore, lighter in winter than the air over the frozen land, may be another cause of our general northwest winds, which blow off to sea at right angles from our North American coast. The warm, light sea-air rising, the heavy, cold land-air pressing into its place.

Heavy fluids, descending, frequently form eddies or whirlpools, as is seen in a funnel, where the water acquires a circular motion, receding every way from a centre, and leaving a vacancy in the middle, greatest above, and lessening downward, like a speaking-trumpet, its big end upward.

Air, descending or ascending, may form the same kind of eddies or whirlings, the parts of air acquiring a circular motion, and receding from the middle of the circle by a centrifugal force, and leaving there a vacancy; if descending, greatest above and lessening downward; if ascending, greatest below and lessening upward; like a speaking-trumpet standing its big end on the ground.

When the air descends with a violence in some places, it may rise with equal violence in others, and form both kinds of whirlwinds.

The air, in its whirling motion, receding every way from the centre or axis of the trumpet, leaves there a *vacuum*, which cannot be filled through the sides, the whirling air, as an arch, preventing; it must then press in at the open ends.

The greatest pressure inward must be at the lower end, the greatest weight of the surrounding atmosphere being there. The air, entering, rises within, and carries up dust, leaves, and even heavier bodies that happen in its way, as the eddy or whirl passes over land.

If it passes over water, the weight of the surrounding atmosphere forces up the water into the vacuity, part of which, by degrees, joins with the whirling air, and, adding weight and receiving accelerated motion, recedes farther from the centre or axis of the trump as the pressure lessens; and at last, as the trump widens, is broken into small particles, and so united with air as to be supported by it, and become black clouds at the top of the trump.

Thus these eddies may be whirlwinds at land, water-spouts at sea. A body of water so raised may be suddenly let fall, when the motion, &c., has not strength to support it, or the whirling arch is broken so as to admit the air: falling in the sea, it is harmless unless ships happen under it; and if in the progressive motion of the whirl it has moved from the sea over the land, and then breaks, sudden, violent, and mischievous torrents are the consequences.

[37] See a paper on this subject, by the late ingenious Mr. Hadley, in the Philadelphia Transactions, wherein this hypothesis of explaining the tradewinds first appeared.

[38] In Pennsylvania.

---

## To Dr. Perkins.

*Water-spouts and Whirlwinds compared.*—Read at the Royal Society, June 24, 1753.

Philadelphia, Feb. 4, 1753.

I ought to have written to you long since, in answer to yours of October 16, concerning the water-spout; but business partly, and partly a desire of procuring farther information by inquiry among my seafaring acquaintance, induced me to postpone writing, from time to time, till I am almost ashamed to resume the subject, not knowing but you may have forgot what has been said upon it.

Nothing certainly can be more improving to a searcher into nature than objections judiciously made to his opinion, taken up, perhaps, too hastily: for such objections oblige him to restudy the point, consider every circumstance carefully, compare facts, make experiments, weigh arguments, and be slow in drawing conclusions. And hence a sure advantage results; for he either confirms a truth before too slightly supported, or discovers an error, and receives instruction from the objector.

In this view I consider the objections and remarks you sent me, and thank you for them sincerely; but, how much soever my inclinations lead me to philosophical inquiries, I am so engaged in business, public and private, that those more pleasing pursuits are frequently interrupted, and the chain of thought necessary to be closely continued in such disquisitions is so broken and disjointed, that it is with difficulty I satisfy myself in any of them; and I am now not much nearer a conclusion in this matter of the spout than when I first read your letter.

Yet, hoping we may, in time, sift out the truth between us, I will send you my present thoughts, with some observations on your reasons on the accounts in the *Transactions*, and on other relations I have met with. Perhaps, while I am writing, some new light may strike me, for I shall now be obliged to consider the subject with a little more attention.

I agree with you, that, by means of a vacuum in a whirlwind, water cannot be supposed to rise in large masses to the region of the clouds; for the pressure of the surrounding atmosphere could not force it up in a continued body or column to a much greater height than thirty feet. But if there really is a vacuum in the centre, or near the axis of whirlwinds, then, I think, water may rise in such vacuum to that height, or to a less height, as the vacuum may be less perfect.

I had not read Stuart's account, in the *Transactions*, for many years before the receipt of your letter, and had quite forgot it; but now, on viewing his draughts and considering his descriptions, I think they seem to favour *my hypothesis*; for he describes and draws columns of water of various heights, terminating abruptly at the top, exactly as water would do when forced up by the pressure of the atmosphere into an exhausted tube.

I must, however, no longer call it *my hypothesis*, since I find Stuart had the same thought, though somewhat obscurely expressed, where he says "he imagines this phenomenon may be solved by suction (improperly so called) or rather pulsion, as in the application of a cupping-glass to the flesh, the air being first voided by the kindled flax."

In my paper, I supposed a whirlwind and a spout to be the same thing, and to proceed from the same cause; the only difference between them being that the one passes over the land, the other over water. I find also in the *Transactions*, that M. de la Pryme was of the same opinion; for he there describes two spouts, as he calls them, which were seen at different times, at Hatfield, in Yorkshire, whose appearances in the air were the same with those of the spouts at sea, and effects the same with those of real whirlwinds.

Whirlwinds have generally a progressive as well as a circular motion; so had what is called the spout at Topsham, as described in the Philosophical Transactions, which also appears, by its effects described, to have been a real whirlwind. Water-spouts have, also, a progressive motion; this is sometimes greater and sometimes less; in some violent, in others barely perceivable. The whirlwind at Warrington continued long in Acrement Close.

Whirlwinds generally arise after calms and great heats: the same is observed of water-spouts, which are, therefore, most frequent in the warm latitudes. The spout that happened in cold weather, in the Downs, described by Mr. Gordon in the *Transactions*, was, for that reason, thought extraordinary; but he remarks withal, that the weather, though cold when the spout appeared, was soon after much colder: as we find it commonly less warm after a whirlwind.

You agree that the wind blows every way towards a whirlwind from a large space round. An intelligent whaleman of Nantucket informed me that three of their vessels, which were out in search of whales, happening to be becalmed, lay in sight of each other, at about a league distance, if I remember right, nearly forming a triangle: after some time, a water-spout appeared near the middle of the triangle, when a brisk breeze of wind sprung up, and every vessel made sail; and then it appeared to them all, by the setting of the sails and the course each vessel stood, that the spout was to the leeward of every one of them; and they all declared it to have been so when they happened afterward in company, and came to confer about it. So that in this particular, likewise, whirlwinds and water-spouts agree.

But if that which appears a water-spout at sea does sometimes, in its progressive motion, meet with and pass over land, and there produce all the phenomena and effects of a whirlwind, it should thence seem still more evident that a whirlwind and a spout are the same. I send you, herewith, a letter from an ingenious physician of my acquaintance, which gives one instance of this, that fell within his observation.

A fluid, moving from all points horizontally towards a centre, must, at that centre, either ascend or descend. Water being in a tub, if a hole be opened in the middle of the bottom, will flow from all sides to the centre, and there descend in a whirl. But air flowing on and near the surface of land or water, from all sides towards a centre, must at that centre ascend, the land or water hindering its descent.

If these concentring currents of air be in the upper region, they may, indeed, descend in the spout or whirlwind; but then, when the united current reached the earth or water, it would spread, and, probably, blow every way from the centre. There may be whirlwinds of both kinds, but from the commonly observed effects I suspect the rising one to be the most common: when the upper air descends, it is, perhaps, in a greater body, extending wider, as in our thunder-gusts, and without much whirling; and, when air descends in a spout or whirlwind, I should rather expect it would press the roof of a house *inward*, or force *in* the tiles, shingles, or thatch, force a boat down into the water, or a piece of timber into the earth, than that it would lift them up and carry them away.

It has so happened that I have not met with any accounts of spouts that certainly descended; I suspect they are not frequent. Please to communicate those you mention. The apparent dropping of a pipe from the clouds towards the earth or sea, I will endeavour to explain hereafter.

The augmentation of the cloud, which, as I am informed, is generally, if not always the case, during a spout, seems to show an ascent rather than a descent of the matter of which such cloud is composed; for a descending spout, one would expect, should diminish a cloud. I own, however, that cold air, descending, may, by condensing the vapours in a lower region, form and increase clouds; which, I think, is generally the case in our common thunder-gusts, and, therefore, do not lay great stress on this argument.

Whirlwinds and spouts are not always, though most commonly, in the daytime. The terrible whirlwind which damaged a great part of Rome, June 11, 1749, happened in the night of that day. The same was supposed to have been first a spout, for it is said to be beyond doubt that it gathered in the neighbouring sea, as it could be tracked from Ostia to Rome. I find this in Père Boschovich's account of it, as abridged in the Monthly Review for December, 1750.

In that account, the whirlwind is said to have appeared as a very black, long, and lofty cloud, discoverable, notwithstanding the darkness of the night, by its continually lightning or emitting flashes on all sides, pushing along with a surprising swiftness, and within three or four feet of the ground. Its general effects on houses were stripping off the roofs, blowing away chimneys, breaking doors and windows, *forcing up the floors, and unpaving the rooms* (some of these effects seem to agree well with a supposed vacuum in the centre of the whirlwind), and the very rafters of the houses were broken and dispersed, and even hurled against houses at a considerable distance, &c.

It seems, by an expression of Père Boschovich's, as if the wind blew from all sides towards the whirlwind; for, having carefully observed its effects, he concludes of all whirlwinds, "that their motion is circular, and their action attractive."

He observes on a number of histories of whirlwinds, &c., "that a common effect of them is to carry up into the air tiles, stones, and animals themselves, which happen to be in their course, and all kinds of bodies unexceptionably, throwing them to a considerable distance with great impetuosity."

Such effects seem to show a rising current of air.

I will endeavour to explain my conceptions of this matter by figures, representing a plan and an elevation of a spout or whirlwind.

I would only first beg to be allowed two or three positions mentioned in my former paper.

1. That the lower region of air is often more heated, and so more rarefied, than the upper; consequently, specifically lighter. The coldness of the upper region is manifested by the hail which sometimes falls from it in a hot day.

2. That heated air may be very moist, and yet the moisture so equally diffused and rarefied as not to be visible till colder air mixes with it, when it condenses and becomes visible. Thus our breath, invisible in summer, becomes visible in winter.

Now let us suppose a tract of land or sea, of perhaps sixty miles square, unscreened by clouds and unfanned by winds during great part of a summer's day, or, it may be, for several days successively, till it is violently heated, together with the lower region of air in contact with it, so that the said lower air becomes specifically lighter than the superincumbent higher region of the atmosphere in which the clouds commonly float: let us suppose, also, that the air surrounding this tract has not been so much heated during those days, and, therefore, remains heavier. The consequence of this should be, as I conceive, that the heated lighter air, being pressed on all sides, must ascend, and the heavier descend; and as this rising cannot be in all parts, or the whole area of the tract at once, for that would leave too extensive a vacuum, the rising will begin precisely in that column that happens to be the lightest or most rarefied; and the warm air will flow horizontally from all points to this column, where the several currents meeting, and joining to rise, a whirl is naturally formed, in the same manner as a whirl is formed in the tub of water, by the descending fluid flowing from all sides of the tub to the hole in the centre.

And as the several currents arrive at this central rising column with a considerable degree of horizontal motion, they cannot suddenly change it to a vertical motion; therefore, as they gradually, in approaching the whirl, decline from right curved or circular lines, so, having joined the whirl, they *ascend* by a spiral motion, in the same manner as the water *descends* spirally through the hole in the tub before mentioned.

Lastly, as the lower air, and nearest the surface, is most rarefied by the heat of the sun, that air is most acted on by the pressure of the surrounding cold and heavy air, which is to take its place; consequently, its motion towards the whirl is swiftest, and so the force of the lower part of the whirl or trump strongest, and the centrifugal force of its particles greatest; and hence the vacuum round the axis of the whirl should be greatest near the earth or sea, and be gradually diminished as it approaches the region of the clouds, till it ends in a point, as at P, *Fig. 2. in the plate*, forming a long and sharp cone.

In figure 1, which is a plan or groundplat of a whirlwind, the circle V represents the central vacuum.

Between *a a a a* and *b b b b* I suppose a body of air, condensed strongly by the pressure of the currents moving towards it from all sides without, and by its centrifugal force from within, moving round with prodigious swiftness (having, as it were, the entire momenta of all the currents $\rightarrow$ $\rightarrow$ united in itself), and with a power equal to its swiftness and density.

It is this whirling body of air between *a a a a* and *b b b b* that rises spirally; by its force it tears buildings to pieces, twists up great trees by the roots, &c., and, by its spiral motion, raises the fragments so high, till the pressure of the surrounding and approaching currents diminishing, can no longer confine them to the circle, or their own centrifugal force increasing, grows too strong for such pressure, when they fly off in tangent lines, as stones out of a sling, and fall on all sides and at great distances.

If it happens at sea, the water under and between *a a a a* and *b b b b* will be violently agitated and driven about, and parts of it raised with the spiral current, and thrown about so as to form a bushlike appearance.

This circle is of various diameters, sometimes very large. If the vacuum passes over water, the water may rise in it in a body or column to near the height of thirty-two feet. If it passes over houses, it may burst their windows or walls outward, pluck off the roofs, and pluck up the floors, by the sudden rarefaction of the air contained within such buildings; the outward pressure of the atmosphere being suddenly taken off; so the stopped bottle of air bursts under the exhausted receiver of the airpump.

Fig. 2 is to represent the elevation of a water-spout, wherein I suppose P P P to be the cone, at first a vacuum, till W W, the rising column of water, has filled so much of it. S S S S, the spiral whirl of air, surrounding the vacuum, and continued higher in a close column after the vacuum ends in the point P, till it reaches the cool region of the air. B B, the bush described by Stuart, surrounding the foot of the column of water.

Now I suppose this whirl of air will at first be as invisible as the air itself, though reaching, in reality, from the water to the region of cool air, in which our low summer thunder-clouds commonly float: but presently it will become visible at its extremities. *At its lower end*, by the agitation of the water under the whirling part of the circle, between P and S, forming Stuart's bush, and by the swelling and rising of the water in the beginning vacuum, which is at first a small, low, broad cone, whose top gradually rises and sharpens, as the force of the whirl increases. *At its upper end* it becomes visible by the warm air brought up to the cooler region, where its moisture begins to be condensed into thick vapour by the cold, and is seen first at A, the highest part, which, being now cooled, condenses what rises next at B, which condenses that at C, and that condenses what is rising at D, the cold operating by the contact of the vapours faster in a right line downward than the vapours can climb in a spiral line upward; they climb, however, and as by continual addition they grow denser, and, consequently, their centrifugal force greater, and being risen above the concentrating currents that compose the whirl, fly off, spread, and form a cloud.

It seems easy to conceive how, by this successive condensation from above, the spout appears to drop or descend from the cloud, though the materials of which it is composed are all the while ascending.

The condensation of the moisture contained in so great a quantity of warm air as may be supposed to rise in a short time in this prodigiously rapid whirl, is perhaps sufficient to form a great extent of cloud, though the spout should be over land, as those at Hatfield; and if the land happens not to be very dusty, perhaps the lower part of the spout will scarce become visible at all; though the upper, or what is commonly called the descending part, be very distinctly seen.

The same may happen at sea, in case the whirl is not violent enough to make a high vacuum, and raise the column, &c. In such case, the upper part A B C D only will be visible, and the bush, perhaps, below.

But if the whirl be strong, and there be much dust on the land, and the column W W be raised from the water, then the lower part becomes visible and sometimes even united to the upper part. For the dust may be carried up in the spiral whirl till it reach the region where the vapour is condensed, and rise with that even to the clouds: and the friction of the whirling air on the sides of the column W W, may detach great quantities of its water, break it into drops, and carry them up in the spiral whirl, mixed with the air; the heavier drops may indeed fly off, and fall in a shower round the spout; but much of it will be broken into vapour, yet visible; and thus, in both cases, by dust at land and by water at sea, the whole tube may be darkened and rendered visible.

As the whirl weakens, the tube may (in appearance) separate in the middle; the column of water subsiding, and the superior condensed part drawing up to the cloud. Yet still the tube or whirl of air may remain entire, the middle only becoming invisible, as not containing visible matter.

Dr. Stuart says, "It was observable of all the spouts he saw, but more perceptible of the great one, that, towards the end, it began to appear like a hollow canal, only black in the borders, but white in the middle; and though at first it was altogether black and opaque, yet now one could very distinctly perceive the seawater to fly up along the middle of this canal, as smoke up a chimney."

And Dr. Mather, describing a whirlwind, says, "A thick dark, small cloud arose, with a pillar of light in it, of about eight or ten feet diameter, and passed along the ground in a tract not wider than a street, horribly tearing up trees by the roots, blowing them up in the air life feathers, and throwing up stones of great weight to a considerable height in the air," &c.

These accounts, the one of water-spouts, the other of a whirlwind, seem in this particular to agree; what one gentleman describes as a tube, black in the borders and white in the middle, the other calls a black cloud, with a pillar of light in it; the latter expression has only a little more of the *marvellous*, but the thing is the same; and it seems not very difficult to understand. When Dr. Stuart's spouts were full charged, that is, when the whirling pipe of air was filled between *a a a a* and *b b b b*, fig. 1, with quantities of drops, and vapour torn off from the column W W, fig. 2, the whole was rendered so dark as that it could not be seen through, nor the spiral ascending motion discovered; but when the quantity ascending lessened, the pipe became more transparent, and the ascending motion visible. For, by inspection of the figure given in the opposite page, respecting a section of our spout, with the vacuum in the middle, it is plain that if we look at such a hollow pipe in the direction of the arrows, and suppose opaque particles to be equally mixed in the space between the two circular lines, both the part between the arrows *a* and *b*, and that between the arrows *c* and *d*, will appear much darker than that between *b* and *c*, as there must be many more of those opaque particles in the line of vision across the sides than across the middle. It is thus that a hair in a microscope evidently appears to be a pipe, the sides showing darker than the middle. Dr. Mather's whirl was probably filled with dust, the sides were very dark, but the vacuum within rendering the middle more transparent, he calls it a pillar of light.

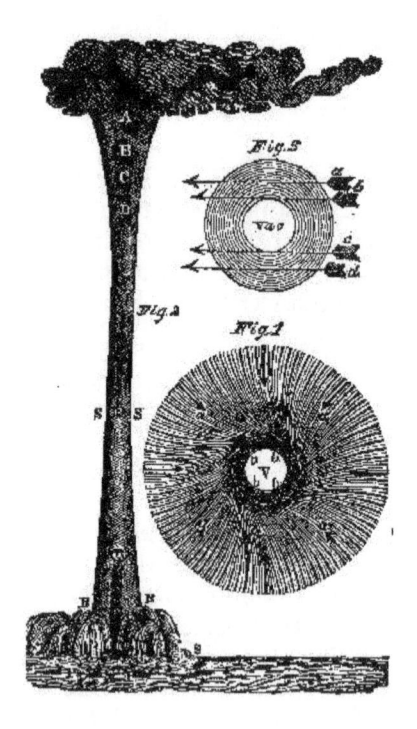

It was in this more transparent part, between $b$ and $c$, that Stuart could see the spiral motion of the vapours, whose lines on the nearest and farthest side of the transparent part crossing each other, represented smoke ascending in a chimney; for the quantity being still too great in the line of sight through the sides of the tube, the motion could not be discovered there, and so they represented the solid sides of the chimney.

When the vapours reach in the pipe from the clouds near to the earth, it is no wonder now to those who understand electricity, that flashes of lightning should descend by the spout, as in that of Rome.

But you object, if water may be thus carried into the clouds, why have we not salt rains? The objection is strong and reasonable, and I know not whether I can answer it to your satisfaction. I never heard but of one salt rain, and that was where a spout passed pretty near a ship; so I suppose it to be only the drops thrown off from the spout by the centrifugal force (as the birds were at Hatfield), when they had been carried so high as to be above, or to be too strongly centrifugal for the pressure of the concurring winds surrounding it: and, indeed, I believe there can be no other kind of salt rain; for it has pleased the goodness of God so to order it, that the particles of air will not attract the particles of salt, though they strongly attract water.

Hence, though all metals, even gold, may be united with air and rendered volatile, salt remains fixed in the fire, and no heat can force it up to any considerable height, or oblige the air to hold it. Hence, when salt rises, as it will a little way, into air with water, there is instantly a separation made; the particles of water adhere to the air, and the particles of salt fall down again, as if repelled and forced off from the water by some power in the air; or, as some metals, dissolved in a proper *menstruum*, will quit the solvent when other matter approaches, and adhere to that, so the water quits the salt and embraces the air; but air will not embrace the salt and quit the water, otherwise our rains would indeed be salt, and every tree and plant on the face of the earth be destroyed, with all the animals that depend on them for subsistence. He who hath proportioned and given proper quantities to all things, was not unmindful of this. Let us adore Him with praise and thanksgiving.

By some accounts of seamen, it seems the column of water W W sometimes falls suddenly; and if it be, as some say, fifteen or twenty yards diameter, it must fall with great force, and they may well fear for their ships. By one account, in the *Transactions*, of a spout that fell at Colne, in Lancashire, one would think the column is sometimes lifted off from the water and carried over land, and there let fall in a body; but this, I suppose, happens rarely.

Stuart describes his spouts as appearing no bigger than a mast, and sometimes less; but they were seen at a league and a half distance.

I think I formerly read in Dampier, or some other voyager, that a spout, in its progressive motion, went over a ship becalmed on the coast of Guinea, and first threw her down on one side, carrying away her foremast, then suddenly whipped her up, and threw her down on the other side, carrying away her mizen-mast, and the whole was over in an instant. I suppose the first mischief was done by the foreside of the whirl, the latter by the hinderside, their motion being contrary.

I suppose a whirlwind or spout may be stationary when the concurring winds are equal; but if unequal, the whirl acquires a progressive motion in the direction of the strongest pressure.

When the wind that gives the progressive motion becomes stronger below than above, or above than below, the spout will be bent, and, the cause ceasing, straighten again.

Your queries towards the end of your paper appear judicious and worth considering. At present I am not furnished with facts sufficient to make any pertinent answer to them, and this paper has already a sufficient quantity of conjecture.

Your manner of accommodating the accounts to your hypothesis of descending spouts is, I own, in ingenious, and perhaps that hypothesis maybe true. I will consider it farther, but, as yet, I am not satisfied with it, though hereafter I may be.

Here you have my method of accounting for the principal phenomena, which I submit to your candid examination.

And as I now seem to have almost written a book instead of a letter, you will think it high time I should conclude; which I beg leave to do, with assuring you that I am, &c.,

B. FRANKLIN.

*Alexander Small, London.*
ON THE NORTHEAST STORMS IN NORTH AMERICA.
May 12, 1760.

Agreeable to your request, I send you my reasons for thinking that our northeast storms in North America begin first, in point of time, in the southwest parts; that is to say, the air in Georgia, the farthest of our colonies to the southwest, begins to move southwesterly before the air of Carolina, which is the next colony northeastward; the air of Carolina has the same motion before the air of Virginia, which lies still more northeastward; and so on northeasterly through Pennsylvania, New-York, New-England, &c., quite to Newfoundland.

These northeast storms are generally very violent, continue sometimes two or three days, and often do considerable damage in the harbours along the coast. They are attended with thick clouds and rain.

What first gave me this idea was the following circumstance. About twenty years ago, a few more or less, I cannot from my memory be certain, we were to have an eclipse of the moon at Philadelphia, on a Friday evening, about nine o'clock. I intended to observe it, but was prevented by a northeast storm, which came on about seven, with thick clouds as usual, that quite obscured the whole hemisphere. Yet when the post brought us the Boston newspaper, giving an account of the effects of the same storm in those parts, I found the beginning of the eclipse had been well observed there, though Boston lies N. E. of Philadelphia about four hundred miles. This puzzled me, because the storm began with us so soon as to prevent any observation; and being a northeast storm, I imagined it must have begun rather sooner in places farther to the northeastward than it did at Philadelphia. I therefore mentioned it in a letter to my brother, who lived at Boston; and he informed me the storm did not begin with them till near eleven o'clock, so that they had a good observation of the eclipse; and upon comparing all the other accounts I received from the several colonies of the time of beginning of the same storm, and, since that, of other storms of the same kind, I found the beginning to be always later the farther northeastward. I have not my notes with me here in England, and cannot, from memory, say the proportion of time to distance, but I think it is about an hour to every hundred miles.

From thence I formed an idea of the cause of these storms, which I would explain by a familiar instance or two. Suppose a long canal of water stopped at the end by a gate. The water is quite at rest till the gate is open, then it begins to move out through the gate; the water next the gate is first in motion, and moves towards the gate; the water next to that first water moves next, and so on successively, till the water at the head of the canal is in motion, which is last of all. In this case all the water moves, indeed, towards the gate, but the successive times of beginning motion are the contrary way, viz., from the gate backward to the head of the canal. Again, suppose the air in a chamber at rest, no current through the room till you make a fire in the chimney. Immediately the air in the chimney, being rarefied by the fire, rises; the air next the chimney flows in to supply its place, moving towards the chimney; and, in consequence, the rest of the air successively, quite back to the door. Thus, to produce our northeast storms, I suppose some great heat and rarefaction of the air in or about the Gulf of Mexico; the air, thence rising, has its place supplied by the next more northern, cooler, and, therefore, denser and heavier air; that, being in motion, is followed by the next more northern air, &c., in a successive current, to which current our coast and inland ridge of mountains give the direction of northeast, as they lie N. E. and S. W.

This I offer only as an hypothesis to account for this particular fact; and perhaps, on farther examination, a better and truer may be found. I do not suppose all storms generated in the same manner. Our northwest thunder-gusts in America, I know, are not; but of them I have written my opinion fully in a paper which you have seen.

B. Franklin.

*To Dr. Lining, at Charleston.*
ON COLD PRODUCED BY EVAPORATION.

New-York, April 14, 1757.

It is a long time since I had the pleasure of a line from you; and, indeed, the troubles of our country, with the hurry of business I have been engaged in on that account, have made me so bad a correspondent, that I ought not to expect punctuality in others.

But, being about to embark for England, I could not quit the continent without paying my respects to you, and, at the same time, taking leave to introduce to your acquaintance a gentleman of learning and merit, Colonel Henry Bouquet, who does me the favour to present you this letter, and with whom I am sure you will be much pleased.

Professor Simpson, of Glasgow, lately communicated to me some curious experiments of a physician of his acquaintance, by which it appeared that an extraordinary degree of cold, even to freezing, might be produced by evaporation. I have not had leisure to repeat and examine more than the first and easiest of them, viz.: wet the ball of a thermometer by a feather dipped in spirits of wine which has been kept in the same room, and has, of course, the same degree of heat or cold. The mercury sinks presently three or four degrees, and the quicker if, during the evaporation, you blow on the ball with bellows; a second wetting and blowing, when the mercury is down, carries it yet lower. I think I did not get it lower than five or six degrees from where it naturally stood, which was at that time sixty. But it is said that a vessel of water, being placed in another somewhat larger, containing spirit, in such a manner that the vessel of water is surrounded with the spirit, and both placed under the receiver of an airpump; on exhausting the air, the spirit, evaporating, leaves such a degree of cold as to freeze the water, though the thermometer in the open air stands many degrees above the freezing point.

I know not how this phenomena is to be accounted for, but it gives me occasion to mention some loose notions relating to heat and cold, which I have for some time entertained, but not yet reduced into any form. Allowing common fire, as well as electrical, to be a fluid capable of permeating other bodies and seeking an equilibrium, I imagine some bodies are better fitted by nature to be conductors of that fluid than others; and that, generally, those which are the best conductors of the electric fluid are also the best conductors of this; and è *contra*.

Thus a body which is a good conductor of fire readily receives it into its substance, and conducts it through the whole to all the parts, as metals and water do; and if two bodies, both good conductors, one heated, the other in its common state, are brought into contact with each other, the body which has most fire readily communicates of it to that which had least, and that which had least readily receives it, till an equilibrium is produced. Thus, if you take a dollar between your fingers with one hand, and a piece of wood of the same dimensions with the other, and bring both at the same time to the flame of a candle, you will find yourself obliged to drop the dollar before you drop the wood, because it conducts the heat of the candle sooner to your flesh. Thus, if a silver teapot had a handle of the same metal, it would conduct the heat from the water to the hand, and become too hot to be used; we therefore give to a metal teapot a handle of wood, which is not so good a conductor as metal. But a China or stone teapot, being in some degree of the nature of glass, which is not a good conductor of heat, may have a handle of the same stuff. Thus, also, a damp, moist air shall make a man more sensible of cold, or chill him more than a dry air that is colder, because a moist air is fitter to receive and conduct away the heat of his body. This fluid, entering bodies in great quantity, first expands them, by separating their parts a little; afterward, by farther separating their parts, it renders solids fluid, and at length dissipates their parts in air. Take this fluid from melted lead or from water, the parts cohere again; the first grows solid, the latter becomes ice: and this is sooner done by the means of good conductors. Thus, if you take, as I have done, a square bar of lead, four inches long and one inch thick, together with three pieces of wood planed to the same dimensions, and lay them on a smooth board, fixed so as not to be easily separated or moved, and pour into the cavity they form as much melted lead as will fill it, you will see the melted lead chill and become firm on the side next the leaden bar some time before it chills on the other three sides in contact with the wooden bars, though, before the lead was poured in, they might all be supposed to have the same degree of heat or coldness, as they had been exposed in the same room to the same air. You will likewise observe, that the leaden bar, as it has cooled the melted lead more than the wooden bars have done, so it is itself more heated by the melted lead. There is a certain quantity of this fluid, called fire, in every living human body; which fluid being in due proportion, keeps the parts of the flesh and blood at such a just distance from each other, as that the flesh and nerves are supple, and the blood fit for circulation. If part of this due proportion of fire be conducted away, by means of a contact with other bodies, as air, water, or metals, the parts of our skin and flesh that come into such contact first draw more near together than is agreeable, and give that sensation which we call cold; and if too much be conveyed away, the body stiffens, the blood ceases to flow, and death ensues. On the other hand, if too much of this fluid be communicated to the flesh, the parts are separated too far, and pain ensues, as when they are separated by a pin or lancet. The sensation that the separation by fire occasions we call heat or burning. My desk on which I now write, and the lock of my desk, are both exposed to the same temperature of the air, and have, therefore, the same degree of heat or cold: yet if I lay my hand successively on the wood and on the metal, the latter feels much the coldest;

not that it is really so, but, being a better conductor, it more readily than the wood takes away and draws into itself the fire that was in my skin. Accordingly, if I lay one hand part on the lock and part on the wood, and after it had laid on some time, I feel both parts with my other hand, I find the part that has been in contact with the lock very sensibly colder to the touch than the part that lay on the wood. How a living animal obtains its quantity of this fluid, called fire, is a curious question. I have shown that some bodies (as metals) have a power of attracting it stronger than others; and I have sometimes suspected that a living body had some power of attracting out of the air, or other bodies, the heat it wanted. Thus metals hammered, or repeatedly bent, grow hot in the bent or hammered part. But when I consider that air, in contact with the body, cools it; that the surrounding air is rather heated by its contact with the body; that every breath of cooler air drawn in carries off part of the body's heat when it passes out again; that, therefore, there must be in the body a fund for producing it, or otherwise the animal would soon grow cold; I have been rather inclined to think that the fluid *fire*, as well as the fluid *air*, is attracted by plants in their growth, and becomes consolidated with the other materials of which they are formed, and makes a great part of their substance; that, when they come to be digested, and to suffer in the vessels a kind of fermentation, part of the fire, as well as part of the air, recovers its fluid, active state again, and diffuses itself in the body, digesting and separating it; that the fire, so reproduced by digestion and separation, continually leaving the body, its place is supplied by fresh quantities, arising from the continual separation; that whatever quickens the motion of the fluids in an animal quickens the separation, and reproduces more of the fire, as exercise; that all the fire emitted by wood and other combustibles, when burning, existed in them before in a solid state, being only discovered when separating; that some fossils, as sulphur, seacoal, &c., contain a great deal of solid fire; and that, in short, what escapes and is dissipated in the burning of bodies, besides water and earth, is generally the air and fire that before made parts of the solid. Thus I imagine that animal heat arises by or from a kind of fermentation in the juices of the body, in the same manner as heat arises in the liquors preparing for distillation, wherein there is a separation of the spirituous from the watery and earthy parts. And it is remarkable, that the liquor in a distiller's vat, when in its best and highest state of fermentation, as I have been informed, has the same degree of heat with the human body: that is, about 94 or 96.

Thus, as by a constant supply of fuel in a chimney you keep a warm room, so by a constant supply of food in the stomach you keep a warm body; only where little exercise is used the heat may possibly be conducted away too fast; in which case such materials are to be used for clothing and bedding, against the effects of an immediate contact of the air, as are in themselves bad conductors of heat, and, consequently, prevent its being communicated through their substance to the air. Hence what is called *warmth* in wool, and its preference on that account to linen, wool not being so good a conductor; and hence all the natural coverings of animals to keep them warm are such as retain and confine the natural heat in the body by being bad conductors, such as wool, hair, feathers, and the silk by which the silkworm, in its tender embryo state, is first clothed. Clothing, thus considered, does not make a man warm by *giving* warmth, but by *preventing* the too quick dissipation of the heat produced in his body, and so occasioning an accumulation.

There is another curious question I will just venture to touch upon, viz., Whence arises the sudden extraordinary degree of cold, perceptible on mixing some chymical liquors, and even on mixing salt and snow, where the composition appears colder than the coldest of the ingredients? I have never seen the chymical mixtures made, but salt and snow I have often mixed myself, and am fully satisfied that the composition feels much colder to the touch, and lowers the mercury in the thermometer more than either ingredient would do separately. I suppose, with others, that cold is nothing more than the absence of heat or fire. Now if the quantity of fire before contained or diffused in the snow and salt was expelled in the uniting of the two matters, it must be driven away either through the air or the vessel containing them. If it is driven off through the air, it must warm the air, and a thermometer held over the mixture, without touching it, would discover the heat by the raising of the mercury, as it must and always does in warm air.

This, indeed, I have not tried, but I should guess it would rather be driven off through the vessel, especially if the vessel be metal, as being a better conductor than air; and so one should find the basin warmer after such mixture. But, on the contrary, the vessel grows cold, and even water, in which the vessel is sometimes placed for the experiment, freezes into hard ice on the basin. Now I know not how to account for this, otherwise than by supposing that the composition is a better conductor of fire than the ingredients separately, and, like the lock compared with the wood, has a stronger power of attracting fire, and does accordingly attract it suddenly from the fingers, or a thermometer put into it, from the basin that contains it, and from the water in contact with the outside of the basin; so that the fingers have the sensation of extreme cold by being deprived of much of their natural fire; the thermometer sinks by having part of its fire drawn out of the mercury; the basin grows colder to the touch, as, by having its fire drawn into the mixture, it is become more capable of drawing and receiving it from the hand; and, through the basin, the water loses its fire that kept it fluid; so it becomes ice. One would expect that, from all this attracted acquisition of fire to the composition, it should become warmer; and, in fact, the snow and salt dissolve at the same time into water, without freezing.

B. FRANKLIN.

---

*Peter Franklin, Newport, Rhode Island.*
ON THE SALTNESS OF SEAWATER.

London, May 7, 1760.

\* \* It has, indeed, as you observe, been the opinion of some very great naturalists, that the sea is salt only from the dissolution of mineral or rock-salt which its waters happen to meet with. But this opinion takes it for granted that all water was originally fresh, of which we can have no proof. I own I am inclined to a different opinion, and rather think all the water on this globe was originally salt, and that the fresh water we find in springs and rivers is the produce of distillation. The sun raises the vapours from the sea, which form clouds, and fall in rain upon the land, and springs and rivers are formed of that rain. As to the rock-salt found in mines, I conceive that, instead of communicating its saltness to the sea, it is itself drawn from the sea, and that, of course, the sea is now fresher than it was originally. This is only another effect of nature's distillery, and might be performed various ways.

It is evident, from the quantities of seashells, and the bones and teeth of fishes found in high lands, that the sea has formerly covered them. Then either the sea has been higher than it now is, and has fallen away from those high lands, or they have been lower than they are, and were lifted up out of the water to their present height by some internal mighty force, such as we still feel some remains of when whole continents are moved by earthquakes In either case it may be supposed that large hollows, or valleys among hills, might be left filled with seawater, which, evaporating, and the fluid part drying away in a course of years, would leave the salt covering the bottom; and that salt, coming afterward to be covered with earth from the neighbouring hills, could only be found by digging through that earth. Or, as we know from their effects that there are deep, fiery caverns under the earth, and even under the sea, if at any time the sea leaks into any of them, the fluid parts of the water must evaporate from that heat, and pass off through some volcano, while the salt remains, and, by degrees and continual accretion, becomes a great mass. Thus the cavern may at length be filled, and the volcano connected with it cease burning, as many, it is said, have done; and future miners, penetrating such cavern, find what we call a salt-mine. This is a fancy I had on visiting the salt-mines at Northwich with my son. I send you a piece of the rock-salt which he brought up with him out of the mine.

B. FRANKLIN.

---

*To Miss Stephenson.*
SALT WATER RENDERED FRESH BY DISTILLATION.—METHOD OF RELIEVING THIRST BY SEAWATER.

Craven-street, August 10, 1761.

We are to set out this week for Holland, where we may possibly spend a month, but purpose to be at home again before the coronation. I could not go without taking leave of you by a line at least when I am so many letters in your debt.

In yours of May 19, which I have before me, you speak of the ease with which salt water may be made fresh by distillation, supposing it to be, as I had said, that in evaporation the air would take up water, but not the salt that was mixed with it. It is true that distilled seawater will not be salt, but there are other disagreeable qualities that rise with the water, in distillation; which, indeed, several besides Dr. Hales have endeavoured by some means to prevent, but as yet their methods have not been brought much into use.

I have a singular opinion on this subject, which I will venture to communicate to you, though I doubt you will rank it among my whims. It is certain that the skin has *imbibing* as well as *discharging* pores; witness the effects of a blistering-plaster, &c. I have read that a man, hired by a physician to stand, by way of experiment, in the open air naked during a moist night, weighed near three pounds heavier in the morning. I have often observed myself, that however thirsty I may have been before going into the water to swim, I am never long so in the water. These imbibing pores, however, are very fine; perhaps fine enough, in filtering, to separate salt from water; for though I have soaked (by swimming, when a boy) several hours in the day, for several days successively, in salt water, I never found my blood and juices salted by that means, so as to make me thirsty or feel a salt taste in my mouth; and it is remarkable that the flesh of seafish, though bred in salt water, is not salt. Hence I imagined that if people at sea, distressed by thirst, when their fresh water is unfortunately spent, would make bathing-tubs of their empty water-casks, and, filling them with seawater, sit in them an hour or two each day, they might be greatly relieved. Perhaps keeping their clothes constantly wet might have an almost equal effect; and this without danger of catching cold. Men do not catch cold by wet clothes at sea. Damp, but not wet linen, may possibly give colds; but no one catches cold by bathing, and no clothes can be wetter than water itself. Why damp clothes should then occasion colds, is a curious question, the discussion of which I reserve for a future letter or some future conversation.

Adieu, my little philosopher. Present my respectful compliments to the good ladies your aunts, and to Miss Pitt, and believe me ever

B. FRANKLIN.

---

*To the same.*

TENDENCY OF RIVERS TO THE SEA.—EFFECTS OF THE SUN'S RAYS ON CLOTHES OF DIFFERENT COLOURS.

September 20, 1761.

MY DEAR FRIEND,

It is, as you observed in our late conversation, a very general opinion, that *all rivers run into the sea*, or deposite their waters there. 'Tis a kind of audacity to call such general opinions in question, and may subject one to censure. But we must hazard something in what we think the cause of truth: and if we propose our objections modestly, we shall, though mistaken, deserve a censure less severe than when we are both mistaken and insolent.

That some rivers run into the sea is beyond a doubt: such, for instance, are the Amazons, and, I think, the Oronoko and the Mississippi. The proof is, that their waters are fresh quite to the sea, and out to some distance from the land. Our question is, whether the fresh waters of those rivers, whose beds are filled with salt water to a considerable distance up from the sea (as the Thames, the Delaware, and the rivers that communicate with Chesapeake Bay in Virginia), do ever arrive at the sea? And as I suspect they do not, I am now to acquaint you with my reasons; or, if they are not allowed to be reasons, my conceptions at least of this matter.

The common supply of rivers is from springs, which draw their origin from rain that has soaked into the earth. The union of a number of springs forms a river. The waters, as they run exposed to the sun, air, and wind, are continually evaporating. Hence, in travelling, one may often see where a river runs, by a long bluish mist over it, though we are at such a distance as not to see the river itself. The quantity of this evaporation is greater or less, in proportion to the surface exposed by the same quantity of water to those causes of evaporation. While the river runs in a narrow, confined channel in the upper hilly country, only a small surface is exposed; a greater as the river widens. Now if a river ends in a lake, as some do, whereby its waters are spread so wide as that the evaporation is equal to the sum of all its springs, that lake will never overflow; and if, instead of ending in a lake, it was drawn into greater length as a river, so as to expose a surface equal in the whole to that lake, the evaporation would be equal, and such river would end as a canal; when the ignorant might suppose, as they actually do in such cases, that the river loses itself by running under ground, whereas, in truth, it has run up into the air.

Now, how many rivers that are open to the sea widen much before they arrive at it, not merely by the additional waters they receive, but by having their course stopped by the opposing flood-tide; by being turned back twice in twenty-four hours, and by finding broader beds in the low flat countries to dilate themselves in; hence the evaporation of the fresh water is proportionably increased, so that in some rivers it may equal the springs of supply. In such cases the salt water comes up the river, and meets the fresh in that part where, if there were a wall or bank of earth across, from side to side, the river would form a lake, fuller indeed at sometimes than at others, according to the seasons, but whose evaporation would, one time with another, be equal to its supply.

When the communication between the two kinds of water is open, this supposed wall of separation may be conceived as a moveable one, which is not only pushed some miles higher up the river by every flood-tide from the sea, and carried down again as far by every tide of ebb, but which has even this space of vibration removed nearer to the sea in wet seasons, when the springs and brooks in the upper country are augmented by the falling rains, so as to swell the river, and farther from the sea in dry seasons.

Within a few miles above and below this moveable line of separation, the different waters mix a little, partly by their motion to and fro, and partly from the greater gravity of the salt water, which inclines it to run under the fresh, while the fresh water, being lighter, runs over the salt.

Cast your eye on the map of North America, and observe the Bay of Chesapeake, in Virginia, mentioned above; you will see, communicating with it by their mouths, the great rivers Susquehanna, Potomac, Rappahannoc, York, and James, besides a number of smaller streams, each as big as the Thames. It has been proposed by philosophical writers, that to compute how much water any river discharges into the sea in a given time, we should measure its depth and swiftness at any part above the tide: as for the Thames, at Kingston or Windsor. But can one imagine, that if all the water of those vast rivers went to the sea, it would not first have pushed the salt water out of that narrow-mouthed bay, and filled it with fresh? The Susquehanna alone would seem to be sufficient for this, if it were not for the loss by evaporation. And yet that bay is salt quite up to Annapolis.

As to our other subject, the different degrees of heat imbibed from the sun's rays by cloths of different colours, since I cannot find the notes of my experiment to send you, I must give it as well as I can from memory.

But first let me mention an experiment you may easily make yourself. Walk but a quarter of an hour in your garden when the sun shines, with a part of your dress white and a part black; then apply your hand to them alternately, and you will find a very great difference in their warmth. The black will be quite hot to the touch, the white still cool.

Another. Try to fire the paper with a burning glass. If it is white, you will not easily burn it; but if you bring the focus to a black spot, or upon letters written or printed, the paper will immediately be on fire under the letters.

Thus fullers and dyers find black cloths, of equal thickness with white ones, and hung out equally wet, dry in the sun much sooner than the white, being more readily heated by the sun's rays. It is the same before a fire, the heat of which sooner penetrates black stockings than white ones, and so is apt sooner to burn a man's shins. Also beer much sooner warms in a black mug set before the fire than in a white one, or a bright silver tankard.

My experiment was this. I took a number of little pieces of broadcloth from a tailor's pattern card, of various colours. There were black, deep blue, lighter blue, green, purple, red, yellow, white, and other colours or shades of colours. I laid them all out upon the snow in a bright sunshiny morning. In a few hours (I cannot now be exact as to the time) the black, being warmed most by the sun, was sunk so low as to be below the stroke of the sun's rays; the dark blue almost as low, the lighter blue not quite so much as the dark, the other colours less as they were lighter, and the quite white remained on the surface of the snow, not having entered it at all.

What signifies philosophy that does not apply to some use? May we not learn from hence that black clothes are not so fit to wear in a hot sunny climate or season as white ones; because in such clothes the body is more heated by the sun when we walk abroad, and are, at the same time, heated by the exercise, which double heat is apt to bring on putrid dangerous fevers? That soldiers and seamen, who must march and labour in the sun, should in the East or West Indies have a uniform of white? That summer hats for men or women should be white, as repelling that heat which gives headaches to many, and to some the fatal stroke that the French call the *coup de soleil*? That the ladies' summer hats, however, should be lined with black, as not reverberating on their faces those rays which are reflected upward from the earth or water? That the putting a white cap of paper or linen *within* the crown of a black hat, as some do, will not keep out the heat, though it would if placed *without*? That fruit-walls, being blacked, may receive so much heat from the sun in the daytime as to continue warm in some degree through the night, and thereby preserve the fruit from frosts or forward its growth? with sundry other particulars of less or greater importance, that will occur from time to time to attentive minds.

B. FRANKLIN.

---

*To the same.*

ON THE EFFECT OF AIR ON THE BAROMETER. AND THE BENEFITS DERIVED FROM THE STUDY OF INSECTS.

Craven-street, June 11, 1760.

'Tis a very sensible question you ask, how the air can affect the barometer, when its opening appears covered with wood? If, indeed, it was so closely covered as to admit of no communication of the outward air to the surface of the mercury, the change of weight in the air could not possibly affect it. But the least crevice is sufficient for the purpose; a pinhole will do the business. And if you could look behind the frame to which your barometer is fixed, you would certainly find some small opening.

There are, indeed, some barometers in which the body of the mercury in the lower end is contained in a close leather bag, and so the air cannot come into immediate contact with the mercury; yet the same effect is produced. For the leather, being flexible, when, the bag is pressed by any additional weight of air, it contracts, and the mercury is forced up into the tube; when the air becomes lighter and its pressure less, the weight of the mercury prevails, and it descends again into the bag.

Your observations on what you have lately read concerning insects is very just and solid. Superficial minds are apt to despise those who make that part of the creation their study as mere triflers; but certainly the world has been much obliged to them. Under the care and management of man, the labours of the little silkworm afford employment and subsistence to thousands of families, and become an immense article of commerce. The bee, too, yields us its delicious honey, and its wax useful to a multitude of purposes. Another insect, it is said, produces the cochineal, from whence we have our rich scarlet dye. The usefulness of the cantharides, or Spanish flies, in medicine, is known to all, and thousands owe their lives to that knowledge. By human industry and observation, other properties of other insects may possibly be hereafter discovered, and of equal utility. A thorough acquaintance with the nature of these little creatures may also enable mankind to prevent the increase of such as are noxious, or secure us against the mischiefs they occasion. These things doubtless your books make mention of: I can only add a particular late instance, which I had from a Swedish gentleman of good credit. In the green timber intended for shipbuilding at the king's yard in that country, a kind of worms was found, which every year became more numerous and more pernicious, so that the ships were greatly damaged before they came into use. The king sent Linnæus, the great naturalist, from Stockholm, to inquire into the affair, and see if the mischief was capable of any remedy. He found, on examination, that the worm was produced from a small egg, deposited in the little roughnesses on the surface of the wood, by a particular kind of fly or beetle; from whence the worm, as soon as it was hatched, began to eat into the substance of the wood, and, after some time, came out again a fly of the parent kind, and so the species increased. The season in which the fly laid its eggs Linnæus knew to be about a fortnight (I think) in the month of May, and at no other time in the year. He therefore advised, that some days before that season, all the green timber should be thrown into the water, and kept under water till the season was over. Which being done by the king's order, the flies, missing the usual nests, could not increase, and the species was either destroyed or went elsewhere: and the wood was effectually preserved, for after the first year it became too dry and hard for their purpose.

There is, however, a prudent moderation to be used in studies of this kind. The knowledge of nature may be ornamental, and it may be useful; but if, to attain an eminence in that, we neglect the knowledge and practice of essential duties, we deserve reprehension. For there is no rank in natural knowledge of equal dignity and importance with that of being a good parent, a good child, a good husband or wife, a good neighbour or friend, a good subject or citizen, that is, in short, a good Christian. Nicholas Gimcrack, therefore, who neglected the care of his family to pursue butterflies, was a just object of ridicule, and we must give him up as fair game to the satirist.

B. Franklin.

*To Dr. Joseph Priestley.*
EFFECT OF VEGETATION ON NOXIOUS AIR.

* * That the vegetable creation should restore the air which is spoiled by the animal part of it, looks like a rational system, and seems to be of a piece with the rest. Thus fire purifies water all the world over. It purifies it by distillation, when it raises it in vapours, and lets it fall in rain; and farther still by filtration, when, keeping it fluid, it suffers that rain to percolate the earth. We knew before that putrid animal substances were converted into sweet vegetables when mixed with the earth and applied as manure; and now, it seems, that the same putrid substances, mixed with the air, have a similar effect. The strong, thriving state of your mint, in putrid air, seems to show that the air is mended by taking something from it, and not by adding to it. I hope this will give some check to the rage of destroying trees that grow near houses, which has accompanied our late improvements in gardening, from an opinion of their being unwholesome. I am certain, from long observation, that there is nothing unhealthy in the air of woods; for we Americans have everywhere our country habitations in the midst of woods, and no people on earth enjoy better health or are more prolific.

B. FRANKLIN.

*To Dr. John Pringle.*
ON THE DIFFERENCE OF NAVIGATION IN SHOAL AND DEEP WATER.

Craven-street, May 10, 1768.

You may remember, that when we were travelling together in Holland, you remarked that the trackschuyt in one of the stages went slower than usual, and inquired of the boatman what might be the reason; who answered, that it had been a dry season, and the water in the canal was low. On being asked if it was so low as that the boat touched the muddy bottom, he said no, not so low as that, but so low as to make it harder for the horse to draw the boat. We neither of us, at first, could conceive, that if there was water enough for the boat to swim clear of the bottom, its being deeper would make any difference; but as the man affirmed it seriously as a thing well known among them, and as the punctuality required in their stages was likely to make such difference, if any there were, more readily observed by them than by other watermen who did not pass so regularly and constantly backward and forward in the same track, I began to apprehend there might be something in it, and attempted to account for it from this consideration, that the boat, in proceeding along the canal, must in every boat's length of her course move out of her way a body of water equal in bulk to the room her bottom took up in the water; that the water so moved must pass on each side of her and under her bottom to get behind her; that if the passage under her bottom was straitened by the shallows, more of that water must pass by her sides, and with a swifter motion, which would retard her, as moving the contrary way; or, that the water becoming lower behind the boat than before, she was pressed back by the weight of its difference in height, and her motion retarded by having that weight constantly to overcome. But as it is often lost time to attempt accounting for uncertain facts, I determined to make an experiment of this when I should have convenient time and opportunity.

After our return to England, as often as I happened to be on the Thames, I inquired of our watermen whether they were sensible of any difference in rowing over shallow or deep water. I found them all agreeing in the fact, that there was a very great difference, but they differed widely in expressing the quantity of the difference; some supposing it was equal to a mile in six, others to a mile in three, &c. As I did not recollect to have met with any mention of this matter in our philosophical books, and conceiving that if the difference should really be great, it might be an object of consideration in the many projects now on foot for digging new navigable canals in this island, I lately put my design of making the experiment in execution in the following manner.

I provided a trough of planed boards fourteen feet long, six inches wide, and six inches deep in the clear, filled with water within half an inch of the edge, to represent a canal. I had a loose board, of nearly the same length and breadth, that, being put into the water, might be sunk to any depth, and fixed by little wedges where I would choose to have it stay, in order to make different depths of water, leaving the surface at the same height with regard to the sides of the trough. I had a little boat in form of a lighter or boat of burden, six inches long, two inches and a quarter wide, and one inch and a quarter deep. When swimming, it drew one inch water. To give motion to the boat, I fixed one end of a long silk thread to its bow, just even with the water's edge; the other end passed over a well-made brass pully, of about an inch diameter, turning freely on a small axis; and a shilling was the weight. Then placing the boat at one end of the trough, the weight would draw it through the water to the other.

Not having a watch that shows seconds, in order to measure the time taken up by the boat in passing from end to end, I counted as fast as I could count to ten repeatedly, keeping an account of the number of tens on my fingers. And as much as possible to correct any little inequalities in my counting, I repeated the experiment a number of times at each depth of water, that I might take the medium. And the following are the results:

|  | Water<br>1½ inches deep. | 2 inches. | 4½ inches. |
|---|---|---|---|
| 1st exp. | 100 | 94 | 79 |
| 2d " | 104 | 93 | 78 |
| 3d " | 104 | 91 | 77 |
| 4th " | 106 | 87 | 79 |
| 5th " | 100 | 88 | 79 |
| 6th " | 99 | 86 | 80 |
| 7th " | 100 | 90 | 79 |
| 8th " | 100 | 88 | 81 |
|  | 813 | 717 | 632 |
|  | Medium 101 | Medium 89 | Medium 79 |

I made many other experiments, but the above are those in which I was most exact; and they serve sufficiently to show that the difference is considerable. Between the deepest and shallowest it appears to be somewhat more than one fifth. So that, supposing large canals, and boats, and depths of water to bear the same proportions, and that four men or horses would draw a boat in deep water four leagues in four hours, it would require five to draw the same boat in the same time as far in shallow water, or four would require five hours.

Whether this difference is of consequence enough to justify a greater expense in deepening canals, is a matter of calculation, which our ingenious engineers in that way will readily determine.

B. FRANKLIN.

## To Oliver Neale.
## ON THE ART OF SWIMMING.

I cannot be of opinion with you, that it is too late in life for you to learn to swim. The river near the bottom of your garden affords a most convenient place for the purpose. And as your new employment requires your being often on the water, of which you have such a dread, I think you would do well to make the trial; nothing being so likely to remove those apprehensions as the consciousness of an ability to swim to the shore in case of an accident, or of supporting yourself in the water till a boat could come to take you up.

I do not know how far corks or bladders may be useful in learning to swim, having never seen much trial of them. Possibly they may be of service in supporting the body while you are learning what is called the stroke, or that manner of drawing in and striking out the hands and feet that is necessary to produce progressive motion. But you will be no swimmer till you can place some confidence in the power of the water to support you; I would therefore advise the acquiring that confidence in the first place, especially as I have known several who, by a little of the practice necessary for that purpose, have insensibly acquired the stroke, taught, as it were, by nature.

The practice I mean is this. Choosing a place where the water deepens gradually, walk coolly into it till it is up to your breast; then turn round, your face to the shore, and throw an egg into the water between you and the shore. It will sink to the bottom, and be easily seen there, as your water is clear. It must lie in water so deep as that you cannot reach it to take it up but by diving for it. To encourage yourself in order to do this, reflect that your progress will be from deeper to shallower water, and that at any time you may, by bringing your legs under you and standing on the bottom, raise your head far above the water. Then plunge under it with your eyes open, throwing yourself towards the egg, and endeavouring, by the action of your hands and feet against the water, to get forward till within reach of it. In this attempt you will find that the water buoys you up against your inclination; that it is not so easy a thing to sink as you imagined; that you cannot, but by active force, get down to the egg. Thus you feel the power of the water to support you, and learn to confide in that power; while your endeavours to overcome it and to reach the egg teach you the manner of acting on the water with your feet and hands, which action is afterward used in swimming to support your head higher above water, or to go forward through it.

I would the more earnestly press you to the trial of this method, because, though I think I satisfied you that your body is lighter than water, and that you might float in it a long time, with your mouth free for breathing, if you would put yourself in a proper posture, and would be still and forbear struggling, yet, till you have obtained this experimental confidence in the water, I cannot depend on your having the necessary presence of mind to recollect that posture and directions I gave you relating to it. The surprise may put all out of your mind. For though we value ourselves on being reasonable, knowing creatures, reason and knowledge seem, on such occasions, to be of little use to us; and the brutes, to whom we allow scarce a glimmering of either, appear to have the advantage of us.

I will, however, take this opportunity of repeating those particulars to you which I mentioned in our last conversation, as, by perusing them at your leisure, you may possibly imprint them so in your memory as, on occasion, to be of some use to you.

1. That though the legs, arms, and head of a human body, being solid parts, are specifically something heavier than fresh water, yet the trunk, particularly the upper part, from its hollowness, is so much lighter than water, as that the

whole of the body, taken together, is too light to sink wholly under water, but some part will remain above until the lungs become filled with water, which happens from drawing water into them instead of air, when a person, in the fright, attempts breathing while the mouth and nostrils are under water.

2. That the legs and arms are specifically lighter than salt water, and will be supported by it, so that a human body would not sink in salt water, though the lungs were filled as above, but from the greater specific gravity of the head.

3. That, therefore, a person throwing himself on his back in salt water, and extending his arms, may easily lie so as to keep his mouth and nostrils free for breathing; and, by a small motion of his hands, may prevent turning if he should perceive any tendency to it.

4. That in fresh water, if a man throws himself on his back near the surface, he cannot long continue in that situation but by proper action of his hands on the water. If he uses no such action, the legs and lower part of the body will gradually sink till he comes into an upright position, in which he will continue suspended, the hollow of the breast keeping the head uppermost.

5. But if, in this erect position, the head is kept upright above the shoulders, as when we stand on the ground, the immersion will, by the weight of that part of the head that is out of water, reach above the mouth and nostrils, perhaps a little above the eyes, so that a man cannot long remain suspended in water with his head in that position.

6. The body continuing suspended as before, and upright, if the head be leaned quite back, so that the face look upward, all the back part of the head being then under water, and its weight, consequently, in a great measure supported by it, the face will remain above water quite free for breathing, will rise an inch higher every inspiration, and sink as much every expiration, but never so low that the water may come over the mouth.

7. If, therefore, a person unacquainted with swimming, and falling accidentally into the water, could have presence of mind sufficient to avoid struggling and plunging, and to let the body take this natural position, he might continue long safe from drowning till perhaps help would come. For as to the clothes, their additional weight, while immersed, is very inconsiderable, the water supporting it, though, when he comes out of the water, he would find them very heavy indeed.

But, as I said before, I would not advise you or any one to depend on having this presence of mind on such an occasion, but learn fairly to swim, as I wish all men were taught to do in their youth; they would, on many occurrences, be the safer for having that skill, and on many more the happier, as freer from painful apprehensions of danger, to say nothing of the enjoyment in so delightful and wholesome an exercise. Soldiers particularly should, methinks, all be taught to swim; it might be of frequent use either in surprising an enemy or saving themselves. And if I had now boys to educate, I should prefer those schools (other things being equal) where an opportunity was afforded for acquiring so advantageous an art, which, once learned, is never forgotten.

B. Franklin.

*To Miss Stephenson.*
METHOD OF CONTRACTING CHIMNEYS.—MODESTY IN DISPUTATION.

Craven-street, Saturday evening, past 10.

The question you ask me is a very sensible one, and I shall be glad if I can give you a satisfactory answer. There are two ways of contracting a chimney; one by contracting the opening *before* the fire, the other by contracting the funnel *above* the fire. If the funnel above the fire is left open in its full dimensions, and the opening before the fire is contracted, then the coals, I imagine, will burn faster, because more air is directed through the fire, and in a stronger stream; that air which before passed over it and on each side of it, now passing *through* it. This is seen in narrow stove chimneys, when a *sacheverell* or blower is used, which still more contracts the narrow opening. But if the funnel only *above* the fire is contracted, then, as a less stream of air is passing up the chimney, less must pass through the fire, and, consequently, it should seem that the consuming of the coals would rather be checked than augmented by such contraction. And this will also be the case when both the opening *before* the fire and the funnel *above* the fire are contracted, provided the funnel above the fire is more contracted in proportion than the opening before the fire. So, you see, I think you had the best of the argument; and as you, notwithstanding, gave it up in complaisance to the company, I think you had also the best of the dispute. There are few, though convinced, that know how to give up even an error they have been once engaged in maintaining; there is, therefore, the more merit in dropping a contest where one thinks one's self right; it is at least respectful to those we converse with. And, indeed, all our knowledge is so imperfect, and we are, from a thousand causes, so perpetually subject to mistake and error, that positiveness can scarce ever become even the most knowing; and modesty in advancing any opinion, however plain and true we may suppose it, is always decent, and generally more likely to procure assent. Pope's rule,

To speak, though sure, with seeming diffidence,

is therefore a good one; and if I had ever seen in your conversation the least deviation from it, I should earnestly recommend it to your observation. I am, &c.,

B. FRANKLIN.

---

*To M. Dubourg.*
OBSERVATIONS ON THE PREVAILING DOCTRINES OF LIFE AND DEATH.

* * Your observations on the causes of death, and the experiments which you propose for recalling to life those who appear to be killed by lightning, demonstrate equally your sagacity and your humanity. It appears that the doctrines of life and death, in general, are yet but little understood.

A toad buried in sand will live, it is said, till the sand becomes petrified: and then, being enclosed in the stone, it may still live for we know not how many ages. The facts which are cited in support of this opinion are too numerous and too circumstantial not to deserve a certain degree of credit. As we are accustomed to see all the animals with which we are acquainted eat and drink, it appears to us difficult to conceive how a toad can be supported in such a dungeon: but if we reflect that the necessity of nourishment, which animals experience in their ordinary state, proceeds from the continual waste of their substance by perspiration, it will appear less incredible that some animals, in a torpid state, perspiring less because they use no exercise, should have less need of aliment; and that others, which are covered with scales or shells which stop perspiration, such as land and sea turtles, serpents, and some species of fish, should be able to subsist a considerable time without any nourishment whatever. A plant, with its flowers, fades and dies immediately if exposed to the air without having its root immersed in a humid soil, from which it may draw a sufficient quantity of moisture to supply that which exhales from its substance and is carried off continually by the air. Perhaps, however, if it were buried in quicksilver, it might preserve, for a considerable space of time, its vegetable life, its smell, and colour. If this be the case, it might prove a commodious method of transporting from distant countries those delicate plants which are unable to sustain the inclemency of the weather at sea, and which require particular care and attention. I have seen an instance of common flies preserved in a manner somewhat similar. They had been drowned in Madeira wine, apparently about the time when it was bottled in Virginia to be sent hither (to London). At the opening of one of the bottles, at the house of a friend where I then was, three drowned flies fell into the first glass that was filled. Having heard it remarked that drowned flies were capable of being revived by the rays of the sun, I proposed making the experiment upon these: they were therefore exposed to the sun upon a sieve, which had been employed to strain them out of the wine. In less than three hours, two of them began by degrees to recover life. They commenced by some convulsive motions of the thighs, and at length they raised themselves upon their legs, wiped their eyes with their fore-feet, beat and brushed their wings with their hind-feet, and soon after began to fly, finding themselves in Old England, without knowing how they came thither. The third continued lifeless till sunset, when, losing all hopes of him, he was thrown away.

I wish it were possible, from this instance, to invent a method of embalming drowned persons, in such a manner that they may be recalled to life at any period, however distant; for, having a very ardent desire to see and observe the state of America a hundred years hence, I should prefer to any ordinary death the being immersed in a cask of Madeira wine, with a few friends, till that time, to be then recalled to life by the solar warmth of my dear country! But since, in all probability, we live in an age too early and too near the infancy of science to hope to see such an art brought in our time to its perfection, I must, for the present, content myself with the treat which you are so kind as to promise me, of the resuscitation of a fowl or a turkey-cock.

B. Franklin.

## LORD BROUGHAM'S PORTRAIT OF DR. FRANKLIN.

The following admirable sketch of the character of Franklin is from a new work by Lord Brougham, recently published in London, entitled "Statesmen in the time of George III." It has not been published in this country:

"One of the most remarkable men, certainly, of our times as a politician, or of any age as a philosopher, was Franklin, who also stands alone in combining together these two characters, the greatest that man can sustain, and in this, that having borne the first part in enlarging science by one of the greatest discoveries ever made, he bore the second part in founding one of the greatest empires.

"In this truly great man everything seemed to concur that goes towards the constitution of exalted merit. First, he was the architect of his own fortune. Born in the humblest station, he raised himself, by his talents and his industry, first, to the place in society which may be attained with the help only of ordinary abilities, great application, and good luck; but next, to the loftier heights which a daring and happy genius alone can scale; and the poor printer's boy, who at one period of his life had no covering to shelter his head from the dews of night, rent in twain the proud dominion of England, and lived to be the ambassador of a commonwealth which he had formed, at the court of the haughty monarchs of France who had been his allies.

"Then he had been tried by prosperity as well as adverse fortune, and had passed unhurt through the perils of both. No ordinary apprentice, no commonplace journeyman, ever laid the foundation of his independence in habits of industry and temperance more deep than he did, whose genius was afterward to rank him with the Galileos and the Newtons of the Old World. No patrician born to shine in courts, or assist at the councils of monarchs, ever bore his honours in a lofty station more easily, or was less spoiled by the enjoyment of them, than this common workman did when negotiating with royal representatives, or caressed by all the beauty and fashion of the most brilliant court in Europe.

"Again, he was self-taught in all he knew. His hours of study were stolen from those of sleep and of meals, or gained by some ingenious contrivance for reading while the work of his daily calling went on. Assisted by none of the helps which affluence tenders to the studies of the rich, he had to supply the place of tutors by redoubled diligence, and of commentaries by repeated perusal. Nay, the possession of books was to be obtained by copying what the art he himself exercised furnished easily to others.

"Next, the circumstances under which others succumb, he made to yield and bend to his own purposes; a successful leader of a revolt that ended in complete triumph, after appearing desperate for years; a great discoverer in philosophy, without the ordinary helps to knowledge; a writer famed for his chaste style, without a classical education; a skilful negotiator, though never bred to politics; ending as a favourite, nay, a pattern of fashion, when the guest of frivolous courts, the life which he had begun in garrets and in workshops.

"Lastly, combinations of faculties, in others deemed impossible, appeared easy and natural in him. The philosopher, delighting in speculation, was also eminently a man of action. Ingenious reasoning, refined and subtle consultation, were in him combined with prompt resolution and inflexible firmness of purpose. To a lively fancy he joined a learned, a deep reflection; his original and inventive genius stooped to the convenient alliance of the most ordinary prudence in every-day affairs; the mind that soared above the clouds, and was conversant with the loftiest of human contemplations, disdained not to make proverbs and feign parables for the guidance of apprenticed youths and servile maidens; and the hands that sketched a free constitution for a whole continent, or drew down the lightning from heaven, easily and cheerfully lent themselves to simplify the apparatus by which truths were to be illustrated or discoveries pursued.

"His discoveries were made with hardly any apparatus at all; and if, at any time, he had been led to employ instruments of a somewhat less ordinary description, he never seemed satisfied until he had, as it were, afterward translated the process, by resolving the problem with such simple machinery that you might say he had done it wholly unaided by apparatus. The experiments by which the identity of lightning and electricity was demonstrated, were made with a sheet of brown paper, a bit of twine, a silk thread, and an iron key.

"Upon the integrity of this man, whether in public or in private life, there rests no stain. Strictly honest and even scrupulously punctual in all his dealings, he preserved in the highest fortune that regularity which he had practised as well as inculcated in the lowest.

"In domestic life he was faultless, and in the intercourse of society delightful. There was a constant good humour and a playful wit, easy and of high relish, without any ambition to shine, the natural fruit of his lively fancy, his solid, natural good sense, and his cheerful temper, that gave his conversation an unspeakable charm, and alike suited every circle from the humblest to the most elevated. With all his strong opinions, so often solemnly declared, so imperishably recorded in his deeds, he retained a tolerance for those who differed with him which could not be surpassed in men whose principles hang so loosely about them as to be taken up for a convenient cloak, and laid down when found to impede their progress. In his family he was everything that worth, warm affections, and sound prudence could contribute, to make a man both useful and amiable, respected and beloved.

"In religion he would be reckoned by many a latitudinarian, yet it is certain that his mind was imbued with a deep sense of the Divine perfections, a constant impression of our accountable nature; and a lively hope of future enjoyment. Accordingly, his deathbed, the test of both faith and works, was easy and placid, resigned and devout, and indicated at once an unflinching retrospect of the past, and a comfortable assurance of the future.

"If we turn from the truly great man whom we have been contemplating to his celebrated contemporary in the Old World (Frederic the Great), who only affected the philosophy that Franklin possessed, and employed his talents for civil and military affairs in extinguishing that independence which Franklin's life was consecrated to establish, the contrast is marvellous indeed between the monarch and the printer."